Over Our Heads

Dear Lovely Lynn,

Thank you so much! For
all your support & love
and wisdom. I
adore you & feel so
blessed that we
met!. Much love,
Andrea.

Canada Council Conseil des Arts
for the Arts du Canada

 ONTARIO ARTS COUNCIL
CONSEIL DES ARTS DE L'ONTARIO
an Ontario government agency
un organisme du gouvernement de l'Ontario

We gratefully acknowledge the support of the Canada Council for the Arts and the Ontario Arts Council for our publishing program. We also acknowledge the financial support of the Department of Canadian Heritage through the Canada Book Fund.

Cover artwork / design: Val Fullard

Library and Archives Canada Cataloguing in Publication

Thompson, Andrea, 1967–, author
    Over our heads : a novel / by Andrea Thompson.

ISBN 978-1-77133-130-2 (pbk.)

    I. Title.

PS8589.H4748O94 2014   C813'.54   C2014-905024-0

 MIX
Paper from
responsible sources
FSC® C004071

Printed and bound in Canada

Inanna Publications and Education Inc.
210 Founders College, York University
4700 Keele Street, Toronto, Ontario, Canada M3J 1P3
Telephone: (416) 736-5356 Fax: (416) 736-5765
Email: inanna.publications@inanna.ca   Website: www.inanna.ca

Over Our Heads

a novel by

Andrea Thompson

Inanna Poetry & Fiction Series

INANNA PUBLICATIONS AND EDUCATION INC.
TORONTO, CANADA

For Mary and Bill McDougall

Heaven is under our feet as well as over our heads.
                                        –Henry David Thoreau

The sun had set and the moon was rising over our heads.
                                        –Virginia Woolf

Nothing ever lasts. It all gets torn to shreds.
If something's everlasting, it's over our heads.
                                        –Jon Brion

1.

LOOKED AT FROM THE SKY, the house doesn't seem special at all. From a plane, flying over on a clear day, all one notices is its proximity to the vast expanse of green that spreads north from the lake. From overhead, High Park looks huge but misplaced, unlike Central Park, with its sprawl of trees feeding the heart of the city. In Toronto, the heart is off to one side, like in a human body.

The park makes it easy to find home from above, though. How many miles above the city would one need to be before the park became a blur, the streets next to it indistinguishable? It doesn't matter because we're not moving further away. We're moving closer.

Parkside Drive runs north and south, along the eastern boarder of High Park, from Bloor Street to Lakeshore Boulevard. Down at the south end, running east off Parkside is Garden Avenue, and two houses in is Indian Road. Number 66 is on the corner where the two streets meet. That's what they're called, Indian and Garden – no kidding. It's only later, after getting some perspective on the whole story that these names begin to seem implausible. But that's what living is like, isn't it? The details that seem the least likely, the most improbable, the coincidences that no one can believe – this is what life is made of.

At the end, looking back, the story of a single lifetime appears perfectly orchestrated, even if while one lives it, it all seems so random and chaotic. That might be one reason why so many young people find it hard to believe in something greater than themselves – God or a higher power, or whatever you want to call it. The young have yet to see a near completed work. How could they fathom the intelligence of the designer who created it? The old, now they are the ones who get to see how life weaves a story together. Call it destiny, fate, providence, or don't call it anything at all. Even the atheists, when pressed on their deathbeds, will admit to witnessing some sort of uncanny progression of events during the unfolding of their lives – even if there is no God, and it's just us behind the wheel. Almost all of us notice, as we get older, an intricate, synchronistic beauty – even with all the tedium, anxiety, heartbreak and suffering. There are some who live out their time on earth without ever noticing the design of their life. It's a shame, though, not to notice. There is so much to see if one keeps one's eyes open.

The house on the corner, for instance. Viewed in terms of its potential market value, or how its upkeep reflects its owner's proclivity to "keep up with the Joneses," it might simply seem a run-down mess. But in terms of structure and integrity of shape and design, nothing can stop number 66 from being beautiful. Not the peeling paint or dangling eaves or the weeds that over-run the garden with giddy abandon.

Most of the other houses on the street are that old stately turn of the century reddish-brown brick. Not number 66. It is made of rock and mortar. Sure, there is likely brick underneath somewhere, but the face of the house is a collage of grey, brown and beige stones varying in size from an apple to a cantaloupe. This makes the house bumpy on the outside instead of smooth, or at least flat, like a brick house. It also makes people want to run their hands over the stone to feel its texture. The house calls out to passersby without them knowing. It stands on the corner, teasing, tempting. *Touch me, touch me, touch me*, it says. *Come home.*

2.

THE FIRST PLACE EMMA REMEMBERED living was by the ocean. Salt was always on her lips, and sand was always all over her face, in her hair. At night, the waves pulsed a wet sloshing heartbeat through her dreams. Some days, the sun would shine on the big white-headed birds that disappeared over treetops. There were whales that moaned in the distance, and rain that beat down on the roof of the tent. Emma remembered the smell of camp stove in the morning, of sweaty bodies and suntan lotion in the afternoon, of singing and laughter in the dark.

Everyone left Emma alone when she lived by the ocean. This was good when her belly was full, and they put her in the shade or inside the tent if it was raining. But sometimes it wasn't so good to be alone. Sometimes they forgot important things, like taking the poo away or giving her a bottle of milk. Emma tried telling them, but nobody heard her at first, because she didn't know how to make her thoughts move outside her head. She realized that her mouth sounds could make them listen, but they still couldn't understand what she was trying to tell them. She knew because when she spoke, they replied with tickling giggly noises or soft purring noises that didn't mean anything at all.

Sometimes they gave her too much food, and it was like a thunderstorm inside that made her belly jump and kick. Sometimes her bum was burning fire, and there was only ocean to put it out and the ocean was gasoline. Sometimes they were gone, gone, gone, even when they were right there sitting with her. Gone inside the coughing smoke or sticky water that made them crazy and sleepy and falling down.

None of them was mother. They were dumb strangers who forgot and pretended and said words that meant nothing. One of the big white-headed birds said so in words that went right into Emma's brain. He told her to suck the salt off her thumb when she was hungry, and to watch him fly when they left her alone too long. So she did. She stared and stared until she went dizzy, then she closed her eyes and wasn't Emma anymore. She was a white-headed bird instead, flying and swooping and looking for a mouse, rabbit, snake, or fish. She spotted one and dove down, knowing nothing could stop her. Soon, her belly would be full. The bird would talk and talk inside her head, and Emma would swoop and search and listen until the sun went down.

The second place Emma remembered living wasn't the second place at all. She lived somewhere before that, between the ocean and the new life. Later, the social workers would tell her that while she was still a baby living near the ocean, someone reported her to the authorities. They took her to the hospital, got her hydrated, and healed her diaper rash, but they couldn't find her mother, so she was taken into custody.

She was in two other homes before they finally got her settled into the house on Columbia Street. Emma didn't remember anything from this in-between time. When she tried, all she could come up with was a memory of being in a car with a man and a woman, and the car stopping because there was something in the middle of the road. The man got out, picked up the thing and brought it to Emma to see.

"It's a turtle," the woman in the car said.

Emma remembered looking at it, and touching the warm, hard shell.

3.

IT WAS MONDAY MORNING. Rachel drove the Benz west along the Lakeshore, toward the Boulevard Club – exclusive haven for the Toronto elite, where she had briefly been a member. The membership was a waste of money, and she knew it at the time, but it was a ridiculous girlhood dream she had felt compelled to fulfill. Since the first time she had seen the expensive cars and well-dressed members that came and went from the club, Rachel had vowed to one day be able to afford to buy a Mercedes and join the ranks of the shore-side select. She had planned to achieve this goal by becoming a famous scientist; however, in the end she had taken a different route to success. A career as a senior actuary for a multi-national insurance company, and a deft combination of long-term and short-term investments, had delivered much the same fiscal results. The fame – a folly of youth, she realized – was non-essential.

Rachel passed the entrance to the Boulevard Club without a second glance. The few times she had attended, she had found the facilities to be impeccable, but still, after a year in the prestigious ranks, Rachel had decided not to renew. Paying for a club she rarely used as a way to celebrate the financial status she'd earned through years of hard work seemed, in the end, to cheapen her accomplishments. The car, however, was different. The car was also practical. It had an excellent safety rating.

Rachel turned the Benz off the Lakeshore and onto Parkside

Drive, holding her breath as she passed under the bridges for the Queensway, Gardiner expressway and CN rail-line. The bridges were low-hanging combinations of steel girders and concrete, and in constant need of repair. When she was a child, Rachel had imagined that one day the old bridges would collapse, leaving crushed cars and corpses in their wake. Although that had yet to occur, Rachel had been awakened on more than one occasion by the sound of metal crumpling against reinforced concrete, as some dozy truck driver who hadn't seen the signs, accidentally smashed his semi right into the side of the first bridge after turning off the Lakeshore. Once, a driver barely made it under, only to become wedged halfway through. It took six tow trucks three hours to finally pull the rig back out. Structurally, the bridges were disasters waiting to happen.

Driving up Parkside, Rachel watched the lake recede behind her in the rearview mirror. When she was in elementary school, she used to pretend that she was doing astronomical research in a remote northern observatory during her summer vacations. It had been simple to imagine that when she was a kid, sitting out on the dock at Sunnyside beach with her dad at night, listening to him name constellations, peering at the stars through his telescope. In those days, Rachel used to convince herself that the lights in the distance were from some fish cannery or rural lakeside resort. Then they started building the CN tower, and the horizon began declaring its urbanism like an exclamation point. There was no pretending after that. Everything had changed that year anyway, so the loss of her northern observatory fantasy was of little consequence.

Rachel drove up Parkside, past Garden Avenue, turned right on Wright Avenue and then right again, onto Indian Road. The huge old oaks and maples had formed their annual canopy, and the wisteria was in full bloom. Spring came early in this part of the city; the combination of the oxygen-rich trees of High Park and the updraft from Lake Ontario made the area relatively temperate. According to her grandmother, the whole neighbourhood had once been considered cottage country, with upscale summerhouses for the urban Hog Town well-to-do. Apparently, Sunnyside was first built to be an amusement park, complete with a roller-coaster, roller-skating rink and bandstand, intended to lure city dwellers out to the western frontier.

"Your grandfather used to go to the Palais Royale every Friday night –it was *the* place to be back then," Rachel's grandmother said every time they passed the old building. "You should have seen him in his Zoot suit, Rach, with his hair all slicked back. He took me to see the Duke there once. All the girls were jealous – a sold out show and all." Rachel would nod during these reminiscences, not wanting to interrupt. Grandma only talked about Grandpa that way when Wanda wasn't around.

That was childhood Grandma – wise, save-the-day Grandma. Grown up Grandma was another story. Slowly over the years, Rachel had watched her grandmother's superhero powers weaken, until she had become like a child, and Rachel had become the adult, left to care for a distant, and increasingly stubborn old woman who was unwilling to admit that her body was failing her. Rachel had begun testing her memory, asking her grandmother what day it was or what she ate for breakfast. Once, she even she showed Grandma a picture of her grandfather, and asked if she knew who he was. But that just set her off.

"My mind is just fine, Rachel!" She yelled. "Now, leave me alone." Rachel was used to it. Ever since Emma had shown up when they were kids, Rachel had become the bad cop. The new Wanda.

Rachel pulled the black car up to the house on Indian Road. Grandma was gone.

It was predictable that it would happen, that her grandmother would die. She had been a very old woman, living alone in a mausoleum of a house full of clutter – clutter that would now need to be removed. Rachel would do the removing of course, along with Emma, who had come back from Vancouver just in time to say goodbye, and ensure that Rachel never got the chance to. Emma had been staying with her old boyfriend, Lester who had a place near Kensington Market. Lester, a man who had briefly, unfathomably, also taken over Rachel's heart and apartment with his sexy, tragic, narcissistic, bohemian voodoo. Emma was en route from his place at that moment, coming to meet Rachel at the house. Emma was back, and there was going to be trouble. Rachel could feel it coming like a thunderstorm.

The house looked pitifully old. All the homes on the street had been constructed at the turn of the century. Not this new century, not the one that had begun with the great non-event of Y2K – but the other century, the one we now have enough distance from to romanticize. They had been built as country estates, but now, at least half of these grand houses had been converted into multiplexes. Still, the area hadn't totally gone downhill yet. Not like Parkdale. The lawns were still trimmed, flowerbeds still attended to. The houses retained the grandeur. Most of them, anyway.

Indian Road. What a terrible name for a street. If city planners could have seen ahead and known the future would render the name politically incorrect, they likely would have thought twice. Instead, they went on an Indian-a-thon: Indian Road, Indian Grove, Indian Road Crescent, Indian Valley Crescent, and Indian Trail. It was excessive. Apparently the proliferation of similar names was explained by an old trading trail that ran through High Park. Still, the repetition and lack of variety was unfathomable, and slightly perverse, considering the fate of the Aboriginal people that originally lived on the land beneath the street signs. It also made the probability that your pizza would wind up blocks away skyrocket to an unnecessarily high level. City planners of the day had not foreseen the future of take-out food either. Hindsight. The only way to see clearly.

4.

WHEN EMMA WAS FOUR YEARS OLD and had learned to talk so people understood her, she was taken to the old wood house on Columbia Street. Inside the house, a giraffe lady and a bear man were waiting. Emma went inside, and they took her to a kitchen that smelled like burnt toast.

The giraffe lady was skinny, with blond hair piled up to the sky and sparkly green powder on her eyelids. The bear man was big and hairy and smelled like dirty feet. They told her she lived in Foster's home now, and that they were Foster's parents. Emma wondered who Foster was, and why his parents gave him a whole house, but didn't ask. The lady and the man didn't give her answers to any of these important questions. Instead, they told her that the giraffe lady's name was Mamma Shirley, and the bear man's name was Jack.

"Just Jack," he said, giving Mamma Shirley a dirty look. "She's not your real mother either, so don't go kidding yourself. And I'm not your father. I'm Jack. Just Jack."

There was another kid in the house too. His name was Jamie Francis. He was ten-and-a-half. Emma could tell right off that he wasn't going to bother her. He had his own room and was mostly busy teaching himself how to play "American Pie" on his guitar. "I'm going to be a big star when I grow up," he said. "Not sure yet what I'll be famous at. I might be a rock star like Elton John, or maybe have my own TV show, like Flip Wilson. I haven't decided yet."

Jamie Francis had a round haircut that Mamma Shirley made by putting a bowl on his head. He also said funny words like "brolly" and "rubbish" instead of "umbrella" and "garbage." It wasn't his fault. He was from England. Jamie Francis told Emma that when he was a teenager, he was going to run away and live with a family like the Partridges where everyone could play a musical instrument.

"I just have to get the chords right for 'American Pie' and then I'm going to learn 'Come On Get Happy'." He told Emma he had a picture of David Cassidy under his bed, and when he practiced in his room, he opened it up and sang to him. Emma didn't say anything at all, but Jamie Francis didn't care. He talked to her like he was alone, not like she was someone.

In the morning, Mamma Shirley made everyone breakfast. Just Jack read the newspaper in his undershirt and track pants, and all the furry black hair on his arms and legs peeked out. After breakfast, Mamma Shirley put everything away, and Just Jack put on the blue shirt with a shiny broach pinned on it. Jamie Francis said that it was a "badge" and that Just Jack needed it so they'd know he wasn't a criminal when he went to work in the Pen.

Emma didn't know what the Pen was, but she knew it wasn't the same pen that you write with. She thought it may have had something to do with Pig-Pen, Charlie Brown's friend with the dust cloud around him. Emma thought the Pen must have been dirty whatever it was. But she wasn't sure, and she didn't ask. She didn't want to talk to anyone there yet. All the air in the house was like a big bowl of cold, gooey porridge. Emma didn't want to breathe it in, didn't want it to get stuck to all her words. She could nod her head for "yes," and shake it for "no." That was enough.

The first real friend Emma made at the house on Columbia Street was Barney, the dog next door. Emma had been out in the backyard, searching the sky for eagles, when she heard a little old man voice in her head. At first it whispered, then grew louder. *Hello, hello, hello,* it said, and made her look toward the wooden back porch in the yard next door.

"Hello?" Emma said out loud.

Something shuffled under the porch, and then a dog came out and walked toward her. Emma crouched down and put her hand through the chain-link fence, reaching out to the graying muzzle. The old dog took a sniff and then looked her in the eyes in a way that made Emma feel like she knew him. She wondered if this little old man-dog would be her friend. *Yes.* The answer went straight from the dog's mind into her own.

Then Emma closed her eyes to see if her new friend had anything else to say. This time there were no words, instead he sent her a picture, like a Polaroid developing inside her brain. The image came into focus: slices of steaming roast of beef in a dog dish. Emma opened her eyes. The old dog looked at her, tail wagging, and for the first time since she came to Foster's house, Emma laughed.

5.

RACHEL PUT THE BENZ into park in the driveway of old number 66. It always shamed her that her grandmother's house was in such a terrible state of disrepair. In photographs of when Grandpa was alive, the house looked respectable, but ever since Rachel could remember, the house had been slowly falling apart. What did that say about her, that she had allowed her grandmother to live that way? Rachel peered through the windshield at the garage door. The paint was so mottled and peeling it looked like army camouflage. Beside the house, the eaves were rusty, dangling from their nails. It wasn't as if Grandma couldn't have afforded to put a little work into the place.

"It's not the money," she'd say whenever Rachel brought up the subject of repairs. "It's the change. I can't stand any more changes. I've had enough for a lifetime. Me and this house are going to fall apart together. And *that's that.*"

It was a shame. Given a little loving care, the place could have stood a chance. Instead, it was an accident waiting to happen, standing in embarrassing contrast to the other houses on the street. Every other dwelling in the area had been given some sort of attention over the years – fresh paint, a new roof or a sandblasting of the dirty old brick. But not number 66. What charm it once held had crumbled. Number 66 was a teardown.

Rachel sat in her Benz in the driveway for a moment to gather her thoughts before going in. There was a lot to do, and she wanted to make sure she kept everything on track. All the clothes needed to be trashed. She could get Emma to do that, as well as tossing out the knick-knacks that littered every imaginable surface. Once the clutter was cleared, Rachel could focus on cleaning. She'd already contacted an estate sale company about the furniture and appliances. They'd pick up whatever was left over from the garage sale on Saturday, and let it go to the highest bidder. Most of the furniture was good quality, some pieces were even antiques. The old mahogany dining room table, scratches and all, would likely bring in at least a grand. The couch and chairs were new, so they'd go pretty fast. The main thing was to get everything cleared out as soon as possible. While most houses show better with a bit of furniture, in this case their best bet was to empty the house out, rather than try to sell it full of Grandma's clutter. In this market, Rachel could likely turn the place over in a few weeks if she could get Emma to pitch in and stay focused. Sam was flying in late tomorrow night, but would be busy with the realtor friend he was bringing by on Wednesday, so he wouldn't be able to help out much. They needed to get started as soon as possible if things were going to stay on track. With both Rachel and Emma working at it over the next few days, it should take almost the whole week to clear the contents, though it would be double that time if Emma lost focus, which was a real possibility.

It was still morning. There was plenty of time to get a head start on things before Emma arrived. There were the insurance people to call. There'd be some money coming in from that, no doubt, but getting it would involve processing time. Her grandmother's account was still active, so Rachel would have to go by the bank to let the manager know. At least she'd been able to call the funeral home over the weekend and talk to them about some of the details. Of course, they had been open. People died seven days a week. The total was more than Rachel had imagined, as she forgot to figure a casket in her calculations. She had chastised herself for that. She was an actuary; it was her job to foresee the probable. Naturally they'd need a casket, even for a cremation. It's not like the body is tossed into a big fire like in some third-world ritual. There'd need to be something for her to be laid in. Then set on fire. Rachel judged herself for thinking it, but thought it all the same. What a waste. And how would anyone know? Chances were, shifty funeral homes claimed to burn the casket, but then reused it instead. Maybe she should make the arrangements with the funeral home first, then close the bank account. She could put the service on Grandma's credit card. Was it wrong to let her grandmother pay for her own funeral? No, it wasn't wrong, or a moral issue. It was a simple matter of accounting. There was plenty in the savings, and the insurance would top the balance back up after the expenses for the funeral came out. It wasn't like Rachel wouldn't be out-of-pocket, waiting for the will to be settled. Someone had to pay for repairs, painters, paint, and landscaping. Rachel would cover the costs for the time being. That was enough. Why should she feel bad anyway? It wasn't like she was asking anyone else to take these things on.

She'd fish out the banking and insurance papers when she got inside the house, and go through the rest of the paperwork in the afternoon. That way she could stay in the dining room, and keep her nose down. She'd put Emma to work on the bedroom closet. That would likely take her half-sister all afternoon. Longer, if she fell apart.

6.

FOSTER WASN'T A REAL BOY, it was just the name they give to a house full of kids with nowhere else to go. When Emma was five, Just Jack finally explained it at breakfast one day. Mamma Shirley had just given them all pancakes, and when she sat down, she told Emma and Jamie Francis that they were getting a big sister. Just Jack put down the paper said, "For Chrissake, Shirley, don't mess with their heads," and explained the whole Foster business once and for all. Then he told Emma she would have to share her room. "She's not your sister though, Emma girl. Not a real sister anyway."

A few days later, Emma's not-real sister arrived. Her name was Nina Buziak, and she acted like a big shot, just because she was twelve and got to wear lipgloss and nylons to school. Emma didn't like her much because she had mean eyes and yellow hair with brown roots, and she wore cheap perfume that made her smell like bacon. At first, Nina wouldn't talk to Emma, which suited Emma just fine because Emma still didn't like talking much to anyone except Barney. Then, about a week after she moved in, Emma heard Nina's voice in the dark just before bed, saying, "What's the matter with you, anyway. How come you don't talk? Are you a retard? I heard Mamma Shirley say she thinks you might be a retard. If you are, then she's gonna have to send you away to go live with all the other retarded kids at Woodlands."

Emma didn't know what "retard" meant, but she knew

it wasn't good, and was pretty sure that she wasn't one, so she said, "I'm not. There's nothing wrong with me," into the darkness, and then felt tricked into talking to bacon-head Nina Buziak. "I just don't talk because," she began to explain, but it was too late. She could hear from the sound of breathing in the room that Nina was already asleep.

After that night, Emma let herself talk more. She even began to believe that maybe she was going to make a friend of Nina Buziak, but Nina set her straight. "I still don't like you, even if you're not retarded, because I don't like dirty Indians," she said. Emma didn't know what she was talking about, but Mamma Shirley who was around the corner listening from the kitchen, piped in. "We don't talk about stuff like that in this house, Nina. Besides, we don't know for sure that Emma's an Indian. She might be a Paki or even a Negro. We don't know what she is. But whatever it is, it isn't her fault, and we don't want anyone upset around here, so we just don't talk about it, understand?"

Emma didn't understand at all, but knew enough not to ask Mamma Shirley what she meant, and no way was she ever going to talk to Nina again. So, instead, she asked Jamie Francis who laughed. "Mamma Shirley's such a square. Nobody says Negro anymore. I don't think you are one anyways, but if you were, so what? Jimi Hendrix is coloured and he's famous. Lots of coloured people are famous. Look at Michael Jackson. Him and his whole family are coloured. Nina's just mad 'cause her mom got rid of her. She's trailer trash. Don't let her bum you out."

Later that day, to cheer her up, Jamie Francis asked Emma if she wanted to see him make Mamma Shirley cry. Emma said, "Yes," just to see what would happen, and because she was a little bit mad about the "Negro" word, even if she wasn't sure why. They found Mamma Shirley hanging up the laundry outside the house, and Jamie Francis yelled out, "Hey Mamma Shirley, are you a foster mom because you can't have kids? Emma wants to know." Mamma Shirley looked at Jamie Francis with horror, then big, fat, black makeup tears fell down her face. Jamie Francis giggled and whispered to Emma that he'd heard Mamma Shirley tell Just Jack one time about how bad she felt 'cause she almost had a baby once, but had had an operation to get rid of it instead. So now her insides were messed up, and she thought God would stop being mad at her about it if she looked after the kids nobody else wanted. Emma's head swam with all this information. What was a baby doing inside Mamma Shirley? And why would she get rid of it? Where had it gone?

Emma felt bad for Mamma Shirley, but the big white-headed bird that still flew overhead and spoke to her sometimes, said: *Don't worry about her, she'll be fine.* He also told her that Jamie Francis felt bad now too, and was going to vacuum the living room for Mamma Shirley when he went inside. That would make Mamma Shirley happy. She liked it when everything was neat and tidy. That was why there was plastic on the couch that made squeaky, crunchy sounds when you sat on it.

Everything stayed like that, with just the five of them in Foster's house on Columbia Street until just after Emma's sixth birthday. The snow had gone, and Just Jack had raked the yard bare of all the winter dirt and leaves. Emma was waiting for the bulbs to bust up with red tulips, when something else happened instead. A new boy came to live with them.

The new boy was four months younger than Emma. He talked a lot and wore silly clothes: fancy shirts, bow ties, and black shoes that looked wet all the time. When she first met him, and looked at his shoes, Emma laughed out loud. When Mamma Shirley told Emma his name was Lester Templeton, Emma laughed even harder, until Mamma Shirley clucked and said, "Shush," and gave Emma the hard eyes. Jamie Francis gave Lester a good looking over before he decided that Lester was all right. "He dresses funny, that's for sure. But he doesn't look mean like the last one." Jamie Francis called Lester "fresh meat," and told Lester if he didn't do anything stupid, he'd let Lester have his clothes when he grew out of them.

While Lester was upstairs unpacking his old, beat-up, Winnie-the-Pooh suitcase in his new room, Mamma Shirley told them that Lester had other clothes he could wear, but that he wore those silly ones because he thought it would make his parents come back. But it wouldn't. Lester's parents had both died in a car crash. Hit and run. Both of them, dead, at the same time. Jamie Francis asked Lester about it later that day, but Lester shook his head. "They're coming back," he said. "You're stupid. You don't know anything!"

Lester started shouting until Jamie Francis said, "Okay, okay, pipe down squirt, will ya?"

Lester stopped yelling, but didn't stop talking. "They're coming back. They *are*! They're just away on vacation, but they're gonna come get me soon," he told them, "So I have to look sharp. I want to look sharp so they'll keep me with them this time."

When Emma heard Lester say this in his silly clothes, with his shoulders slumped down, she thought to herself, Lester Templeton is the saddest boy in the whole world. He was like the baby bird that Emma had found one day, flopping and crying: *Help me, help me*, in the middle of the backyard. Barney had said the little bird was a goner, but Emma had picked it up and kept it in a box with Kleenex stuffed in it. She'd fed the little bird worms from the garden, and had left the box in the branches of the crab apple tree, leaving the lid open in case the mamma bird came looking. One morning Emma had noticed the box lay empty on the ground, little bits of Kleenex scattered like snow in the grass. Barney had said he thought Puffy the cat down the street got it, or maybe a raccoon. "No," Emma had told him when Barney came to look. "It flew away to be with its family." She'd said the words, but didn't believe them. That night, she had dreamt of a snake slithering though the grass with a bulge in its middle.

Standing in the living room with Mamma Shirley and this new little boy, Emma thought about the bird. She took a breath, closed her eyes and opened them again. Little Lester was still smiling, and full of silly hope. She wanted to tell him to smarten up, but she couldn't. Looking at Lester made her too full of love to scold him. It wasn't his fault he thought stupid things. He was just a sad little boy. He didn't know anything. He was only five-and-a-half years old.

By the time the sound of crickets filled the hot summer air, Lester and Emma had become inseparable. Nina and Jamie Francis were out of school, and Mamma Shirley said that things were getting too crazy with all the kids underfoot. Just Jack had some vacation time from the Pen coming to him, so he offered to take Jamie Francis and Lester camping in the Kootenays. Emma was supposed to stay home with Mamma Shirley and Nina, but when they told her, she ran to her room and cried until Mamma Shirley said, "Geez Louise, okay, okay. You can go camping with the boys."

They all slept in a big tent that smelled like a basement for two weeks that summer, and ate baked beans warmed up in a dirty old pot. They swam in the lake every day, even when it rained. Lester got poison ivy, and Jamie Francis got a fishhook stuck in his finger, but nothing bad happened to Emma. Even when she had to go to the outhouse at night, and Jamie Francis told her that if she peed too loud, bears would come and eat her, Emma wasn't afraid. Once, when they went to the woodlot next to the dump, they did see a bear. The bear didn't want to eat them, but it still wasn't happy they were around. It didn't say so out loud or anything, but Emma got a feeling in her belly when she looked at it, and then words came into her head that weren't hers. The bear said that it didn't want anything to do with the stupid campers, and then showed Emma a movie of people driving fast past cubs in cars that sounded like thunder. The bear also said it hated the way the humans teased them with snacks they could smell, but couldn't get their paws on.

One night, when Jamie Francis was poking the fire with part of a fallen branch, and Lester was trying to get everyone to sing "99 Bottles of Beer," Just Jack drank his Molson Golden and made everyone roast marshmallows on a stick because it was fun. Later, when the beer made his words sound like his mouth was full of mashed potatoes, Just Jack decided to tell them all about the Pen. He didn't want to at first, but Jamie Francis kept asking, so finally he gave in.

"It's not the sort of place you want to go to unless you had to. I'm lucky I work in the piggery and not inside the old skookum with the rest."

"Skookum?" Jamie Francis asked. Just Jack laughed.

"Yeah, that's what they call it, the skookum house. It's Indian for 'big house.' That's what they call it in Indian language. There's a lot of Indians in there," Just Jack said, turning his head just enough for Emma to catch him looking at her in the light of the campfire. "Lots of other types too, and all of them bad. Bad to the bone."

"But you don't get to hang out with any of the criminals? I mean you just sit around with the pigs all day instead?" Jamie Francis asked.

"I'd rather be with pigs than criminals any day!" Lester added.

Just Jack laughed. "I don't blame you, Les. But no, James, I still have to spend time with the men in the piggery. They do the feeding, cleaning and grunt work, and I supervise them. It's no picnic, though, don't get me wrong. Those fellas, even them that are some part decent, some part not totally eaten up by evil thoughts, well, they still turn hard after a while in the Pen. There's something about being locked away that messes a person up. Takes his manhood away. That's what makes them really dangerous, the fact that they've already been to hell. They've got nothing to lose."

Jamie Francis asked Just Jack to tell him about the cells the men lived in, and what sort of crappy food they had to eat. Just Jack kept telling his stories, but Emma didn't want to listen anymore. She could hear noises in the forest, so she decided to go see what was going on. On the other side of the tent, a family of raccoons asked her if she had anything to eat. Emma said no, and the raccoons said, *In that case, don't come any closer.* She sat and listened to them for a while, until Lester noticed she was gone, and Just Jack called her back to the campfire to listen to more stories of bad men and pigs that apparently didn't say anything at all.

That night, Emma decided that when she grew up she wasn't going to bother with a house. She'd get a tent instead, and drive around and live wherever she wanted. When she told Just Jack the next day, he laughed and said Mamma Shirley would get a kick out of that one. Emma didn't give a hoot. "I don't want to go back home," she said. "Can't we just stay here?"

Just Jack stopped laughing when he saw Emma's eyes well up. "Sorry girl. No can do Emma-boo. But, we'll be back next year. For sure."

Chapter 7

RACHEL WAS STILL SITTING in the car on the driveway of number 66, the engine running. How long had she been there? She had been thinking about thermodynamic systems and lost all sense of time. It had started with the house, or the walls to be precise. As Rachel looked through the windshield, she began to see the collection of smooth stones that formed the exterior of the building as a boundary or membrane that had kept them all contained – as a family, as an isolated system attempting the unattainable state of perfect equilibrium. And the area – the neighborhood, park, and lakeshore had been their environment, their reservoir.

Perhaps it wouldn't have been so bad if she had stopped there, but instead, Rachel's idling mind took it one step further. Next, she began to imagine each of them within the family as their own individual system. This led, quite embarrassingly, to thinking about the four fundamental laws of thermodynamics, and who in the family most resembled each principle.

Wanda was clearly the first law. Regardless of her transformation from mother to question mark, her total matter and energy had been conserved, and her effect on her family remained constant. While Grandma would be a natural choice for the second law, with her recent embodiment of the process of decay, it was obvious that Emma also did a good job of embodying entropy. She was a natural-born measure of ever increasing disorder, of the inevitable evolution of an isolated system out of balance.

Rachel shook her head and turned off the engine. What the hell was she doing? The notion of comparing one's family to fundamental laws of physics was ridiculous. Worse, even, than the latest trend of these principles of hard science being applied to individuals, under the dubious guise of "human thermodynamics," or the even more esoteric "sociological thermodynamics," both of which were examples of pseudoscience of the worst kind. Let the bored sociologists and new age fitness gurus use their own terminology for their explanations of social structure and metabolism. A human being was an open, non-equilibrium system, with unknown values, which meant that there was no way to predict the amount of energy that could be either gained or lost. So, naturally, conservation laws could not apply to either individuals, or social configurations. It was impossible, nonsensical – the whole stream of thought. Every minute Rachel had spent on the ridiculous analogy, with the engine running no less, had been a complete waste of time. Rachel unbuckled her seatbelt and took a deep breath. She needed to remain focused. There were too many details to attend to.

They'd have to go through the formalities of the reading of the will in a couple of days, although that shouldn't be a problem. Sam was coming back home from Florida. He'd keep Grandma's condo there, no doubt. That was to be expected. He had been living in it for years now. Hustling. That's what he had said when Rachel asked how he was managing to pay the maintenance fees all this time.

"You know me, Rach," he'd said with a wink the last time he was up for Christmas. "I'm a survivor. A little bit of this, a little bit of that. I make ends meet."

Rachel knew what that meant. It meant don't worry and don't ask unless you really want to know. Whatever business he was into would be shady, for sure. Just this side of legal, though likely sliding over the line every now and then. But

Rachel didn't worry much about Sam. When they were kids, he'd always reminded her of Bugs Bunny. A smarty pants – a wise guy with a good heart. Whatever he was up to, Sam always knew how to land on his feet.

Rachel turned off the ignition, gathered her briefcase and purse, and opened the car door. Then she stopped abruptly, leaving the door open, as she settled back down in her seat.

Wanda. Rachel couldn't see her grandmother including Wanda in the will at all. It had been years since Wanda had taken off, and as far as Rachel knew, Wanda hadn't bothered to keep in touch in all that time. Grandma had long ago reached a point where she had just given up on her daughter.

"Even if she comes back, I'm not having her in this house again," is what Grandma had said one year at Christmas. "You don't abandon your daughters, so sometimes you've got to draw a line," she had said, removing the plate from the place Emma had set, punctuating her statement with the three words Grandma always used to let people know that regardless of was being talked about, the subject was closed, "And *that's that.*"

Rachel swung her legs around, got out of the car, closed the door with her hip, and walked briskly up the driveway to the house. The cracks in the concrete of the front steps looked wider than the last time she had been there. How long did concrete last before it crumbled? Hopefully, it wouldn't happen when some unsuspecting potential buyer was on their way in for a showing, disintegrating steps sending them lurching forward and landing face first.

The money from the house would either be split three ways, or more likely would be left to Rachel and Emma. That would be fair, as the Florida property would be more than likely in Sam's hands. Getting number 66 liquid was the number one priority. Rachel didn't imagine it would be hard to get Emma on board. They had their differences, that was for sure. Even at first glance, a stranger could have seen that Rachel and

Emma were as polarized as night and day. And, physical appearances aside, they had completely contradictory natures and inclinations.

The old cliché that distance made the heart grow fonder was definitely true for Rachel when it came to Emma. Everything between them seemed to smooth out as soon as Emma left Toronto and moved back out west. But they were going to be spending a lot of time together in the coming week, so Rachel had to remember to try to not lose her patience. Emma always seemed to forget all the times Rachel had been there for her, had bailed her out. It went with the sensitivity, Rachel supposed. Emma had the typical artist's temperament – full of mistrust and pointless suffering. She'd be a mess, no doubt, without Grandma around, and would want to hold on to every last piece of memorabilia. Sentimentality would take over. There would be tears. That's where Rachel would come in to keep her on track, to take care of the details, and get things sorted out for them both. At least after the house was sold, Emma would have some money in her bank account.

Rachel looked at the clock on her phone as she stood in front of the door to the house. Emma would be late, as always. That way she could make an entrance and make sure that, for a moment, she got that hit of attention she seemed to crave. At least she'd given up her fantasy of being a rock star. Emma hadn't made a cent on that whim, even though she had plugged away at it for years. Even if she had the talent, the odds were against her, as the chances of a person without money or connections making a success of life in the music business were slim to none. But now, with her newest venture, it seemed that Emma had completely lost her grip on reality. God only knows why she chose the evening of Grandma's passing to make her big announcement. They had been sitting at Rachel's dining-room table, having take-out from Amato's Pizza.

"I've finally found my calling," Emma had announced, as

Rachel divided up the roasted garlic that had come with their salad. "Now, you're going to think it's stupid, but I just want you to know that you're not going to have to worry about me any more. You know, with money," she said. "Really Rachel, this is it. To tell you the truth, I'm surprised it took me so long to realize what I should be doing with my life. In hindsight, it's so obvious. It's not quite enough now to cover my rent, but my clientele is growing by the day. I know, I mean maybe this isn't really what we should be talking about now. But in a way, you know, it sort of makes sense. Like it's some sort of Lazarus moment. The whole phoenix from the flames thing, you know?" Emma added, in a tone that had reminded Rachel of old black-and-white movies, as she'd pushed her clove across her plate, through a field of mixed greens. "I feel it tonight. Maybe it's grief or the wine talking, but I feel like this day, with Grandma going to spirit, because that's all it is really, just a transformation of forms from solid to spirit. Well, now – it's sort of like she's left us both with a space in our life. A vacancy that we can now fill with whatever we want. You know what I mean?"

Rachel had nodded, making the appropriate sounds to indicate listening and comprehension. She'd known better than to think Emma was drunk. Nope. Only half a glass had been consumed over the last hour. Nachos and salsa before the pizza came. Two slices. Salad. Nope, this was Emma sober, beaming her esoteric light from the far reaches of her home planet, Woowoo 7.

Rachel stood on her grandmother's porch, remembering that night. She searched her purse with annoyance for the key to the house, thinking that in hindsight, this last statement of Emma's must have been a set-up – a way to set the stage for the announcement of some sort of normal vocation. That and the use of the word "clientele." Sneaky Emma. Naturally, it had been a relief, for that brief moment, to believe that at long last, Emma had stopped floating around the stratosphere of magical thinking, and had settled back down to earth. But no – *pow* – sucker-punch.

"I'm going to be a pet psychic," Emma had said, with an inappropriate glee.

"A what?"

"Don't laugh, Rachel."

"I'm not laughing, Emma." Rachel popped a bud of garlic into her mouth, and sucked on it. She *had* wanted to laugh. Instead, she'd tossed the clove over, from one side of her mouth to the other, trying to give her cheeks something else to do. "Pet psychic? So you're going to read minds now? Dog and cat minds? And birds? Are you going to do birds, too, or is it more a mammal-focused sort of practice? Would you call it a practice, or maybe more an art form? So you're going to be a psychic for pets? Huh. Didn't see that coming. Though come to think of it, there was that time at the zoo with the apes." Rachel reached for another clove of garlic, and popped it in her mouth. She'd thought it best to keep her tongue busy.

"No," Emma said, looking hurt – her forte. "I mean, yes. Yes and no. I mean, it's not really being psychic. Animal Communicator is what I'm going to put on my business cards. I mean anyone can do it. Animals talk to us all the time."

Rachel glanced up at the clock.

"No really, Rachel, it's scientific. Our thoughts create electromagnetic brain waves that travel through the air, and that we can pick up on. Everyone can sense it, but most people tell themselves they can't, so when it happens, they excuse it away." Emma had started talking faster, as if speed would somehow make her more credible. "It's not magic. It's just paying attention, or inter-species communication if you want to get technical about it. That's what my poem 'Listen' was about. I was going to record it for our next lit-pop fusion CD but then the band broke up for a while. Plus, Lester was driving me crazy. Sorry."

Thinking about that conversation as she stood on the porch of the house, Rachel started to sweat. The key to her grandmother's house was not in its usual compartment. She felt around inside her purse for a while, eventually dumping it out on the patio chair beside the door. The key rattled to the ground, along with the rest of the contents.

It must have been shock, Rachel thought of Emma's rambling that night. There had been not one mention of the fact that Emma had never called from the hospital when she should have. Instead, she had gone on and on about this pet psychic nonsense. Nothing about what happened that night with Grandma. No explanation at all.

Emma had played with her salad. As soon as she had stopped, Rachel cleared the plates, loaded the dishwasher, and called it a night. She asked Emma if she wanted to stay over. Told her she could if she wanted. Suggested she maybe would prefer to go back to Lester's. Rachel didn't care anymore. Lester had been in Toronto for years now. He said he needed to be away from his old friends, who were still using in Vancouver, but Rachel knew better – he needed to get away from Emma, her endless needs and the way she kept Lester handy like a loyal lap-dog.

"Anyway, I got the inspiration for the poem from a time when I was out in the backyard at Grandma's, lying in the grass and listening to the birds. I just stayed there until all the thoughts emptied out of my head, and then all of a sudden I heard them," Emma said.

"Who? You heard who?" Rachel asked. At least Emma entertained when she rambled. She was a born performer. A regular Judy Garland. Just don't laugh at her. Then she'd be upset. Then the tears would come.

Emma laughed. Rachel turned away.

"The birds! I heard the birds. I mean, they were there all along of course, but with all the noise in my head, I couldn't hear them until I emptied my mind. I used to be able to hear them when I was younger, but I'd forgotten about it. I'd forgotten how to listen."

"So the birds spoke to you in the backyard one day, and now you want to get people to pay you to tell them what their pet is thinking?" Rachel had no need for the garlic anymore. The urge to laugh had vanished. Instead, something inside went quiet. The word "charlatan" had come to mind. Likely Emma didn't see it that way. More probable was that Emma believed she really was helping people with her magic extrasensory powers. It made Rachel nervous to watch Emma veer so close to the edge of rational. One more step and – what? What would happen if Emma lost it completely? Why did that thought still fill Rachel with dread? It wasn't just because she'd be the one to have to look after her. No, it was more than that. It was a feeling that if Emma strayed too far from sane, it would be the loose piece of yarn pulled, the mistake realized too late, until the whole sweater unravelled.

"Well no. Not that time. Not in words or pictures or anything. But yes. I mean yes, the birds did sort of speak to me, you know. Just in birdsong. They were calling back and forth to each other. They were talking, exchanging information. They gossiped, they giggled. It was beautiful." Emma had beamed, like the events of the day had never happened. Was it Joanne Woodward who played Sybil in that movie? No. Sally Field. Woodward was the psychiatrist. It was in *The Three Faces of Eve* that Woodward had played the starring role of the nut-job.

"So the birds told you to be a pet *psychic*?"

"*Animal Communicator*. Now listen, Rachel, it's not as crazy as it sounds. I mean, it's not like I think I have magic powers or something. I'm sure anyone could do it if they really put their mind to it. It's just that for me it comes naturally." Emma had said, her voice wavering slightly.

Rachel was about to open the door to old 66, when she remembered the mail. She hadn't checked the box when she was at the house last Friday. Do it now, she told herself, before you forget. Rachel had a lot of details to attend to, and something like retrieving the mail could easily fall through the cracks. Maybe there was an overdue bill Grandma hadn't paid, or some infomercial jewellery she'd ordered – which Rachel would have to return, of course. She checked the mailbox. It was empty.

Rachel supposed that she should count her blessings that at least Emma hadn't fallen apart that night at her condo. And it had sounded like people were willing to pay for her "special skills." Her clientele were crazy cat ladies, no doubt. Not that Rachel wanted to dwell on the topic. Light conversation, that's what she thought they'd have that night. Having dinner together had made sense at the time. They were the ones that had been left behind. The bereaved descendants of the dearly departed.

"You think you can read minds? That doesn't sound a little crazy to you?" It had come out more cutting, crueler than Rachel had intended.

"It's not crazy," Emma had replied, defiantly. "I've already had six sessions, and all my clients have been thrilled. They've written references. I've posted them on my website. Really, it's not anything magical. Anyone could do it if they tried, but people think it's not possible, so they don't bother – don't listen to what they're being told. For me, the information doesn't often come in words. Usually I just get this sense, more of an overall impression. Sometimes I see images, like I'm being sent a snapshot of some incident. And sometimes it's like a movie clip – I'll see the whole scene unfold until it becomes clear what the problem is. Like for instance, there was this dog, George, that kept peeing on the rug, well it turns out..."

"You have a website? A pet psychic website?" Rachel was getting nervous. If this was how Emma planned to support herself, she'd burn through her inheritance in no time. Wasn't losing Grandma enough to deal with in one day? Rachel had tried to be positive. It could be worse, she'd supposed. Emma could be claiming to communicate with the dead or with UFOs. Yes, it could have been worse. Most likely, Rachel had thought, it was only a flash in the pan, a whim that Emma would abandon with time.

"I'm not sure when I'll be going back to Vancouver. I might just stay here for a while," Emma said, lowering her eyes as if looking for approval.

Rachel was silent. Grandma was gone, and there had been no chance for goodbye. Emma hadn't given her a good enough reason why. And instead of talking about that elephant stampeding across the room, they were discussing the secret reason that George the dog peed on the rug. Rachel wanted to laugh.

"Well, there's this symposium here next month," Emma said.

"Symposium?"

"An Animal Communication Symposium. It's part of the Psychic Fair at the CNE."

"Oh, for God's sakes. You're kidding."

"No Rachel, and please try to be supportive okay? It wouldn't kill you."

She tried, but the day had delivered too much to be able to handle Emma and her fairy-tale new-age world on top of it all. Nothing is funny today, Rachel thought. Let her talk about her stupid pet psychic kick, and then, when she was done, Rachel could ask her again – why she didn't call when she knew Grandma was about to die?

"That's wonderful Emma," Rachel had said. "Congratulations."

Emma had frowned.

Rachel stared at the door to her grandmother's house. At the best of times, it took effort to not become impatient with Emma's flakiness. The things she would come up with were ridiculous. Rachel wondered how her sister had made it this far in life with such a loose grip on reality. At least she hadn't asked Rachel for another loan in the last couple of years. What a laugh. As if Rachel would ever see a cent of that money again. She had to do it though. It was up to her to keep Emma off the streets. If she didn't look out for her, who would? Sure, Sam could likely afford to help her too, but he'd never think to offer. She envied Sam for that. It may have been selfishness on his part, or maybe it was his ability to be oblivious to the obvious. Either way, Sam floated through life. Always had. Never felt the pressure of responsibility, of obligation that Rachel always felt. Why should he? If there were a fire, Rachel would put it out long before anyone else even smelled the smoke.

Rachel breathed deeply before opening the door to number 66. The house had been closed up since Grandma had gone into the hospital. Inside, the air would be stale, so better get a lungful of fresh air while she could. She opened the door, and stood staring into the musty darkness of the house. She stepped over the threshold and reached for the hallway light, flicking it on. Nothing. She flicked it off, then on again. Still nothing. She stood in the darkness with a sinking, jittery feeling in her belly. Don't be an idiot, she told herself, it's just a burnt out light bulb. No big deal.

She headed towards the kitchen as her eyes adjusted, and reached for the light switch. She flicked it on. Light filled the room. She flicked it off again, then on again, then off again. Three times. She knew better than this old trick, but she was alone so what the hell.

Rachel tried to remember when it started, the triple light switch flicking, and the illogical feeling of security that followed. Who was it that first told her about that friend whose house had gone up in flames one night? Not having a light switch solidly flicked to either "on" or "off" hadn't been enough to make the electricity jumpy in the walls. It hadn't caused it to shoot all through the house, as those inside slept unaware, later burned to a crisp. It had been a lie. How long had it been after she heard this urban legend that Rachel had discovered the truth? She couldn't remember. All she knew was that she was never really able to shake the feeling that a switch that was neither on nor off, but left somewhere in-between, could destroy everything.

Rachel took the list out of her purse and posted it on the fridge with a magnet. It wasn't for her. She remembered every item, every step they would need to take to get the house sorted and sold. The list was for Emma, to keep her on track, to remind her of why they had come here, and what they had to do. The more quickly they could get things settled, the better. The market was good and the area was prime. They could turn it over quickly if they focused. One step at a time, and soon it would all be sorted, and Rachel could get back to her life. It wasn't as if her grandmother had chosen the moment when she'd finally let go, but really, the timing couldn't have been worse. Rachel was in over her head at the office with the aftermath from year-end reports.

Picking up the pieces after someone dies is a full-time job if you're the executor. Back when it was her dad, it had been Grandma who swooped in like a superhero to save the day, and pull Rachel out of the dark bullet hole in the middle of the kitchen floor. Wanda had been around at the time, sure. But as usual, Wanda hadn't been much help. Grandma had been the one to arrange everything. But this time, it was Rachel's turn to take the helm.

Rachel felt an emptiness in her belly start to swell, start to bully its way toward her eyes. There's too much to do, she thought. I don't have time for this. Hold it together.

8.

WHEN RACHEL WAS NINE YEARS OLD, the police came to the door right in the middle of the pilot episode of *The New Original Wonder Woman*. Dad was on the road and Sam had gone out without telling anyone where again. Mom tried asking him, but Sam said, "Don't hassle me," so Mom said, "Screw it," and decided to spend the night on the couch, playing the drinking game Rachel had invented for the two of them. Mom had her rum and Tab, and Rachel had her chocolate milk, and every time someone said the word "Wonder Woman," they'd take a sip. Two sips when Wonder Woman used her Lasso of Truth, and three sips when she deflected a bullet with her Indestructible Bracelets. They were both laughing a lot because they had played the game during the *Six Million Dollar Man*, too, taking sips at the mention of the word "bionic" and whenever anything was done in slow motion. Mom was just starting to get loaded, but wasn't yet at the point when Rachel would have to watch her cigarette.

If it wasn't for the fact that it was right at the part where the Amazon warrior women were shooting at each other in the big "bullets and bracelets" contest to see who would be allowed to take the handsome air force man back to America, it would have been Rachel who let the cops in. She was always the one who went when someone came to the door. She didn't know why, but whenever she heard the doorbell she'd jump. Sam would always laugh and call her "Pavlov." Rachel didn't know who Pavlov was, and Sam never clued her in, but she could tell from the way he'd shake his head after he said it that it wasn't a compliment. Rachel wished she had been Pavlov that night though. If she had been the one to let the cops in, it would have been different. She would have seen the bad news in their eyes, and would have told Mom herself instead of them.

Cops always made Mom shaky, but Rachel knew how to handle them. When cops came to your house you had to be cool. You had to not tell them anything and act stupid, like you didn't know what was going on. Once they got you to open the door, they'd try to trick you by asking you things like if your older brother had any secret hiding places in his room, or if he had a lot of friends drop by who didn't stay very long.

The pigs always lied, Sam had told Rachel after that time they came looking for him. That was the first thing you had to know when you got busted, he said. Usually Sam wouldn't talk to her about important things like that, because she was a stupid kid who listened to the Bay City Rollers and AM radio. Sam had long hair and a leather jacket with fringes down the arms and would never be caught dead listening to anything but CHUM FM, where they played cool music like David Bowie and Frank Zappa, so Rachel understood. Sam had been extra nice to her though, because she told him she had found a joint on the floor in the kitchen one day and she hadn't wanted him to get in trouble, so she'd hid it in his guitar case before Mom found out. After that, Sam told Rachel she was all right, and that he was going to give her seventy-five bucks for her birthday. He told her he would have to pretend to only give her twenty-five bucks though, and would slide the rest to her later so nobody would start asking him a lot of stupid fucking questions.

Seventy-five bucks was a lot of bread, and Rachel had no idea what she would do with it, so she had decided she'd stash it in her Easy-Bake Oven. It was the perfect place to hide things. Rachel was disappointed when she got it for Christmas that year. She had wanted a chemistry set, but instead, her parents gave her a fire hazard. Rachel had said thank you and smiled, but never once plugged it in. She knew the money would be safe there until she came up with a plan. It was important to have a plan, Sam said. Like when you climbed up on the high school roof to drink beer with your friends, you had to come up with fake names and phone numbers for all the guys beforehand in case some asshole heard the bottles smashing and called the cops. That way, if you got busted, and the pigs tried to tell you that your buddy ratted you out, you'd know they were trying to pull a fast one on you.

Pigs were always trying to pull a fast one. So, when Mom opened the door that night, and Rachel saw the two dark uniforms standing in the shadow of the carport, she knew she'd need some back up. She went to the door, and stood next to Mom, when the dark haired cop with the bushy sideburns asked, "Are you Mrs. Robert Stewart?"

Mom started to sway a bit. She was still holding her rum and Tab. "Yes," she said, "that's me." Rachel started thinking: off, on, off, on, and reached up for the light switch. Without even turning to look at her, Mom swatted Rachel's hand away.

Most of the time Rachel would only check the lights when nobody else was around, cause she knew that if Mom saw her, she'd get mad, and if Sam saw her he'd call Rachel a nut-job. She had tried to explain it to Mom once, but Mom hadn't taken her seriously.

"It's so the house won't set on fire," Rachel had told her.

"That's ridiculous," Mom said.

Then Rachel had told her how Marcia Miller said at recess one day that her cousin's next-door neighbour's house burned down because they hadn't turned the lights off properly.

"The electricity got loose and just shot right through the walls into the living-room and set the drapes on fire. Then the whole house went up in smoke. Just like that," Rachel had said, snapping her fingers. "So, I'm just making sure that they're either on or off because in between is dangerous."

"Turning the lights on and off won't stop the house from setting on fire Rachel," Mom had replied. "Leave the bloody light switches alone."

Mom invited the cops in and everyone stood in the hall and didn't say anything for a minute. Rachel started thinking about the guitar case, and whether they'd go up to search Sam's room, and find the joint still in there. She was about to go up the stairs and check, when they all looked at her, and the cops asked if they could speak to her mom alone. Mom said sure and told Rachel to go back in the living room, and tell her how *Wonder Woman* ended. Then the other cop, the one with the dark circles under his eyes like a raccoon said, "Ooh, I had wanted to watch that." Rachel felt like kicking him.

Rachel pretended to go back to the TV room, but went to the dining room instead, and crawled under the wooden buffet that had come with the dining room table. There was just enough room underneath for her to lie flat on her belly. She didn't really like being under there, because if the bottom of the buffet fell out all of a sudden, all the dishes inside would fall out on top of her. She thought about the sound her ribs would make if she was crushed, and held her breath.

From there, on the floor, Rachel peeked around the corner so she could see the cops and her mom in the kitchen. The cops made the fridge look small and stupid, and left puddles on the floor from the snow melting off their boots. Mom was sitting on the stepladder she used to get the stuff off the top shelf when Dad was on the road, which was all the time those days. At least that was what Mom told him whenever he came home and they started fighting again.

Mom said the fights were because Dad had sex with other ladies when he was away. One time she even said that she wouldn't be surprised if he had a whole other family stashed away somewhere. But Rachel knew the truth. She knew the fights were really because they all lived in Grandma's house instead of their own place. Dad had told her once, when she was helping him work on the basement renovations. She had been watching him put the drywall up over the concrete, when he sighed and said, "I wish I could buy us all our own house, Rach, I really do. I think that would help your mother. If I could get her away from here, she'd get better. It's not good to stay in this place with all those memories." Rachel hadn't asked what was wrong with her mother that she had to get better or what memories she had to get away from. Not right away, anyway. She hadn't wanted to ask because that moment with her dad was so rare. It wasn't like him to sigh, or to talk to her like she could hold his secrets. So she hadn't wanted to startle him into realizing what he was doing. She figured that if she stayed quiet, he'd tell her everything she wanted to know. She figured there was plenty of time.

Sam said that Dad wouldn't bother to have a whole other family, because it was cheaper if he just went to see whores when he was on the road. Rachel didn't believe any of it. To her, Dad was the good parent, the solid one who remembered their birthdays every year, and always kept track of when they had doctors' appointments or were going on school trips. She couldn't see him doing any of the sneaky stuff that Mom always accused him of.

"You never know," Sam said. "He does have all those *Playboy* magazines in his sock drawer. It's not like he doesn't like to look."

Rachel didn't need Sam to tell her the magazines were there. She knew where everything was kept in Mom and Dad's bedroom. She remembered the first time she did an inspection, she was in the hall and noticed Mom going through Dad's drawers like she was looking for something, but couldn't find it. So later, when Mom had gone out, Rachel decided to see if she could find it – whatever it was – instead. Mom's inspections were messy. She'd leave Dad's underwear unfolded and all the pockets of his pants turned inside out. She'd go from his suits in the closet to his papers in the desk by the bed in bursts. Mom's inspections were a series of sprints that always ended up with her standing still with her hands on her hips, chewing on her lip.

Rachel's inspections were silent, orderly marathons. She'd wait till Mom was out somewhere, or had passed out on the couch before beginning so she'd have a lot of time; then, she would go from the far corner, slowly around the room. She looked in places Mom didn't bother with, like behind the drapes. She'd even peek behind the painting of the lady in the chair with the blue bonnet and the eyes that followed you no matter where in the room you were standing. Dad had always hated that picture. He said it gave him the creeps.

Rachel peered into the kitchen from under the buffet, wishing that her dad were there now, or at least that the cops would get to the point. She was thinking about all the good stuff she was missing in *Wonder Woman*. Finally, the cop with the bushy sideburns started talking. "I'm sorry," he said. "There was an accident. Your husband was in a collision on the Don Valley Parkway. There were several vehicles involved. Unfortunately his injuries were fatal. I'm sorry," the cop said again.

Then both the cops just stood there, as if they didn't know what to do next. It made them look stupid, with their big belts and walkie-talkies. They had guns sticking out of their belts too, and for a minute – just a minute because Rachel wasn't a wacko – she wanted to jump out, grab the gun and shoot something. Not a person, just something. Maybe just a little hole in the floor. But then Rachel forgot all about the guns, when the cops told her mom that it wasn't the accident that killed her dad, but the thing that happened after the accident when he got out of his truck.

As soon as the cop said the word "decapitated," Mom dropped forward, like she was going to pick something up off the floor all of a sudden, or like if there really was a gunshot hole in the floor right beneath her and she wanted to peek into it. She went so far forward that her bum lifted up the step of the stool, and Rachel could see right down her top. But then the cop with the bushy sideburns stepped forward and pushed her back into the chair.

Mom's head snapped back in a way that looked like it would give her a sore neck later, and everyone just sat there breathing for a minute. The cops asked if she was all right and if they could call someone. Mom said, "No, no, no." Then she started to laugh, and said, "He lost his mind!" She put her hands over her face after that and didn't say anything, even though her shoulders were going up and down.

Rachel didn't know why, but for some reason, right at that moment she started to think about when her dad had told her that their cat, Cindy, had climbed up in his semi one night to keep warm by the engine, and he saw her fall out in his rear-view mirror when he hit the turnpike. He had told Rachel that she hadn't suffered at all and there were lots of mice in kitty heaven. Rachel hadn't believed him, and had told him she hated him and would never ever speak to him again.

Watching her mom, and thinking about Cindy, Rachel almost started to cry as well, but just then Mom looked up, toward the doorway of the dining room. She looked right toward where Rachel was, and she would have caught her peeking if Rachel had been standing up instead of lying under the buffet. Mom kept looking too high up, as Rachel pushed herself away from the door, then rolled over quick out from under the buffet, then jumped up and ran to the couch like she was bionic. The stupid raccoon-eyed pig came back in the living room, but he was too slow, and didn't know Rachel had heard everything. She really wanted to say something that would get her in trouble, like calling him a "pig" out loud or a "motherfucker" even. Rachel had never said the word "motherfucker" before, and for a minute she was sad about that and mad at herself too for being such a stupid kid and listening to the Bay City Rollers. She wished Sam would come home and talk to Mom even if he was stoned or drunk or something.

But Rachel didn't say anything. Even when the cop asked her what was happening with Diana Prince. She ignored him, and stared at the TV instead, which she knew was rude, but she didn't give a shit.

By the time Sam came home Rachel had already gone to bed. The next morning, Rachel and her mother were up already when he came in the kitchen. He looked at them and asked: "What happened? Is it Dad?"

Mom said, "Yes," and then told him that Dad didn't have time to know what hit him. She didn't use the word "decapitated." Rachel never heard her say that word to anyone. Still, it was as if Sam could see the same movie Rachel saw, with the sheets of metal from the truck slicing Dad's head right off and sending it rolling down the road. Sam's face went white, and he sat down fast with a thud.

"Shit," he said. "Holy shit, what are we gonna do now?"

Mom didn't answer him. Just turned away and went to pour some more rum and Tab in her coffee cup and get the Captain Crunch out of the cupboard.

Nobody said anything else all through breakfast. It was like they couldn't think of anything to talk about anymore. After breakfast, Mom got the newspaper from the carport and put it on the table. She stared at the headline about how the new CN Tower was about to be completed and that it was going to be the highest freestanding structure in the world. For a while Rachel thought she was reading the article, but after a while she realized that her mom's eyes hadn't moved across the page at all.

By the time Rachel was ready for school, Sam had already shovelled the driveway. All the driveways on the end of their street had been shovelled so that a pair of small snow hills stood at the side of the bottom of each one. Rachel walked to the end of the driveway and climbed one of the piles of snow, then slid down the other side. Then, she went up and down the snow hills beside the end of the driveway of the house next door. She stopped and looked at all the hills at the foot of all the driveways down the street, and decided that if she was going to climb some of them she should climb them all.

By the time Rachel got to school, class had already started. Miss Bertrand raised a surprised eyebrow, and asked her what time she had left her house that morning. When Rachel told her, both her eyes got small and squinty, and her lips made a hard flat line. Rachel didn't care. She thought of maybe calling Miss Bertrand a "motherfucker," to see what would happen, but instead just laughed out loud. Rachel didn't say anything else to anyone till afternoon recess. Then she found Marcia Miller and played jumpsies and pretended to be bionic like everything was normal. She started talking between jumps, and didn't want to stop. She talked about Miss Bertrand and how mean she was. She talked about who she liked in the class, who she didn't like, letting all the stupid words just fall out of her head. She talked about anything that came into her mind, saying any word except "accident" or "Dad" or "dead."

For the next three days nobody talked about Dad at all, so Rachel didn't either. Sam stayed in his room all the time and Mom just stared off into space. Everything in the house was quiet, and even when Rachel decided to put Mom's Simon & Garfunkel record on, the air in the house seemed to eat all the happy up from the music before it could get in her ears.

The day before the funeral, Grandma arrived, back from her condo down south. Rachel hadn't seen her for a long time. Not since that Christmas when Dad was on the road, and Grandma had come and given Rachel a Malibu Barbie and that snowman card with five bucks in it. Rachel thought it was great to have Grandma there with them, but Mom had yelled at her and told her to leave before New Year's. "As if you would know the first thing about being a mother," Mom had shouted, shaking. "A mother is supposed to protect her daughter, not turn a blind eye. So, if you don't like the way I live my life, then you should go back to Florida."

Grandma told Mom to pull herself together, and that the drinking in the morning was out of hand. Then Mom told Grandma to mind her own bloody business, because it wasn't like people could turn their lives around on a dime, and forget everything that had happened to them.

"Okay, Wanda. I'll go." Grandma said when Mom's shaking had finally stopped. "But remember, it's not me you're fighting with. It's yourself."

9.

EMMA STOOD ON QUEEN STREET, waiting for the 501 streetcar to take her west, back to the old house on Indian Road. She pulled out her phone to check the time. She was early, a rarity. Rachel would be amazed. Lester had wanted to walk her to her stop, but she told him no. He almost didn't listen, but she stopped him before he could get his other shoe on. He was only trying to help, but he didn't understand. He'd only been a kid when he lost his parents. He thought that Emma's desire to be alone was somehow abnormal, another case of macabre Emma wallowing.

"You need to at least go for a walk, Emma," he'd said, when she came back from Rachel's the night after grandma went to spirit. "You need fresh air and to have some sort of mental stimulation. At least listen to some music." He had clicked on the old transistor radio in the kitchen of his Kensington Market apartment. The Steve Miller Band's "The Joker," a song from their Columbia Street days, filled the room. Lester had looked at Emma and smiled.

Emma hadn't replied. She could try to explain, but she knew he wouldn't understand. Lester was a typical Taurus, always sure that his way was best, stubbornly refusing any invitation to see the world through any but the most comfortable, familiar perspective. She had tried to smile back at him, but only her mouth moved. Her eyes remained lifeless.

Lester's smile slid from his face, and his shoulders slumped.

Emma gave up, went into the kitchen and clicked the radio off, too tired to explain that she didn't want anything else to digest, not even music. Her body already held too much. Her belly was too full of chewed-up feelings and memories. Funny how loss can do that to you, how it took away a person who lived in the middle of your body and filled that gaping hole with a stew of uncooked emotion. Cold potatoes that Lester had wanted her to drag around town. Emma had walked toward him, eyes down. She'd held him to her for a moment, and then left without a word.

It had been early Saturday morning when Grandma went to spirit. Emma had called in to work to let them know that she wasn't sure when she'd be back in Vancouver again. Not her real work – her soul's calling – but that other work, the one that paid the bills. The manager of the Java Hut on Water Street in Gastown had given her a hard time.

"What do you mean you don't know when you'll be back? You expect me to just hold your job open for you? I mean I'm sorry you lost your grandmother and all, but shit, Emma, it's peak cruise ship season down here. We need everyone on board. Come on, just get yourself together," he'd said, adding, "It's not like it was your mother or something."

Emma hadn't meant to tell him to go fuck himself, but she said it anyways. So, that was that for the coffee shop job. But the upshot was that it had given her a full week to go back to the old house on Indian Road and help sort it out. She didn't want to stay at Lester's place in Kensington Market, watching him moon over her. She needed to go back home to number 66 for a while. Besides, she knew that Rachel was in a hurry to pack up the old house and everything in it, and auction it off to the highest bidder. Done and dusted, like nothing had happened – just another item to cross off her to-do list.

The 501 pulled up in front of her before Emma noticed. She climbed on, shuffled to the side of the aisle by the driver. Half a dozen passengers boarded behind her. While she fished in her pockets for fare, they all seemed to be scowling as they pushed past her. The driver sighed. Emma wanted to tell him to go fuck himself too. Anger. Kübler-Ross's second stage. At least she wasn't stuck in denial. Emma dropped her change into the coin box and gave the driver a weak smile.

The streetcar rattled down Queen, past Bathurst and the kitschy mix of hip restaurants, fabric stores, and boutique clothing shops, past the old Prague Deli and Terroni's. Past the old Queen Street Mental Hospital, which had been all re-done now. The name had also been changed to the more holistic and respectful, Centre for Addiction and Mental Health. There were new buildings as well, and a huge sign with their new slogan in bold print: *Transforming Lives.*

The Sadhus, India's Hindu holy men, called death "the great transformer." They believed that the human soul died and was reborn again and again for eternity in a cycle called Samsara. The Buddhists also used the word Samsara when they talked about reincarnation, except in Buddhism it was possible to end the cycle through enlightenment. Amazing how geography had such a drastic effect on how people viewed the end of the line. Christianity had its moments of resurrection, sure, but they were extreme scenarios only achievable by big name players like Jesus or Lazarus, and not an everyday occurrence. Emma liked the Eastern versions better. The idea of transformation seemed more in tune with nature.

The streetcar stopped in front of one of the remaining dingy old Parkdale bars. Everything was getting gentrified along this strip. First came the campy antique stores, then Stella Luna's funky second-hand clothing shop, and once the retro café Easy moved into the hood, with its black and white posters of Peter Fonda and Dennis Hopper on old Harley-Davidsons – the hipness factor of this end of Queen West became firmly established. Artists. It was the artists who kept a city's neighbourhoods alive – until the developers would catch on, of course, and commodify the whole thing. Then the culture-pollinating, bohemian butterflies would have to find a new downtrodden pocket of the city to call home.

The streetcar squealed to a stop outside St. Joseph's hospital. A wild-eyed woman with greasy, grey hair plastered down the side of her face, and a dirty oversized winter parka dangling off one shoulder, ran toward the bus. She got on, and Emma right away could see the crazy in her eyes, which darted from side to side like she was watching a horror movie only she could see. Emma knew it wasn't drugs, she could feel drugs a mile away. Coke vibrated through a person with a jagged, cocky, please-love-me or I'll-kill-you desperation. Heroin seeped into a user's skin, into their bones leaving a smell like old socks and sulphur. When they were high, junkie's faces were blissful and dopey, and when they were jonesing, they were pouty and resentful like a child on the verge of a tantrum. Either way, being near them always felt like drowning. Once, Emma had crossed the street to get away from a guy in front of a bowling alley who zigzagged across the pavement with a mania that felt to Emma like a hundred razor blades under her skin. It wasn't until she got home, and had the deadbolt firmly locked, that she figured out what she had felt was methamphetamine.

No, this wasn't a drug, it was something else. Something more deeply disconnected. More permanent. It was the woman's eyes that said crazy first, but you could also tell it from the rest of her body. Her hands and arms shook uncontrollably. She's not being taken care of by anyone, Emma thought. The woman shuffled down the streetcar, muttering to herself as she walked past. She smelled rank of psoriasis and clothes gone stiff with filth. Once at the back of the streetcar, she started drumming on the seat in front of her with an empty green pop bottle. Her muttering grew louder over her own din.

Emma closed her eyes, and imagined that the woman was an incognito Shaman, issuing secret chanting prayers over the inhabitants of the area. Who knows? It could happen. If some saintly, wise person were to suddenly appear in the midst of

Parkdale, they'd be just as likely to show up as a bag lady as looking like Jesus in sandals and a flowing robe. And what else would such an angelic being do besides bless the lost and tragic masses on the westbound Queen car? Apparently the Dalai Lama once blessed Lake Ontario, so that peace would flow out of the water taps and into the bodies of everyone in the city. At least that's what Emma remembered reading somewhere. Anything was possible, of that she was certain.

The wind picked up, and blew the woman's stench through the streetcar. Emma wanted to cover her nose, but resisted. The chanting wise-woman fantasy was becoming difficult to maintain. If the song was right, and God really was one of us, surely she'd bathe. Only one more stop till the Parkside overpass. With her free hand Emma pulled the yellow cord. The bell rang, and as she rose and moved toward the door, the volume of drumming and muttering grew.

"Oh, I know what you're all thinking," the woman yelled at no one in particular. "You think I'm crazy. You think I'm just some lunatic who doesn't know anything. That's fine. I don't give a shit, because I know what I know. I know all kinds of stuff about all kinds of people. That's why they lock me up. They don't want to know the truth. They're afraid, so they say it's me who's crazy. Ha! Look around at this world – it's the people who run it who are really fucked up. They'll tell themselves anything just so they don't have to look in the mirror. That's what I am, a walking, talking mirror in a fucked up world."

The streetcar stopped. Emma pulled her foot up from the sticky floor and stepped down. Just get me off this thing, she thought, get me away from this woman, with her bad smells and bad vibes. This time the woman screamed.

"You're one to talk. You think you're all high and mighty, but I'm not so different from you, you know. I bet your mother's just as crazy as I am. You'll see!"

Emma looked back, and the woman's eyes grabbed on to her.

"Yes, I'm talking to you! " She yelled, pointing, then started to laugh.

Emma stepped down. The streetcar doors opened. Without looking back, she ran along the platform, then down the concrete staircase that led to the street below the overpass. At the bottom, she stopped and steadied herself against the wall, thinking she might throw up. She tried to put the streetcar woman out of her mind, and continued to walk down Parkside Drive, and right along Garden Avenue. It wasn't the mental instability of the woman that had scared Emma, it was the foreboding of her prophecy – and right after Emma had imagined Shamanic powers. Be careful what you wish for.

The turning in Emma's belly stopped as soon as she saw the backyard of number 66. She turned the corner onto Indian Road, and went up to the front walk of the old 66. Her sister's black Mercedes gleamed in the driveway. Yellow tulips at the edge of the weedy garden rounded the house like a moat. Emma pulled out her phone to check the time. It was only three minutes after two o'clock. Good thing she had caught the early bus from Lester's place. She was almost right on time. She knew Rachel would assume she'd be late. That would give her sister time to get into the closet first, and then who knows what she might hide away. Not that she would want or need anything. She'd do it on principle. She'd decide that Emma didn't deserve this, or wouldn't know how to take care of that.

The prodigal granddaughter, that's what Rachel had called her the day Grandma left her body behind. Emma had spent that last night in the hospital. She had known Grandma's travelling was coming to an end, and that she was about to arrive at her destination on the other side. The doctor in palliative care told Rachel that Grandma had at least a couple more days, but Emma knew better. The night before that last night, she'd had the dream where all her teeth fell out. The cots in the palliative ward could be pulled out, in case family decided to stay with their loved one as they departed, so before she had gone to the hospital that morning, Emma had packed a bag.

She wished she wasn't thinking about that last night with Grandma as she stood on the front porch of the house, steeling herself to see her sister again. It had only been a couple days since they'd last seen each other. After Grandma had departed, Emma called her half-sister, and she came to pick Emma up from the hospital. From there, the two of them went back to Rachel's place in Yorkville. That was a bad idea. Rachel was angry, and on her own turf. She hadn't been there, that last night in the hospital, and she had questions. Why hadn't Emma called? Because it had happened too fast. One minute she had been asleep on the cot, and the next minute the nurse had woken her up and said, "It's time." Emma tried to explain this to Rachel, but her words seemed to hit some invisible wall. Rachel was hurting, and she didn't want to be. She would rather be angry.

Emma would rather have gone back to Lester's place that night, but she didn't want to rub it in. Rachel still had a thing for Lester. Emma could feel it whenever she mentioned his name. No, Rachel was fragile enough as it was. Like ice over a puddle in spring, Rachel seemed solid, but was prone to cracking. Emma should have known Rachel would need to numb herself out. At least she had let Emma sleep for a while when they got back to Rachel's place. It was still morning when Emma lay down on the pancake flat futon in Rachel's guest room, and dark outside by the time she woke again.

"You know, you could have called me," Rachel had repeated after Emma woke up, and they'd ordered a pizza. Rachel was on her second vodka tonic by then. At least the second one that Emma had seen her pour. "It's not as if it would have taken me long to get there."

Emma was sitting in the living room trying to get comfortable, but the furniture in Rachel's condo was too sparse, too modern, and too cold. Every piece of furniture was more for show than comfort. Everything screamed affluence, other than the tattered old futon Emma had slept on. That, Rachel had inexplicably kept since her university days. The white leather of the couch she sat on felt chilly beneath Emma's thighs. There were no throw blankets to be seen. There was a fireplace, but Rachel never used it. She said it was a hazard, and filled it with bricks.

"It's amazing, you know, how you just waltz in at the last minute," Rachel had continued, when it's been me holding down the fort, handling the doctors, paying Grandma's bills. And then you show up, and all of a sudden I'm the one left out in the cold." Rachel pulled two square-shaped blue plates out of her immaculate white kitchen cupboards, and placed them with an unnecessary firmness on top of the white cotton place mats that sat on her glass dining room table. Then she was back to the kitchen, fishing around loudly in the cutlery drawer. Utensils retrieved, she smashed the drawer closed, took a long sip of her drink, and then left it there on the counter as an emergency reserve.

"You were the last one she spoke to, Rachel," Emma finally managed. "When you left that night, after she said goodbye to you, she didn't say anything at all." Emma didn't tell her about the moans that came later, or how they gave Grandma morphine to calm them as that night turned to morning. She didn't mention the death rattle in the back of Grandma's throat that came with the dawn, or how her breath became deceptively soft again after that, then, following one last gasp, stopped altogether. She didn't tell Rachel how in that moment, she put her hand over their grandmother's chest until she felt the heart beat for the last time.

Rachel was at the sink, running water as Emma spoke. She wheeled around and walked into the dining room. The glasses of water in her hands sloshed over slightly as she brought them down hard on the cotton mats. Emma thought she would blow then, but instead it looked like Rachel started to laugh, then, changed her mind. She's losing it, Emma thought. Finally.

"You could have called. I didn't even get to say goodbye." Rachel's voice was a whisper. She's forgotten, Emma thought. Rachel doesn't remember Grandma's last words to her, when she told Rachel she loved her. It was incredible to Emma that Rachel couldn't seem to remember any of it. Grandma had held Rachel's hand, looked in her eyes, said she was sorry, and then said goodbye.

Emma sipped her glass of chardonnay slowly. She didn't want her mind to get sloppy and slip into thinking about Grandma picking at the sheets, moaning, and searching the room as if looking for the exit. She had to control her thoughts, or the tears would come. That would send Rachel over the edge for sure. Like a light switch, she'd flip from cool and composed in a flash if Emma started blubbering, as if Emma's display of normal human emotion were one more thing she personally would have to take care of.

Thinking back to that night at Rachel's, Emma took a breath to steady herself, as she stood in front of the door of the three stories of mortar and stone that she used to call home. She had forgotten to bring her key from Vancouver. She rang the bell and waited. Somewhere in the trees above the house, the machine gun knocking of a hungry woodpecker announced her arrival. Emma looked up to try to spot it, but the woodpecker stopped, as if self-conscious at being noticed. Rachel took her time coming to the door. When she opened it, she looked fresh and efficient. Emma felt dishevelled, her clothes sticking to her from the heat, and her eyes still puffy from crying. Rachel ushered Emma into the house, not speaking until they were both in the kitchen.

"Would you like something to drink?" Rachel asked, as if Emma were a stranger. As if she had never lived there and helped create the air that the house breathed in and out every day. Emma nodded. Rachel got a glass from the cupboard, turned on the tap and poured Emma some water. In a second, it seemed, the glass was in Emma's hand without her remembering how it got there. She lifted the glass to her lips and drank. Grandmother water, give me strength. Rachel's taken over already. Here we go.

"So, I made up a list to help keep us on track." Rachel pointed toward the fridge. Emma looked at list on the fridge, but was too far away to read what it said. She didn't bother taking a step forward. The words remained scribbles. She felt like a rebellious teenager. A rebel without a cause. Or, without a cause she'd explicitly stated. She didn't plan on being difficult. It was a pattern between her and Rachel that was born of natural instinct, a result of the clash of their totem animals. Rachel was a rabbit – always in a rush, and Emma, a turtle, wanting to take her sweet time.

She could just tell Rachel she didn't want to sell the house. That would be more direct, but would also likely lead to confrontation. Emma took a step forward and looked at the list. "Hmm," she said. "Okay. This looks doable."

Rachel turned toward the doorway, and began walking down the hall without a word. Emma followed her into their grandmother's bedroom. Grief, she reminded herself, is sneaking its way through both of us.

Rachel slid open the faux wooden shutter doors of the clothes closet. Grandma filled the room.

"It smells like her," Emma said, wrapping her arms around herself.

"Of course it smells like her. It's full of her clothes. Please, Emma, get a grip. Let's not have a scene today, okay?" Rachel took a garbage bag from under her arm, and unfolded it.

Emma let go of herself. "All I said is that it smells like her in here. Which it does, does it not?" Emma took a breath, and reminded herself to be patient.

"It's not a big deal. It's putting clothes into garbage bags. Simple." Rachel licked her thumb and forefinger to pull the plastic apart, then shook the bag open with a fluttering of air.

Emma stepped toward a row of dressing gowns. Sam got her

one every Mother's Day, and Grandma never had the heart to throw any of them out. Emma reached out to a deep purple terry-cloth bathrobe, as old as Emma's memories on Indian Road. She brought its sleeve to her nose and inhaled.

"We're not getting rid of everything are we? I mean is that what you had in mind? Because I thought we'd be going through stuff, you know? See what we want to keep for ourselves."

"You're kidding me. Most of her clothes are in tatters. I already threw out all those polyester-blend pants in the dresser. Every single pair were altered by hand or just left hanging. And those elastic waistbands she used to cut when her back was hurting? Oh, but you wouldn't know that would you? You weren't around for that part."

Emma turned her back on Rachel and her garbage bag. Her voice was a whisper. "Some of these sweaters are nice."

"I bought her most of those. She never wore them. So if you want something with sentimental value you've got nothing there with those. But keep them if you want. They're all good quality. Brand names, every one. At least better than the stuff she usually got from K-Mart or wherever it was she used to shop. I don't think any of this stuff will fit me anyway, so if you want to go through it, fine. I'll be in the dining room."

"No. I mean, don't you even want to look at her hats or scarves or something? I could give you first pick of those if you want." Emma looked at the garbage bag dangling in Rachel's hand as if it were a gun.

"First pick. How generous of you, Emma. No, you go ahead." Rachel thrust the garbage bag toward her. Emma left her hands at her side, and took a step back. Of course Rachel would take out her anger on Emma. Where else could it go? Rachel had to think of herself as the rock. It was the only way she knew how to stay solid, by telling herself that it was everyone else who was falling apart. It was an old trick, and Emma had seen it a million times. It was a reprise of the "Ballad of Rachel the Martyr."

Emma should know better than to let it get to her. Still, there was that old feeling again, that mild itch of violence crawling under her skin. That impulsive reaction that made her want to throw something, a glass or a cup no one wanted. She wanted to smash something – hear it shatter when it hit the ground. At least she could acknowledge it, this urge. But Rachel? With Rachel, everything was held in tight, only coming out in ways that were twisted.

Rachel let the bag go, turned and left the bedroom. The black plastic trembled to the ground.

10.

AT HER FATHER'S FUNERAL, there were pictures where Rachel's dad should be, and a vase that Sam said was full of his ashes. The vase was a rusty silver colour and Rachel wondered if they found his head and burned that too. She looked up at the ceiling of the room they were all sitting in. It was like a church inside but more boring, and without the stained glass windows. The ceiling was yellow with wooden crossbeams that had been painted yellow as well. Rachel imagined what would happen if the ceiling caught on fire with all of them inside, which of the beams would fall down first, and in what order. She wanted to check the light switches she saw at the back of the hall, but just put her hands under her bum instead. There was a preacher guy at the front of the room telling everyone about her dad. The preacher said Dad had been a good provider and liked to do gardening. He said he had liked astronomy and had loved his family. Rachel didn't like the preacher, and the way everything he said about her dad was in the past tense. His hair was bald on top and parted way down on the side, like he was fooling anyone. Some of his hair was going the wrong way, flopping down over his ear, waving at them. Rachel wanted to laugh and for Sam to laugh at it too, but Sam was just looking down at his hands. He hadn't taken his gloves off yet. Rachel started to whisper to Sam about the waving hair, but he wouldn't look up. "Fuck-off, Rachel," he said.

Rachel knew that when terrible things happened, everyone was supposed to be sad and all messed up, but that's not what happened in their house. Grandma didn't let it. After the funeral, she decided that she was moving out of her condo in Florida and moving in with them for a while. She took over everything, even the air. She wore lavender perfume, watched *The Bob Newhart* show, and played ABBA and Sonny & Cher albums way too loud on the living-room hi-fi. Once, she threatened, to pour all of Mom's rum down the drain, so Mom had to hide it in a suitcase under her bed after that. You could still smell it on her, but Grandma let it go. Likely because, other than the drinking, Mom did what Grandma said. She acted like a little girl, one who talked to herself out loud. "It's only grief," Grandma said. "It's normal."

After she was done bossing Mom around, Grandma got two men with big muscles and tattoos who rode up on motorcycles to take Sam's secret trunk right out of his room and put it in their van. Sam came home just as they were getting it out onto the front lawn.

"What the fuck?" he yelled.

Then the bald muscleman walked over to Sam and said, "Watch your mouth, boy. It's time to grow up. Be a man and look out for your family now or I'll be back so we can talk about it some more, you understand?"

Sam looked at him, then at the ground. Grandma stood in the doorway nodding, before she went back inside to get dinner going.

As for Rachel, Grandma pretty much left her alone during the first few weeks after the funeral, even when she caught Rachel messing with the light switches. The first time Grandma saw her go through the on, off, on, off routine, she just stopped sweeping the floor and stared at Rachel with a sad look on her face.

A few weeks later, Grandma decided that Rachel should have a party since she didn't do anything for her real birthday, other than eating ice-cream in bed and trying not to scratch.

"You only turn nine once," Grandma said. "And if you spend your birthday with the chicken pox, you should be allowed to have a do-over."

Rachel was allowed to invite as many people as she wanted to her not-birthday party, and there were balloons and cake, and Marcia Miller won a deck of cards and some sea monkeys for being the best at pin the tail on the donkey. Grandma gave Rachel a book called *The Secret Garden*, and Mom even got her something; a longhaired calico kitten Rachel called Diana Prince, who slept in her dirty clothes hamper. Sam gave Rachel twenty-five bucks cause he was only washing dishes at the Burger Chef now.

"I'm sorry, Rach," he said. "I'm lying low for now, so the cash flow's tight. I'll get you the other fifty bucks when I'm back in the game." He winked, and Rachel told him thanks and that twenty-five bucks was excellent. She never did figure out what she'd do with seventy-five whole dollars anyhow, and was happy to get anything since Sam had found out that Rachel had scratched his Ziggy Stardust album.

After her birthday, Grandma told Rachel, "In a couple of weeks, you and me are going to clean up that backyard of yours." They had to wait a while for the frost to stop coming in the morning, but when that finally happened, they went out with rakes and cleaned up all the bits of paper and plastic and tin cans. Then, they found a spot by the fence where a flowerbed had grown over.

"We're going to make a special spot for you here, Rachel," Grandma said.

When they were finished preparing the soil, they planted some forget-me-nots and other seeds, and Rachel made a sign: "*Rachel's Secret Garden. KEEP OUT!*"

Nothing happened for what seemed like ages, even though Grandma made Rachel water the dirt every morning before school. Then one day, Rachel went out with Diana Prince and saw that tiny blue flowers had burst out all around the edges of the grass.

"Those are crocuses," Grandma told Rachel. I planted those the year your Grandpa died. And that bush over there is lavender, that'll be blooming as soon as it warms up. The forget-me-nots won't come up until next year, but you've got sweet peas in there too. Your mother planted those. She used to insist that we put them on the table. She never would tell me why." Grandma said, shaking her head. "They don't bloom until summer, those ones, but they'll still be fragrant when you head back to school in the fall. Trust me, it'll be sweet, you'll see."

11.

EMMA WORKED HER WAY through her grandmother's closet. Each piece of clothing called to her, had a story to tell. But she knew better than to dawdle, Rachel was on a schedule. There was a list to contend with on the fridge, a mission to be accomplished. Rachel needed her lists. They were her security blanket.

Emma stuffed all the sweaters and dresses into the garbage bags at her feet. There were already three full bags ready to go to the Sally Ann, and one almost-full bag of things Emma wanted to keep for herself. Her eyes had puffed up again. Her mascara was smudged and smeared on her wet sleeve. When she came to her grandmother's dressing gowns, she lifted the hanger that held the purple terry-cloth one up off the rack. Her legs buckled as the smell of it wafted over her, and she crumpled down, settling cross-legged on the floor. The bathrobe landed in her lap. It was her grandmother's favourite, the one she had decided to bring when she went to the hospital that last time. It was the only thing Emma had taken from her grandmother's room that night. Rachel must have brought it back and hung it up.

Rachel had told Emma that she had gone to visit Grandma that last morning before work and found her sitting on the bathroom floor. "She wasn't upset, wasn't crying or calling out when she heard me come in. She was just sitting there like it was the most natural thing in the world." Rachel had tried to help her back on her feet, but Grandma said, "Don't bother love, these legs of mine are done for. Call your sister now, will you dear? I want her to do my hair."

"It's the most ridiculous thing I've ever heard," Rachel said, when she got Emma on the phone. "You should see her. She hit the sink on her way down. The bruises on her ribs are already purple. She really needs to go to the hospital, but she won't let me call an ambulance until you come. She said she wants you to do her hair. Can you believe it? I really shouldn't even listen to her, but you know how stubborn she is. She said she's not going anywhere till you get here. So I've booked you a flight from Vancouver. It leaves in two and a half hours. You can pick up the ticket at the counter. Then take a cab from the airport. I'll give the driver the fare when you get here."

Emma had hung up and wiped the sleep out of her eyes. Outside it was still dark, her window with a view of the mountains, a black square on the wall. All she had said to her sister during the call was, "Hello, okay and goodbye." Emma had been expecting the news. She had already known that Grandma had started travelling. Lucy, from the Java Hut had told her that's what they called it in the Caribbean – travelling. Moving from the land of living to the land of spirits apparently didn't happen in a flash, it was a journey.

Emma remembered hearing about a cat in a nursing home that would sense when someone's soul started travelling, and would sit on the person's bed with them until they passed on. Or about the man in great health, who suddenly decided one day to write out his will and get his affairs in order, then died immediately afterward. It was if someone's actual death was like thunder, nothing more than an echo of something that had already occurred.

Emma had first felt her grandmother embark on that journey a week earlier, when she had dreamt of a snake losing its skin. It was the same dream she'd had before Barney died. The next morning, she had done her laundry and called the cat sitter. Then she'd had a dream that all her teeth fell out of her head. She knew about that one from a translation of Artemidorus's *Interpretation of Dreams,* a book Lester had bought her for her birthday one year. Even in second-century Greece, losing a mouthful of teeth meant the death of someone you knew was likely. The morning after that dream, Rachel had called.

When Emma's cab arrived at 66 Indian Road later that day, Rachel and Grandma were in the bedroom. Grandma was sitting on the edge of the bed in her purple terry-cloth bathrobe. Rachel was standing, scolding her for not using her walker.

"I mean this is why I got it for you." She spoke as if Grandma were deaf, or a foreigner.

Emma stood in the doorway watching for a moment, then said, "Rachel, could you kindly give us a moment so I can do her hair?" Rachel looked stunned for a second.

"Oh you're here. Sure, fine – whatever. Go ahead," she said, and left the room. Grandma laughed.

"Emma! Come here and let me see you, love." Emma patted the air around her grandmother, who seemed smaller than she had remembered her being when she last saw her at Christmas. Emma asked to see the bruise. Grandma lifted her shirt. Emma drew a breath, but didn't say a word.

"You don't have to be so hard on her. She does a lot for me you know," Grandma said, as Emma plugged in the curling iron.

"I know Grandma. We all know. We are constantly reminded." Emma took a tube of hand cream from her purse. Grandma held out both her hands. Emma squeezed a dollop of cream onto each, and massaged it into her grandmother's skin.

"You want pink or clear?"

"Pink." Grandma leaned forward to survey her choices, then winced.

"It hurts, eh?" Emma said as she took a bottle of pink polish off the dresser top, then sat across from her grandmother in a chair.

Grandma nodded, placed her hands on Emma's knees, fingers stretched out and shaking.

"Bad?"

"Bad enough. It's better than it was though. Rachel gave me some Advil. Don't worry. We've got all the time in the world, love. I'm just glad you're here."

Emma gently patted one of her grandmother's hands down on her knee. It stilled. The other she held as she painted on the polish.

"You know I heard that in the Caribbean they call it travelling. You know what I mean, Gram? Like, when someone's getting ready to go. Travelling. I like that, don't you?"

"Yes, I like that too, love. Travelling. That's good."

Footsteps approached in the hall. Emma and Grandma both looked up to see Rachel standing in the doorway, looking at Grandma's hot pink nails.

"Oh for God's sakes, you're kidding me. You're giving her a manicure?"

Emma used her foot to kick the door closed. The footsteps retreated.

After Emma was finished with Grandma's nails, she curled the thin crispy wisps of grey into orderly waves. It wouldn't have to last long, just a couple of days in the hospital at most, and maybe enough of the shape would hold till the end.

Emma took out her make-up bag. "Just a bit of blush for the lady, what do you think?"

"Why not?" Grandma replied, her eyes softening.

12.

EMMA WAS SIX-AND-A-HALF, and it was almost time for school to start. She knew because all the commercials showed shiny clean children buying binders and pens and new jeans. Jamie Francis kept talking about how he was going to see all his friends soon, and Nina went to the drug store to spend her allowance on blood-red back-to-school nail polish. It was time for Emma and Lester to finally go to school now too, but nothing was happening. Mamma Shirley wasn't buying them anything, or saying anything at all. Jamie Francis told Emma that six was the age when you have to go to school, or you got thrown in the Pen. He was going to junior high school that year, and could name all the provinces and territories. Nina already knew how to speak French, but Emma didn't know anything. She didn't even know how to read. She had never been inside John Robson Elementary School; she'd only hit tennis balls against it with Jamie Francis a couple of times. Lester didn't know much either, but he didn't give a hoot. He said he didn't have to worry about school, because his parents would be back to get him before it started. He still wore his shiny shoes and his bow tie. Jamie Francis said the other kids were going to make mincemeat out of him. Emma vowed she wouldn't let that happen, and planned to put some willow branches in her schoolbag, just in case she needed something to swing at someone.

Mamma Shirley said there was plenty of time and moved through the house too fast for Emma to be able to ask her anything else. She was the Tasmanian devil twirling around and around, cleaning everything all the time, telling Emma and the other kids that she was too busy for their foolishness. Everything seemed to be foolishness to Mamma Shirley those days. She had a new job, now that Just Jack was home all the time. She worked at Woodlands where the bad kids go. Emma thought that Woodlands was a pretend place that Nina had made up to scare her, but no. It was a real place all right, not only for retarded kids, but ones who were so bad and crazy that they got sent away, even if they had real parents. Emma had figured out that "retarded" meant not smart like normal people, but it wasn't nice to say it out loud because nobody could help the way they were born. Sometimes Mamma Shirley had to work late and there was no dinner, so Jamie Francis or Nina got it. Toast with peanut butter or mini-pizzas, usually. That was okay because Emma knew why everything was different. It was because Just Jack was gone now. His body was still there, but the rest of him was gone.

It had started at the beginning of the summer. One day out of nowhere, everything changed. Just Jack stopped wearing his blue shirt with the badge on it. They weren't allowed to ask him why he wasn't going to work or say anything at all about the Pen, which was hard because it had been all over the news. One day Just Jack himself had been on TV, walking fast, looking scared, with his hand pushing the camera away. The announcer had said that he was one of the accused. That meant he was one of the men who had shot the lady hostage. She'd been a chef, at least she had been until Just Jack or one of the other guards at the Pen shot her dead.

Jamie Francis said it was an accident, and that they meant to shoot one of the bad guys, but that the lady was in the way. "There was a goddamned riot, Emma! Imagine all those criminals running around like crazy taking over the place. We're lucky he got out of there alive!"

Mamma Shirley had gotten mad at the dead lady. She smacked her fist on the table and yelled, "Well what the hell did she expect? Did she think she was working in Disneyland? Things happen sometimes. It's no place for a woman to have been working. What did she expect? I don't understand why you can't go back. Everyone knows it wasn't you. You could go back, you know. There's no shame in it." And *poof*, Just Jack was gone. He'd grabbed his coat, gone out the door, and stayed out till way after they all had gone to bed.

"They have to do an investigation," Jamie Francis said. "That's why he's not allowed to go back to work at the Pen. They have to ask everyone what happened, and see whose bullets ended up in the lady. Then they're going to have a big trial like on *Perry Mason*."

So, all Just Jack did that summer was wait for the investigation to start. Emma had hoped there would be another camping trip to the Kootanays, but Jamie Francis said there was no chance in hell. Just Jack had stayed glued to the television, watching the news, re-runs of *Adam 12* and episodes of *The Rockford Files*, and eating Pop Tarts and Spaghetti-O's right out of the can. When they had forgot he was there, and made a ruckus in the living room, he'd tell them to bugger off outside.

Mamma Shirley would stand in front of the TV when she got home and tell him to go mow the lawn or run to the store to get milk. "I should be so lucky," she'd say, "I'd love to sit around all day and watch my soaps. Who knows what's happening in Genoa City now. The TV *Guide* says this might be Katherine Chancellor's last season. That'd be just my luck."

Emma wanted to ask someone about kindergarten, but she was afraid because of what Nina Buziak said about Woodlands. Nina had said that a girl named Suzy Sinclair from her old foster home used to live there. "Suzy was my best-friend, so I got the real-deal low down on what it's like there," Nina said.

"Well if your best-friend used to live there, then she must be retarded, too."

Nina laughed. "They didn't send Suzy to Woodlands because she's retarded, Emma. They sent Suzy to Woodlands because she doesn't take shit from anyone, and because she stuck a fork in her foster dad's arm while he was sleeping on the couch one day."

"Why?" Emma asked, eyes wide.

Nina sighed, "Well if you must know, Emma, it's because he kept trying to fuck her and she'd had it with him. Before that she tried to set the house on fire. Poured vodka all over his bed, and tossed a lit match on top. Burned up the whole bedroom." Nina laughed. "Suzy Sinclair is a bad ass, that's why she got sent to Woodlands, not because she's a retarded little Indian like you."

Nina said the "f" word. And her best friend had stabbed her foster dad in the arm with a fork. Emma didn't know what to say next. So, she walked out of the room, slow and backwards to the sound of Nina's laughing.

The investigation into the shooting at the Pen led to a big trial that took place on the first day of kindergarten. Just Jack had to go to the trial, and Mamma Shirley was going too, so Nina was supposed to take Emma and Lester to their first day at school. That morning, after everyone had their breakfast, Emma tried to tell Mamma Shirley that she could find her own way there, but Mamma Shirley said she was sorry, and that it was time for Nina to help.

Mamma Shirley, Just Jack, Jamie Francis and Nina all went upstairs to get dressed and showered. Lester was playing truck driver in the backyard. Emma knew because she heard him say "10-4 good buddy" into the garden spade. He was still in his pajamas. Emma went outside for a while to try to convince Lester to get ready for school, but Lester said, "No way, José. Keep on truckin'," and tooted on an imaginary horn.

Emma went in the house and got a pair of Lester's jeans, a

plaid shirt, and his Superman underwear. "You better put these on," she told him. "Everyone knows that this is what all the truck drivers wear. You can't drive a truck in your pajamas, you know." Lester bought it, and stripped down right there in the backyard.

After that, Emma went to find Jamie Francis to see if he could tell her how to get to the little kids' school. But she was too late, he'd gone already, and so had Nina. Emma was pretty sure she knew the way, but decided that she should have a map just in case. She went into the garage, and got into the car to see if she could find one in the glove compartment.

While she was bent down looking, Emma heard the garage door open and close. Then she saw Just Jack come in and root around under the garbage bag in the trash can. Then, as Emma peeked over the dashboard, he pulled out a bottle and Emma knew there was booze in it by how sneaky and relieved he looked. He drank and drank and drank, then sat down on the cement step and started to cry like a little kid. His big shoulders shook up and down, until he finally stopped. Then he rubbed his hands across his face, stood up and went back inside.

Emma stayed in the car until she'd counted a hundred Mississippis. She knew if Just Jack caught her in there, watching him cry like a baby, she'd be in trouble for sure.

Finally, Emma slipped out and went into the backyard. She'd forgotten to bring the map with her, but didn't care about that anymore. She'd find her way. She had to talk Lester into coming with her to school. "Maybe your parents will be waiting for you there," she told him.

Lester looked at her with big eyes and a smile. Emma felt like a heel, but she knew she had to do it. If Lester didn't go to school, he might be thrown in the Pen, or worse, if he opened his trap and started yakking about his dead parents coming back they might think he's loony and send him to Woodlands. Emma knew that Lester would be disappointed when his parents didn't show up that day, but it was better than Emma losing him forever.

Emma and Lester made their way down Columbia Street, further than either of them had ever been without having Just Jack, Mamma Shirley or Jamie Francis with them. Emma led them down the street and around the corner until they saw the school. Just the sight of it made Emma feel smarter. There were no kids outside playing. The schoolyard was deserted. Emma knew they were late, and that now they were going to get in trouble. She'd have to come up with a good excuse. While she was standing there thinking, Lester walked over to the side of the building, and peered into a ground-floor window. At that moment, an old man with long grey hair, holding hands with a little girl walked up to where Emma was standing by the doors. Lester ran over to them.

"What are you doing out here, you two?" the old man asked. Emma thought he was going to give her heck, but instead his dark, wrinkled face opened up into a smile.

"I'm um – um – " Emma started, but then stopped. What could she say? What was she doing still standing outside anyway?

"Nice to meet you Um Um. And who's your side kick there?" the old man asked. The little girl giggled. She was about Emma's age, with long dark hair and skin the colour of maple syrup. "Shouldn't you be inside though Um Um? I mean, I'm not an expert or anything, but I think they teach the classes inside the school, not outside." The little girl giggled again.

"I'm Jenny," she said. "And this is my Grandpa."

Emma introduced herself, and Lester, who was standing in front of Jenny's grandfather, staring at his long hair.

"Are you an Indian?" Lester asked before Emma could stop him. The old man laughed.

"Do I look like I come from India? I'm Chinook. What are you a cowboy or something? You gonna try to run me out of town on your horse?"

"I'm a truck driver," Lester said. "If you could see my superman underwear you'd know."

Jenny and her grandpa both started laughing then. The grandfather laughed so hard that little tears squeezed out of his wrinkly eyes. Emma was about to say something to try to explain Lester, so they wouldn't make fun of him, but a teacher came out of the doors and looked at the four of them standing there.

"What's going on here?" she asked. "I'm Miss Higgins. These kids should be inside, not out here fooling around." She gave Jenny's grandpa a cold stare. "School starts at nine a.m. Sharp."

Then she looked at the two of them, "Are you Emma and Lester?"

Emma nodded.

"Well, your foster mother called to make sure you made it to school. I had to say no. Now I'll have to leave a message for her at the courthouse so she knows you're okay. She was worried sick. She said your sister was supposed to take you to school and pick you up today."

The teacher looked at Jenny. "You're Jenny, right?" Jenny nodded her head, gripping tight onto her grandpa's arm.

"Okay then. All three of you, in you come." Then she looked at Jenny's grandfather again. "Nine a.m., sharp," she said, turning to open the door.

Emma went in first. Already, she'd decided that school was not going to be any fun. She wished that she could stay and laugh with the old man some more, but no. Inside they went. Jenny took hold of Emma's hand, and Emma held on to Lester's.

"Wait! My parent's won't know what room I'm in," Lester started, but Emma gave his arm a quick yank, and he shut his trap. Jenny turned to wave to her grandfather. There were tears in her eyes.

Jenny wasn't the only Indian in the class. There were two others, little boys who kept their dark eyes down when Miss Higgins spoke to them. Emma tried to ask them if their grandfathers were medicine men too, but Miss Higgins told her to not be such a nosy-pants and to sit down. Miss Higgins wasn't so mean after all. After recess, she let them draw a picture of their favourite animal. Emma decided to draw Barney, and was putting glitter on his head to show all the words that he would say to Emma that nobody else could hear. Jenny leaned over to look and told Emma her picture was skookum. Emma dropped her crayon.

"Skookum means jail. Just Jack told us," Emma said.

"No, it doesn't. Skookum means great. Extra super-duper great. It's not a white people word. It's an Chinook word, so I should know," Jenny said defiantly.

Emma thought about arguing with Jenny, but now she wasn't so sure. What if Just Jack got it wrong? Just Jack wasn't an Indian, so what did he know?

At the end of the day, Miss Higgins told the class that they were wonderful and bravo for their first day at school. Now they had to wait till their parents came to get them. Jenny's grandpa was the first to come take her home. Jenny gave Emma a big hug and called her Cheechako, and then giggled. Jenny told Emma that the word meant new friend, but also kind of meant that Emma didn't really know much. Emma didn't mind, because she knew from the love in her eyes that Jenny was only teasing. Her grandpa gave Emma a high-five, winked at Lester, then took Jenny's hand and walked toward the playground.

While they waited for Nina to show up, Emma and Lester watched all the real parents come to get the other kids and take them home. Emma was worried, but she pretended to be listening to Lester, who was telling Emma that his parents were probably going to come get him anyway, and how he'd ask them to give her a ride back to Columbia Street. Miss Higgins kept looking at the clock and then making little *tsking* noises and shaking her head. After a long time had passed, and the school was quiet except for Emma and Lester, Miss Higgins gave a big sigh and said, "Okay you two. It looks like I'm going to have to take you home myself." Then she got up and headed to the door. "Come on then," she said. "I don't have all day."

Emma and Lester walked outside with Miss Higgins toward the parking lot. Emma kept quiet, and tried to keep Lester quiet too. She knew Miss Higgins wasn't happy to be taking them home. Twice, Emma thought. It's only the first day of school, and already she and Lester had been in trouble two times. Emma was wondering what Miss Higgins was going to say to Mamma Shirley and whether it was Nina's fault because she was the one who was supposed to pick them up, when she saw Jenny and her old grandpa heading over to them from the playground.

"I can take them home if you like," he said, pointing to Emma and Lester, his wrinkly face turning up around his mouth and his eyes going all crinkly and kind.

Miss Higgins looked at him, and then at Emma and Lester, then said slowly, "Well, I guess that would be okay." Miss Higgins looked toward the school, and then around the parking lot. For a minute, it looked like she was going to say something else, but then it was as if she were a balloon that just had all the air let out of it, and she stopped talking, and smiled. "That's very nice of you to offer Mr –"

"Olemm," said Jenny's Grandpa. "Last name's Olemm, Miss. But you can call me Jim."

"Well thank you, Jim. Are you sure that it won't put you out?"

"Nope. I'm happy to do it, Miss Higgins," Jenny's grandpa said.

"Okay, Jim," she said, looking around the schoolyard one last time. "That's very kind. They live in a house down at the other end of Columbia – "

"I know where my house is Miss Higgins. I can show him," Emma said.

"Looks like we're all good here then, Miss. Don't worry. I'll get these kids home safe," Jim said.

Miss Higgins said okay again, got in her car and drove away.

Jenny's Grandpa looked at Emma and Lester. "Don't you worry, you two. Everything's skookum."

Emma decided right then that she loved Jenny's grandpa, and wished that he was her and Lester's Grandpa too. On the way home, Jenny and Lester walked up ahead, and took turns kicking a tin can down the street. Emma dawdled behind so she could talk to Jenny's grandpa. "Um, Jenny's grandpa," she started hesitatingly. "Can I ask you a question?"

"Sure, Emma. You can call me Jim. Or Big Jim, it's up to you. So what did you want to know?" he asked.

"Well, I wanted to ask you – how do you know for sure that you're an Indian?" Emma asked.

"Not Indian, Chinook." Jenny's grandpa replied.

"Sorry," Emma said. "I mean I know that you know for sure that you're a Chinook, and Jenny knows for sure that she is because her parents are and stuff, but I'm wondering, for the kids who don't have parents anymore, how would they know if they were Indian, and not something else. Like a Paki or coloured or something."

"Those are bad words, but a good question, Emma." Big Jim looked serious for the first time since Emma had met him. He looked at Emma for a long time, then said, "Well, there's no way to know for sure what someone is if they don't know their parents, or where their parents are from. But my guess is that you're not Chinook, or from any Nation, Emma. You may have some in your blood, who knows, but from the looks of it, you've got something else mixed in there too. People like you, in my language, we call them 'Sitkum Siwash'. That means you're a mix of different cultures. You have white people in you I think, and another part something else, maybe Black. Can't tell unless you see the parents. And even then sometimes it's hard to know for sure," Jenny's grandpa laughed.

Emma was disappointed. She had hoped that she was at least part Chinook or some kind of Indian, even though it would make Nina be even meaner to her. Emma didn't say much after that. It wasn't that she was mad at Big Jim. He called her a name, but Emma didn't get the feeling it was a bad name. As with Jenny, his eyes told her the truth.

When they got to Emma and Lester's house, the driveway was empty. Emma started wondering if she was going to get in trouble when Mamma Shirley and Just Jack came home. Emma thought about Just Jack in the garage that morning, drinking and crying, and wondered what happened to him at the trial. What if he got sent to the Pen? Would they be allowed to stay with Mamma Shirley? Then what would happen? The questions filled up all the space in her head, churning till her ears started to ring.

Just then, Nina yelled out through the kitchen window.

"Emma! Lester! Get your asses in here, dinner's ready."

Emma looked at Jenny and her Grandfather. All the happy that was in everybody's face before was gone.

"Mesachie," Big Jim said under his breath, as he nodded at the window Nina's yelling had just come out of, his eyes looking dark like just before it rains. He looked at Emma and Lester, and said, "Keep on truckin', you two." Lester beamed at that one.

Inside, Nina and Jamie Francis were already sitting at the kitchen table eating their mini-pizzas. Nina looked at Emma with a face that would have looked friendly if it had been on someone else.

"Come and join us, Emma," Nina said. "Lester, I made your favourite."

Lester smiled and sat down at the table, but Emma knew that something was up. Nina was never nice to anyone unless she had to be. Emma stayed quiet as she sat in her seat.

"Cat got your tongue, Emma?" Nina asked. "Okay then, suit yourself."

"I'm done," Jamie Francis said, put his plate in the sink and left the kitchen without another word. Emma started eating, picking the pepperoni circles off her pizza, giving them to Lester.

"Oh, and by the way," Nina said as she put her own dish in the sink. "If Shirley asks how you got home today, you tell her that I came to pick you up, okay? We don't want anybody's parents getting the wrong idea, do we?" Nina walked out of the room.

Lester stared after her in horror, then looked down at his mini-pizza. Little drops fell from his face, and onto his plate. Emma didn't want to lie, and knew that Nina was the one who'd get in trouble if they told the truth, but she didn't want to get Mamma Shirley mad either. She was trying to decide what to do, when Jamie Francis yelled from the living room. "It's him! It's him! Just Jack is on TV!"

Emma, Lester and Nina ran to join Jamie Francis on the couch, just in time to hear the announcer say that the trial was over, and that it was Just Jack's gun who shot the chef lady at the beginning of the summer. The announcer said that they had footage from the courthouse that afternoon, and then the screen showed Mamma Shirley and Just Jack walking to the car. Mamma Shirley had her hard eyes on, and Just Jack looked like he was going to cry again. When Jamie Francis saw that part, he didn't say anything. Lester went up to his room, watching Nina out of the corner of his eyes. Nina laughed, and looked back at the television.

"Oh," she said. "Now he's in for it. Just Jack is gonna be in big trouble now. You can't go around shooting people, you know. Just Jack is a criminal! They're gonna throw him in the Pen, for sure," she said, and laughed again.

Jamie Francis turned away from the television and shot Nina a look like he wanted to punch her in the nose, or yell at her or something. But Emma knew that he was afraid of Nina, even though he never said so. Instead he went to his room and put on his Jimi Hendrix album really loud. You could hear him screaming along with the music. "Hey Joe, where you going with that gun in your hand?" It wasn't singing Jamie Francis was doing, it was angry yelling and loud noises like he was moving all the furniture around.

"Jamie Francis is a fag," Nina said, turning of the television. "Everyone at high school knows it. I know you think he's this cool guy, Emma, but you don't know what goes on when you're in high school. You can't go around having a faggy name like Francis without all the other kids making fun of you. He's gonna get his this year, you'll see. I heard Brian Swanson say so in homeroom. He said, "That Francis kid with the bandana, he's done for!" Nina said.

Emma hated bacon-head Nina Buziak more than she had ever hated anyone before in that moment, and was going to tell her so, when Just Jack and Mamma Shirley came through the door. Nina and Emma looked at them, waiting for them to tell the two of them all about it, even though everyone already knew what happened, but neither Mamma Shirley or Just Jack said anything. Mamma Shirley didn't even give Emma heck for walking to school without anyone in the morning. Instead, she just asked if they had eaten anything yet. Emma nodded, and Nina said, "Yes, I made mini pizzas for everyone." It was like she wanted Mamma Shirley to be proud of her or tell her how grown up she was and what a big help, but all Mamma Shirley said was, "Good," and then she went in the kitchen and started opening and closing the fridge and smashing pots around. She was making dinner for Just Jack and her, without telling anyone anything about the trial or the investigation or saying anything about the chef lady at all.

Just Jack slumped down in his chair in the living room, and watched TV. He didn't even yell up to Jamie Francis to tell him to turn his hi-fi down. He pretended to be watching *Jeopardy*, but Emma could tell he was gone.

13.

WITH EMMA BUSY SORTING the clothes in Grandma's closet, Rachel went back to the dining-room table, which was covered with paperwork. Before Emma arrived to help go through their grandmother's things, Rachel had made piles for the important papers like the deed to the house, unpaid utility bills, and letters from the insurance company. Rachel had created a filing system for her grandmother a few years ago. All her important documents had been given a slot in the neatly labeled accordion files that were left piled in the corner of the living room.

Months ago, after she had come to the house one day to help her grandmother write out the monthly checks, she discovered an unfilled prescription note and a cable bill in the folder marked "death certificates." When she had confronted her, her grandmother had said, "Oh, Rachel, really. I'm ninety-six years old. I might pop off anytime now, and I'll be damned if I spend my last afternoon sorting one little piece of meaningless paper from another." The result was a jumble of documents, stuffed haphazardly into the accordion files. So, Rachel had to dump the contents of the files on the dining-room table in order to start over again. She knew Emma wouldn't be any help. She wasn't surprised when her sister made a beeline to the walk-in. Rachel couldn't care less about hats and sweaters. The accordion files now sat on the empty dining room chairs, waiting to be properly filled.

On top of the pile was a letter from Veterans' Affairs about her grandmother's Benefits for Survivors, money that the government sent every month to widows of service-men. Rachel's grandpa was already dead by the time she was born, but she'd heard some stories. Grandpa had been in the RCAF, stationed in England during the war. Back in the old days, when Rachel was a kid, before Mom became Wanda, Grandma had told the two of them that she didn't know what had hit her when all of a sudden all these young Canadian boys in their crisp foreign uniforms filled the streets of York, replacing the local boys who had gone off to fight.

"We were all going out with the Canadians back then," she'd told them. "They'd have these dances on Friday nights. That's where I met your grandfather. Oh, he tried to get away, though! He asked me to dance, and once we were out on the floor he stepped on my foot. Oh, he was really embarrassed, like." Whenever Grandma told the story, her Yorkshire accent would thicken. "I just laughed and said don't worry. Everybody knows that Canadians can't dance. You should have seen his face! He was beet red, and tried to storm off the floor. But I wouldn't let him. Grabbed his hand and made him dance with me again."

Whenever Grandma had talked about what it was like to live through the war, the same stories had flowed out of her. She told them about the ration books, and how everyone needed to carry identity cards. She told them that since nobody had any money, it wasn't a big deal. Things were the same for everyone.

"None of the girls could afford stockings, so if we were going down to the dances or the pub – we always had shandy or a glass of sherry back then – we'd draw black lines on the back of each other's legs. And every once in a while the air-raid warden would walk down the street yelling: *lights out, lights out!*"

Rachel had asked if she was scared, if she remembered being afraid of getting blown-up. Grandma had said no; it wasn't like that back then.

"To tell you the truth, it was kind of exciting," she said. "We had a bomb shelter in our backyard, you know, our family. And one night your Grandpa and I saw a plane break open in the sky. It happened right in front of us. Enemy aircraft, it was. After that, whenever your Grandpa had to fly out on a mission, he would tip his wing as he flew over the city. That was his way of telling me I didn't have to worry about anything. Your Grandpa was always looking out for me, he was. He was a good man, no matter what anyone says. And *that's that*."

Rachel tried to imagine what it would look like to see a plane break open right before your eyes. What it would be like to be that girl from Yorkshire, and to get on a ship and sail halfway around the world to start a new life with a man you married because he had looked good in his uniform. It was unfathomable

Underneath a two-year-old phone bill, Rachel found a postcard of Rosie the Riveter, with her red headscarf and flexed muscle under the words "We Can Do It!" Rachel laughed out loud, then covered her mouth.

"Your grandfather used to call me Rosalyn the Riveter," her grandmother would say proudly to anyone within earshot. "Us girls, we did our part while our boys were away. Everybody had a wartime job, unless you were a cripple or something. Your Auntie Dolly worked for the Women's Auxiliary Air Force. They did office work in the hangars. And there was another one, another group for women. What did they call it again? They looked after the fields while the farmers were away. I was with the girls in the munitions factory. We did counter-sinking. You know, with that machine that punches holes in things for the screws to go into. I know it doesn't sound very interesting, but we used to have a laugh, us girls. And the heels! You should have seen the heels we wore in those days. That's why my feet are so bad now. It was all for the boys," Grandma had said with a laugh.

There were more photos under the postcard. Rachel fanned them out on the dining room table, pushing the rest of the papers aside. There were a few of her grandfather in uniform, standing alone or with a group of similarly dressed fresh-faced young men. Rachel looked at his face and tried to feel something. She could see a little of Wanda in him, around the eyes. His uniform looked sharp, though. It gave his young, rebellious stance an air of purpose. Grandma had said that was why she married him. "He was always very sure of himself," she said. "Sure, he ran around with other girls sometimes, but he always came back to me," she told Rachel one afternoon, after a glass of sherry. "You don't understand. It was different in those days," she said, taking a long slow sip. "Everything we did was for our boys."

14.

AFTER THE INVESTIGATION, everything in the house on Columbia Street changed. Just Jack never did get thrown in the Pen for shooting the chef lady, but he didn't go back to work at the piggery either. He didn't go to work anywhere. Mamma Shirley hardly bothered to talk to him at all. When she did, she'd say that he was a lazy, no-good bum. She had to say this to him at dinner, because he didn't get up with everyone for breakfast anymore. He stayed in bed till Mamma Shirley was gone, and he was still in his housecoat and track pants, with his hair all standing up all over and his chest fur sticking out, when they all got home from school.

Sometimes, after dinner, Just Jack would go out for the night and Mamma Shirley would put on her Elvis record and play it so loud the windows rattled. Some nights Mamma Shirley stayed in and watched *Happy Days* with Emma and Lester on the couch, and some nights she packed up her pink suitcase and wheeled it around the subdivision, to sell Avon makeup to all the neighbour ladies. Mamma Shirley said she had to keep an eye on her inventory because Nina had slippery fingers, so when she wasn't using it, she kept the suitcase locked in a trunk in the garage.

Nina said that Avon was crap for raisin-faced old ladies. Nina didn't have a lot of makeup, but she said that she didn't give a rat's ass, 'cause she had good skin, and only needed lip-gloss, eyeliner and mascara. In the mornings, and after dinner, she put it on fresh, making her lips look slick and gooey, and her eyes caved in and sneaky, like a raccoon.

After a few months like that, things changed. Emma starting noticing that as soon as Mamma Shirley left to go sell Avon, Just Jack and Nina would go out together in the car without saying goodbye. One night, they were still out when Mamma Shirley got home, and didn't come back until long after everyone went to bed. The next morning, Mamma Shirley paced in the kitchen, stirring her coffee like she was mad at it, until Nina got up and came down for breakfast.

"Hey!" Mamma Shirley said as soon as Nina walked into the kitchen. "Where were you last night?"

"None of your damn business," Nina shot back, her eyes still puffy and smudged with black eyeliner from the night before. She pushed past Mamma Shirley, and put a slice of bread in the toaster.

"Yes it is my business!" Mamma Shirley yelled, popping the bread back up, and standing in front of the toaster, so Nina couldn't pop it back down.

"Okay, Jesus," Nina said. "If you must know, Just Jack took me out for driving lessons."

"Driving lessons?" Mamma Shirley said, blinking like there was something in her eyes. "But you're too young. You won't even be able to get a learner's permit for at least another year."

Nina laughed. Not a happy laugh, but the one that meant that she thought everyone was an idiot, except for her. Then she left the kitchen, shouting behind her, "Keep your fucking toast." Mamma Shirley gave her a dirty look as she left the room, and was about to yell something after her, when Just Jack came in. Mamma Shirley started talking to him instead, telling him that he shouldn't be taking Nina out in the car, because she was too young, and it was illegal.

"That is if this whole driving lessons story is true, which I'm really not sure about at all," she said, pouring Just Jack a cup of coffee like she always did in the morning, though this time, she held on to his cup – like it was a hostage.

Just Jack rolled his eyes up to the ceiling and rubbed his head. "What the hell else do you think we were doing?" he asked. And then said, "Do you think I could just have my coffee now, Shirley? For God's sakes, I try to help the girl, do a good deed, and all I get is hassled."

Mamma Shirley looked down into the coffee cup. She looked like she was going to get mad again for a minute, then she looked like she was going to cry. But instead, she said, "Sorry Jack. I don't know what I was thinking."

Just Jack took the coffee cup out of her hand, and Mamma Shirley left the kitchen to go get ready for work. Emma went upstairs too after that, to get ready for school. Nina was in their room, looking at herself in the mirror, rubbing her makeup off with cotton-balls and baby oil.

"You should be nicer to Mamma Shirley," Emma said, before she could stop herself. "Even though she pretends to be happy, she's really not, and when you're mean to her it makes her cry when she's alone in the bathroom."

Nina wheeled around and threw her hairbrush in Emma's direction.

"Can you shut your trap for one second?" She yelled after it.

The brush flew by Emma's head, and left a dent in the wall.

After that, Emma didn't say anything when she saw something bad happening. Instead, she became a frozen statue, invisible, silent, dead. Possum.

Jamie Francis hardly ever spoke to anyone. When he was home, he stayed in his room practising his guitar or listening to records. He threw David Cassidy away and said John Denver was for kids. He had posters of KISS in their scary makeup and platform shoes, and one of Angie Dickinson in her Police Woman uniform. He stopped letting Mamma Shirley cut his hair, so it was long and hanging down in his eyes. He wore a blue bandana all the time to hide the pimples on his forehead. He told Emma he wore it so he could look like Jimi Hendrix and Robert Plant. He said Zeppelin was "heavy," and Hendrix was "off the hook." Emma wondered what hook, but didn't ask. "Nobody ever messes with those guys, not even that Freddie Mercury from Queen. And he wears makeup and everything," Jamie Francis told Emma once when he was in a good mood and decided to let her in his room. "Francis is only for a girl when it's a first name," he said. "And besides, you spell it differently for girls."

Even Lester was different that year. That was because of the skunk they saw on the way to school one day.

"Oh Jesus," Mamma Shirley said when she saw it, all mashed up with its guts spilling out like hamburger on the side of the road.

"What happened to it?" Lester asked, walking over to get a better look. There were flies on the hamburger and a bad rotten smell all around it.

"The poor thing must have been in an accident. Likely a car just smacked into it and drove right off. Sheesh. The least they could have done was call the city and get someone to clean it up. It looks like it's been here all weekend."

"A hit and run?" Lester asked, his eyes wide. "The skunk was in a hit and run?"

"Yes, Lester, Jesus, come on now. It stinks," Mamma Shirley said, holding her nose.

Lester didn't move. He stared at the heap of skunk guts till Emma came and pulled him away by the arm.

"Not all car accidents are like that though, Lester," Emma told him.

Lester didn't seem to hear Emma, but he let her lead him back to the sidewalk anyway.

After that, Lester stopped dressing up in his bow tie and shiny shoes, stopped playing truck driver with the garden spade, and never talked to anyone at Foster's house about his parents coming back to get him again. At school it was a different story though. At school, Lester started telling everyone that Emma was his real sister, and that their parents were away on parents' day, doing big important jobs. Once he said that their dad was an astronaut, and their mom worked in a newsroom like Mary Tyler Moore. Another time he said that their parents were big stars in Hollywood and were going to have their own TV show soon, just like Sonny & Cher.

Emma didn't call Lester out, or say he was a liar right in front of everyone, but if any of the other kids asked her afterwards if it was true, Emma would whisper, "No. Lester's mixed-up. We don't have the same parents. His parents are dead, but he doesn't like to talk about it. Hit and run." As for Emma's parents, she didn't have much to say on that because she didn't know where they were. Mamma Shirley said, "Beats me," and that nobody in the office at the place where she got Emma knew either. Emma wondered sometimes if Lester was right, and maybe her parents were still alive doing something super cool out there somewhere in the world. Emma thought she remembered her mom though, and didn't think that she was really Cher, or anybody else on TV, just a normal lady. As for her dad, Emma had no idea who or where he was. She had a feeling though, that he was the reason she was so brown and different from everyone. Emma wished whoever her dad was, that he was someone else instead. Someone more like a normal person.

15.

AN HOUR INTO THE PAPERWORK on her grandmother's dining room table, Rachel took a break. It was time to try to get caught up on her phone calls. It would be only a few days before the funeral. She pulled out her cell, but at the same time that she noticed it was dead, she realized that she had forgotten to bring her charger with her. She'd been doing too much forgetting lately. I need to be sharp now, she thought. Time to smarten up. She was about to pick up the house phone, an old dial-up model that Grandma had refused to give up in spite of Rachel's protestations.

"But you can't use any Touch Tone services with this phone, Grandma. What about when you're calling the bank or something and have to deal with an automated system?"

"Then I wait Rachel, and eventually a real human being comes on the line and says hello. I'm not getting a new phone. There's nothing wrong with this one. *That's that.*"

In the morning, before she had started in on her paperwork, Rachel had left a message at the funeral home about coming in to sign the contract. She had wanted to get that done as soon as possible, before they found any other new charges to add on to the bill. The clunky old receiver was in her hand, and her finger ready for the workout of dialing, when the doorbell rang.

"I'll get it," Rachel yelled, though she doubted Emma heard and didn't know why she bothered anyway. She was always the first to the door. Old habits die hard. She looked through the peephole and saw a burly man in a black leather jacket standing outside with the screen door wedged open. He had on some sort of uniform that Rachel didn't recognize, so she decided to shout through the door.

"Hello?"

"Delivery," the man said, holding up a sealed white envelope in his hand.

The probability of being robbed in the middle of the afternoon, in full daylight, on a quiet downtown street in a nice neighbourhood was likely in the single digit percentile. Rachel opened the door. Without a word, the man handed her a clipboard to sign. Rachel glanced at the paper. It was a typical delivery receipt, nothing out of the ordinary. She signed, took the envelope, and the man turned and walked down the driveway.

As she closed the door, Rachel recognized the return address in the corner. It was from the estate attorney. She called him the day Grandma passed, while Emma was napping. George Robertson was his name. Rachel had met him already. He had helped with the paperwork that gave Rachel power of attorney when Grandma's health started to go downhill. He had said it would be simple sorting out the estate – a straightforward allotment of assets. Rachel tore open the envelope as she walked down the hall to the bedroom.

Emma was lying on the bed in Grandma's purple bathrobe. Rachel couldn't see her face, but knew she was crying from the sound. Dear god, it had been less than an hour, and already Emma was crumbling. Rachel looked at the closet, expecting to see the rest of the clothes still hanging there. Instead, the hangers were empty, all except one, from which hung a plastic grocery bag. Rachel took the letter in her hand out of the envelope. Emma rolled over quickly, seemingly startled.

"What? Nothing," she said, though Rachel hadn't said anything. "I'm just resting my eyes a minute. I know. There's more to do. I know. I just took a minute okay?" Emma wiped her eyes, and Rachel couldn't help but feel for her for a moment. What would it be like to be so skinless? To walk around the world letting everything that happened touch you so deeply that you were left unable to function? Rachel had seen Emma cry at the oddest things. A sunset. The moon. What an existence. Really, it was to be pitied. Rachel vowed to try harder, at least in these early days, at least until after the funeral and garage sale. Then they would be done with each other for a while, and each could go back to their comfortable existence halfway across the country from each other.

Rachel sat down on the bed, and was about to read over the letter when Emma got up and bounded toward the closet.

"This is for you," she said, handing over the plastic bag, on the side of which was written in black marker, *for Rachel*.

Rachel took the bag from Emma's hand, and Emma took the letter from Rachel. As she opened it, Rachel smelled something escape with the air inside like an exhale. Before her brain made sense of it, her nose delivered the message: *garage sale, goodbye, tuna-fish sandwich. Wonder Woman.* As her mind brought the jumble of words and olfactory triggers together, her eyes delivered the final clues. Inside the bag was her grandmother's sun visor, the white one with the green see-through brim. The poker player, wheeler-dealer, *what you see is what we get, and that's that* visor. Rachel had looked for it a couple of times over the years – rummaged around in the basement to see if she could find it. She never thought to look in here. Never thought that her grandmother would have put it aside for her all these years.

Rachel wanted to put the bag to her nose and get more of it, but she resisted. She'd wait till she was alone. She wished she were alone now, instead of with Emma, who just stood there, watching Rachel with an expression of concern. Rachel didn't have the energy to explain. She closed her eyes. If Emma tried to hug her, she didn't know what she'd do. Likely nothing, but it would take effort to overcome the urge to either laugh or slug her. Rachel felt the weight of her sister as she sat on the bed next to her. She knew she should open her eyes. Get up, go to the bathroom, and splash some cold water on her face. Just a moment of privacy, Rachel thought, and she'd be fine.

"Oh wow," Emma said and Rachel's eyes flew open to look at her sister, who now held the letter open in her hand. Her face had gone white, or at least a paler shade of brown. Oh wow, what? What now, for god's sakes?

Emma handed the letter over to Rachel, who read it while the other hand held the visor pinned down to the bed.

Wanda. It was about Wanda. There had been an earlier version of the will. Of course there had. Wanda had been included in that one, listed as an heir to the house. According to the letter, the house wasn't covered in the new will at all. Yes, the insurance, and the bank accounts, the Florida apartment, and even the beat-up old furniture had been mentioned. Oversight, the letter read, as if that were a sufficient explanation for Mr. Robertson's obvious ineptitude. How could he have not noticed? So now, the house could not be settled without Wanda's consent.

"It looks like we're going to have to find her, Rachel." Emma was using her soft, empathetic voice. Like she was talking to a baby or a kitten.

Rachel stood up, and brushed off her lap as if it were full of crumbs. "This is bullshit," she said. "I'll get him on the phone. Sort it out. How the hell can we wait till Wanda shows up? It's been thirty-five years. Who knows where she is, or even if she's alive at all anymore? No. I'll get Mr. Robertson on the phone. Sort it out. He just doesn't understand the situation. It'll be fine." Rachel turned away, feeling Emma's eyes on her back as she walked to the door.

"I'm pretty sure she's still alive," Emma said. Rachel turned back

"You've heard from her?"

"No. Well yes, sort of. I thought I saw her in Gastown once.

But it could have been someone else." Rachel waited. "No. I haven't heard from her. Not really." Emma's face went blank. Rachel knew better than to press the issue. Any sentence of Emma's that began with both "yes" and "no" would always end with confusion and a baffling lack of both clarity and facts. Rachel shook her head, and left Emma without asking her to explain further.

Back in the dining room, Rachel picked up the phone again, and dialed the number for the law office. The dial mechanism took forever to click through the numbers. How did people have the patience for this back in the day? Finally the line connected, but it was an automated answering machine. Press one for this, two for that. Rachel waited for the message to end, and for the operator to come on to direct her call. Nobody. Nothing. Just an option to repeat the message, then dead air.

Rachel could hear Emma in the kitchen. Maybe she had a cell on her? Emma never had a cell phone that Rachel knew of, but it was worth a try.

She walked to the kitchen, but stopped short in the doorway. Emma was staring at the list on the fridge. Rachel took a step back, out of sight. She wanted Emma to finish reading before she came in the room. She waited, but Emma continued to stand and stare. The handwriting was legible enough. What was taking her so long?

Rachel watched as Emma's legs buckled and she collapsed on the floor. This is a put on, Rachel thought, another episode of the *The Emma Show*. But Emma hadn't known she was being watched, so what was the point? Emma was down on her knees in front of the fridge, as if she was praying to a monolithic stainless steel God.

"Emma!" Rachel hadn't meant for her voice to be so sharp when it left her, but once outside her head, she knew it sounded like a bark.

Emma snapped her head around towards the doorway. Her

eyes were streaming. She looked like she wasn't right in the head. Grief is one thing, but –

Emma used the refrigerator handle to pull herself up.

"Don't say anything, okay?" Emma used her own stern voice now. "Not a word. I'm not a robot, Rachel. It's normal. Happens to people all the time. Emotions get too heavy and pull you down. Legs go out all of a sudden. Whoopdy-do for you that you can hold it together. I don't think it's healthy, but it's your business. Just no commentary, okay? To each her own."

Rachel left it alone. At least her moment of rebellion had brought Emma's backbone out. Hopefully, it would help keep her standing.

"So the basement then?" Emma asked.

"What?"

"The basement. It's the next item on your list. I'm done with the closet, so the basement is next. Let's box up the basement," Emma said, this time leaving Rachel standing in the middle of the kitchen as she headed toward the stairs.

16.

EMMA AND LESTER were in the first grade now. Jenny was in a different class from them, but she was still Emma's best friend. After school, Jenny's grandpa picked them all up, and they all walked home together. That was the best part of the day for Emma. Everything was okay; no matter what happened during the rest of the day, as long as Emma got to walk with Big Jim, and listen to him tell her things. Sometimes he told her with words that were inside her head, if it was a something that only she needed to know, and sometimes he talked out loud, so Jenny and Lester could hear as well. It reminded her of being with Barney, and just like with Barney, when Emma spoke without making a sound, Big Jim could understand.

"You see those two peaks up there?" Big Jim said, pointing at the mountains over North Vancouver one day during their walk home. "Everyone calls them the Lions, but that's not their real name. They're called the Two Sisters. That's the name we gave them a long, long time ago."

Jenny piped in, solemn. "The Sisters remind us that family is the most important thing in the world."

Lester looked down for a moment, but only Emma noticed. Big Jim was looking at Jenny, laughing.

"And what about animals?" Emma blurted.

"Animals are important, but they're not as important as family," Jenny replied, though Emma was barely listening.

Instead, she sent the rest of her message right to Big Jim, inside his head.

Big Jim looked at her for a long moment, nodding his head, before he said anything at all. And then he told her, in his silent voice that was just for her.

"Yep, I talk to animals all the time. They use me, move through me when I go to heal people. I sit with the sick person, and after a while an animal comes – not just his voice, but his whole spirit. He sends his brand of spirit healing from that place of being, his fox medicine or turtle medicine like you have, and it goes through me and into the person to heal them. Animals aren't like people. They like to share, and I'm an open channel. A middle-man," he said, and began laughing out loud.

Lester was startled, and jumped, which made Jenny start laughing as well, and made Big Jim laugh harder. Emma didn't laugh, just looked up at the mountains, glad to finally know their real name.

That was one of the last times they all walked home together, because in grade two, you're old enough to walk home from school by yourself. It's also old enough to know that some things you talk about, and some things you keep under your hat. Like talking to people or animals in your head, Emma didn't tell anyone about that. She hadn't even told Lester, in case he told someone else by accident.

Emma especially didn't want Mamma Shirley to know. Nina had already told Mamma Shirley that Emma was retarded, so there was no point in adding crazy to it too. That was the kind of trouble Emma didn't need. She'd had enough to deal with since that sitcom *Good Times* came on TV. Ever since then, Johnny Craymore started calling her Buffalo Butt.

"Hey Emma, did you watch *Good Times* last night?" Johnny asked in the schoolyard at recess. "They all look like you on that show. Is that what you are? A Buffalo Butt? Look like one to me."

Emma couldn't think of anything to say. All she could think of was how the kids playing dodge ball stopped and listened to Johnny, and how, if he kept yakking away, soon everyone would be looking, and would guess that she wasn't an Indian after all. Then the trouble would really start.

"Well, what have you got to say for yourself, BB?" Johnny sneered.

Emma was frozen. Possum. She wished she were invisible. Jenny grabbed her arm, and pulled her away to the other side of the dodge-ball court.

That night, Jenny must have told her grandpa what happened, because the next day he was there at the school when they all got out.

"Which one of them is calling you names?" he asked, looking at Emma from under his brown cowboy hat.

Emma pointed at Johnny, who was coming out the school doors. Big Jim didn't say anything. He just stood there in his hat and fringed leather jacket, his grey-and-black hair long and flat down his back. He looked at Johnny Craymore as if he was a bad smell. Johnny turned around all of a sudden, like he got the feeling someone was watching him. Then he got this scared look on his face. He looked at Emma, who was still pointing at him, then he turned and started running, disappearing around the corner of the school.

Emma looked at Big Jim, and was about to say thanks, when he said, "Don't sweat it, kid."

After that, Johnny left Emma alone. She was still nervous though, and waited for something else bad to happen. Mamma Shirley always said that bad things came in threes. Most of the time Emma wouldn't pay attention to the things Mamma Shirley said, cause Mamma Shirley was too busy with her job and Avon at night to know what was really going on. Like how Just Jack and Nina were still being sneaky when Mamma Shirley was at work, and how Nina hardly ever went to school at all anymore.

"I'm gonna blow this pop stand soon anyway," Nina told Emma one night while she was putting on her raccoon eyes to go out. "Just Jack's gonna give me his car, and I'm gonna drive to California and start a rock band. But you keep your mouth shut about it, you hear? Cause I'll beat you black and blue and send you to Woodlands myself if you mention a word of it to anyone."

Emma nodded. There were no words in her brain, no words in her mouth. She crawled into bed and pulled the covers over her head until she heard Nina leave the room, closing the door with a slam. That night Emma dreamt that a snake was caught under the tire of Just Jack's car. The snake winked at Emma, then slithered out of its skin, leaving the old skin under the car as it glided through the grass toward where Emma was standing. Emma wanted to pet the snake, but before it reached her, her teeth started to come loose, and suddenly all of them fell out of her mouth. She was on her knees in the grass looking for them, when she woke up in her bed.

17.

B Y THE TIME RACHEL WAS BACK at school, after the summer after her dad died, the sweet peas really were in full bloom, sending wafts of Grandma all around the neighbourhood. Everything seemed to be back to normal. Not normal like when Rachel's dad was alive, but a new kind of normal, where Grandma took the place where Dad used to be. Grandma would sit in his chair, and Sam would sit opposite her. Mom sat at the side of table like a kid, waiting for Grandma to serve her. Rachel didn't trust this new mom. She wanted to tell her to snap out of it. It wasn't that Rachel didn't like having Grandma in charge, because she did. Grandma in charge meant that things got done. Little things, like vacuuming and feeding Diana Prince, the cat, at the same time every day, but also big things too, like having a garage sale.

"Nobody ever wants to deal with the belongings of the dead," Grandma told Rachel as she went around the house putting price-tags on all of Dad's things. "But it has to be done, or else you end up living in a house full of ghosts."

Rachel and Grandma were in Mom and Dad's room, going through Dad's clothes. "Some of these suits are worth putting out on a rack, don't you think?" Grandma asked.

Rachel said, "Yes," but wasn't really thinking about whether they'd make any money from the suits. She was trying to connect them with the man who used to wear them. Rachel's dad used to call them "monkey suits," would only wear them when he had to, and would take them off as soon as he got home. He wouldn't wear jeans and sweat shirts like other dads, though. He said jeans were for bikers and hippies, and always wore slacks and shirts instead. When it was cold he would wear one of his sweaters with the leather patches on the elbows. Mom would always laugh when he wasn't around and say they were his pretend professor sweaters, and that he should go back to Gilligan's Island. Mom said that Dad tried to be a square so he could act like he was smart. She called him a throwback to the fifties, and would call him "Mr. Cleaver" sometimes. She'd say there was no way in hell she was going to be his June, so he could just forget it. She said it would be a cold day in hell when she'd go fetching his slippers and getting him a drink when he came home from the road. She had said these things out loud to Rachel and Sam, but would only roll her eyes to the sky when Dad was around.

Looking at the row of black and grey suits hanging in the closet, Rachel realized that her dad hadn't only been a parent to her and Sam, but that he had been like a father to Mom too. Now that Grandma was here, it was as if she was the only grown up in the house.

Grandma took Rachel's father's suits off the rack and laid them one on top of the other on the bed. The rest of his clothes she began to put into black garbage bags.

"We'll just donate these. Suits are one thing, but shirts are too close to the skin to pass on," Grandma said.

Rachel reached up, delicately removed a white cotton shirt from the rack, crouched down and stuffed it into the bag. She stayed crouching, her eyes avoiding her grandmother. She thought about trucks with cats hidden underneath them, smashing into bridges. She thought about bullet holes in wood, and how far away the shooter would have to be to make them clean – and from what distance splintered.

"How about I take them from the rack and you put them into the bag then?" Grandma said. Rachel nodded, but didn't look up. Her grandmother took a handful of shirts off at once, and dropped them on the floor.

"I'm going to get a job." Mom's voice was suddenly behind them. She had come in while they were facing the closet, her footsteps silent on the deep shag rug. She sat on the bed stroking one of Dad's suits like it was a cat.

Rachel's grandmother turned around and stood with her hands on her hips facing her daughter. "Well, that's good news. I was just thinking that it would be good for you to get into some sort of routine. You can still type, right? Rachel and I can look for an old Underwood for you to practice on –"

"No, I mean I got a job already. It's not secretarial work, though, Mom, it's cooking, in a shelter for homeless people off Yonge Street," Rachel's mom said, then took a breath, readying herself for Grandma's reaction. For some reason hearing her mother use the word "Mom" made Rachel clench her fists.

"What? You got a job cooking for a bunch of derelicts? You can't cook. And where off Yonge Street? It's the longest street in the world." Grandma's voice spilled out her annoyance.

"It's downtown," Rachel's mother said.

"Downtown! Why do you want to go down there? It's seedy now. What are you thinking, Wanda? Are you looking for trouble again?" Rachel's grandmother was shouting. Her mother stood up from the bed and strode toward her own mother defiantly.

"Look, there's nothing wrong with the place, okay? They serve food to people who need it. It's not like I don't have a plan. I've been thinking of going back to school eventually. And anyways, I already went down and they hired me so *that's that.*" Rachel's mom stood like a mirror to her own now, with her hands also on her hips. Neither of them spoke. They looked at each other as if the other were about to do something terrible. Rachel still sat on the floor by the closet, surrounded by her father's shirts. She prayed her mother and grandmother would forget she was there, that they would get past their bickering, and get down to whatever the real truth was, and finally allow it to come bursting out from behind their crossed arms. A woodpecker began hammering away on a tree outside the bedroom window, breaking the trance the three seemed to be held in. Rachel cursed it under her breath.

"You go to your job downtown then. What the hell. Do what you want. You always have." Grandma walked past Mom, and dropped the shirts she still held onto the bed. Mom's arms dropped to their side.

"You know what, Mom?" Rachel's mom said, picking up one of the shirts. She folded it quickly, and put it back down. "I'm done. No more pretending. No more covering everything up. I'm not like you. I'm willing to make sacrifices for my children. I understand what it takes to be a mother. You'll see that one day."

"I don't expect you to be me, Wanda," Grandma said, picking up the shirt Mom had just finished with, and folding it again. "I just expect you to take responsibility for the choices you make in life." She placed the neatly folded shirt down on the bed.

"That's what I'm trying to do here. I'm getting a job so I can feed my family and start saving money for school," Wanda replied, picking the same shirt up again, wadding it up into a ball, and lobbing it into the corner of the room.

"Don't be dramatic, dear. You know you'll never lack anything as long as I have any say in it," Grandma said, suddenly looking toward Rachel where she sat on the floor.

"That's it exactly."

"What? What's it exactly?" Grandma's voice grew louder and frail, as if her vocal cords were being stretched along with her patience.

"Whether or not you should have any say in it. In anything. This may be your house, but it's my family, not yours. You had your chance." Rachel's mom was tearing up now.

"Please, Wanda, get a grip." Grandma sighed.

"You!" Wanda wiped her eyes with the back of her hand, and then pointed at Grandma. "*You have neither kindness, nor faith, nor charity beyond what serves to increase the pleasure of the moment. You desert the fallen.*"

"Jesus, have you been drinking again?" Grandma asked. It was the final spark that ignited Mom's anger into a crackling fire.

"No mother, I haven't been drinking. Not that it would be any of your business if I had. I'm an adult you know. You should treat me like one." Mom was full out crying now, her body shaking and her eyes red and swollen.

"An adult doesn't make the choices you've made, Wanda."

"Huh," Mom said. "You're one to talk."

"Don't try to change the subject."

"It always comes down to this, doesn't it? You're the good mother and I'm the bad one. Your whole life is just this *tissue of vanity and deceit*!" Wanda's voice was gravel. She was a wounded animal, cornered.

"Fine," Grandma said. "Suit yourself. It's your mess, so I'll just leave you to it." Grandma picked up the suits and walked out of the bedroom.

Rachel and her mom looked at each other as if neither was sure who the other was anymore.

The next morning was the garage sale, so Rachel and Grandma hauled the price-stickered suits, golf clubs, power tools, and other unused stuff out to the front of the house. Grandma sat in a lawn chair at a card table with a metal box on it, wearing a visor with a green see-through brim. She looked like she was getting ready to play poker with the mailman.

"Don't let them give you less than we're asking for Rachel," she coached. "You gotta stand firm. If they see you're willing to haggle, you're done for."

Rachel nodded solemnly.

Throughout the day, neighbours came by to check the wares. Every once in a while, Rachel's Grandma would announce, "This is a haggle-free zone, folks! All prices are fixed as marked. What you see is what we get!" Then she would laugh her head off.

Around noon, Grandma told Rachel to go wake her brother up. "It's a beautiful day, and that boy needs to lend a hand. We need all hands on deck here, girl!" All hands apparently did not include Rachel's mom who was nowhere to be found all morning. When Rachel asked where she was, Grandma's lips made a hard flat line as she said, "Your mother's still annoyed with me about our conversation yesterday. She thinks she's punishing us, but she's really punishing herself." Grandma's mouth softened. "Never mind that girl. She'll be back. She always comes back eventually. Just go wake your brother up all right?"

Rachel went up to Sam's bedroom, and yelled his name outside the door.

"What?" Sam's voice was still groggy with sleep.

"It's garage sale day, and Grandma says you have to come help," Rachel told him, then returned to join her grandmother. Shortly after, Sam appeared in his track pants and the Rolling Stones T-shirt with the big red tongue and lips on it. His hair was sticking up, and he blinked in the sunshine.

"The prince has arisen!" Grandma said, getting up out of her seat, and ushering Sam into her place. "I'm going to make us some sandwiches for lunch. Tuna? You want tuna?" she asked, without waiting for an answer. "Okay then, tuna it is! Rachel, you tell Sam the drill. No haggling," she said, then turned to the rest of the yard where strangers fondled their belongings. "You hear that shoppers? Don't even think about it. Ha, ha!" With that she disappeared into the house.

"Argh," Sam said when she was out of earshot. "Tuna. I hate tuna. Where's Mom?"

Rachel repeated what Grandma had told her earlier, word for word.

"What the hell does that mean?" he asked. "She's not taking off again, is she?"

"What do you mean *again*?" Rachel asked, surprised that

Sam seemed to be able to make sense of their grandmother's cryptic comments.

"Like she did the last time," Sam said, using his finger to crush an ant that had made the unfortunate decision to crawl across his foot. Rachel waited. "You don't remember? You know, that time when Mom took off for a while. She was gone for a long time, months I think. You remember that first time Grandma came to stay with us?" he said, unaware of the effect his words were having.

"What the hell are you talking about? Mom took off? Took off where? Where was I? Are you bullshitting me?" Rachel found it hard to breathe.

"You don't remember? That's weird. Well I guess you wouldn't have been very old," he said, looking up into the air above his head and nodding to count the years. "Oh yeah, you would have just been a baby then." Sam raised his hand to shade his eyes from the sun. "Geez, it's hot out. You think she'll bring out some lemonade with those sandwiches? God. I hate tuna fish."

Sam rambled off a commentary on the neighbours, how Julie Martin looked like she was getting fatter by the hour, and Mrs. Lewis' pants were so tight she had a camel toe. Rachel sat very still, digesting the words that had spilled out of Sam's mouth, and matching them up with those exchanged between her grandmother and her mother the day before.

The only surprise was how she missed it, how she could see everything around it like a halo, but not the event itself. Not that she would have remembered.

She asked Sam how old she would have been, and he said, "You hadn't been around that long. You were a baby. Come to think of it, I remember at the time wondering why Mom would leave when she had a brand new kid." Sam looked at Rachel then. He was finally awake, his voice softening on his last word. Rachel asked him what else he knew.

"That's it. All I remember was she split and then came back. I don't know where, why, nothing. You know what it was like when Dad was around. Nobody talked about shit. I don't even remember Grandma saying anything. Fuck, I don't know, Rachel, I was just a kid myself."

Grandma came out with lunch. Rachel took a sandwich and did inventory, moving the items scattered across the driveway and lawn closer together.

Her mom was going to leave again. Rachel knew it in her bones. Suddenly, she realized she had always known. The awareness of her mother's looming departure had been buzzing inside her for years, filling her up without her realizing. It was like when someone leaves a television set on somewhere, and that high-pitched monotone burrows into your brain without you noticing until someone turns it off.

Rachel's mom didn't leave all at once. At first it was just nights at the homeless shelter, coming home late, and sleeping in all day. When Rachel would see her mom in the afternoon, she would look at her and think: on the outside she is Mom, but on the inside she is Wanda. Wanda equals question mark.

Then came the nights when her mom wouldn't come home at all. First, one night, then two, then a whole week away someplace else. Question mark gone AWOL. Grandma stopped asking Wanda where she had gone, and instead became resigned, folded in on herself. Even the air, once occupied by the sheer power of Grandma's will, grew thin and tired. The hi-fi in the living room became eerily silent.

It took a while for them to realize that Wanda was gone for sure, but after a month without her returning, the finality settled around them all. A relief, an exhale followed by a breath into the space left behind. Small blessings, as Grandma would say, that Wanda's slow departure made adjustment not such a difficult task. Rachel's mom had long ago left the rhythm of the household. She had slipped through a crack in the wall like the wind.

18.

EXHAUSTED, EMMA HEADED DOWN her grandmother's rickety basement stairs. She was worried her knees might buckle again, so she gripped the banister. She was tired deep down in her bones. It had been a day of sorting and organizing, and checking things off Rachel's to-do list. Her goal was to just get through the night.

"This weekend? You still want to do the garage sale this weekend? I mean, isn't that a bit soon? Especially since we have to find Wanda now," Emma said over her shoulder as she reached the basement's cement floor.

Rachel was right behind her. "Don't worry about Wanda. I told you. I'll sort it out. I'll call Robertson in the morning. It's just an administrative error. Besides, Sam will be here tomorrow night, and will be meeting with the real estate agent Wednesday. Yes, Emma, we've got to get the house cleared out if we're going to be able to show it next week."

So Wanda had a week. How would they find her? Rachel said she didn't care, but how could she not? Wanda was her mother, too, and she'd been her mother longer than Emma's. Should they hire private detectives, or was that only done in the movies? If Wanda wanted to keep the house, Rachel would have a fit. Get rid of it pronto, that's all Rachel cared about. Bury the past and make a profit in the process. Why not keep it? Emma could move in, and pay rent toward the upkeep and taxes. Not that she was in a hurry to leave Vancouver.

There were no eagles in Toronto, no ocean, and the vegetarian restaurant selection was pitiful compared to out west. She'd made a name for herself there with her band, Koko and the Talking Apes, even if the members had changed over the years. Maybe Lester could leave his place in Kensington and move in with her – at first on a trial basis to see how it went. As long as Rachel was cool with it. They could turn it into a duplex, and rent out the extra apartment to some quiet, non-smoking vegetarian.

"Okay, so I brought price tags. There's a roll for each of us. And markers," Rachel said, pointing at the metal card table set up next to the bottom of the stairs. There was packing tape on rollers with tear-off serrated plastic edges. Scissors. Newspaper. Cardboard boxes leaned up against the side of the wall. Rachel picked up a black marker and a roll of stickers and passed them to Emma.

The sight of Rachel's brisk efficient movements sent a sound like the ocean whooshing through Emma's ears. She put her hand flat on the cool cement wall.

"I don't know why she never got this basement finished," Rachel said. "My dad –" Then she stopped talking. Stopped moving and stood still for a moment. Blinked. "My dad was working on getting it finished when he died. He put the studs in to divide it up into rooms. Did the drywall and panelling in the laundry room and our play – in that big room over there. It was just the furnace room and this entrance area he didn't get to. That, and the floors."

Then it went dark for a minute. Emma had been expecting it. She saw Rachel put her hand out to the wall and reach toward the light switch. It was unconscious. Rachel didn't know she had done it. She had watched Emma place her own hand on the wall, and then when her dad talk started to bring up the weight of those old feelings, she reached out to steady herself. At that point, flicking the light switch was simply reflex.

Darkness.

Only for a moment though, then Rachel caught herself, flicked the lights back on, and went back to giving instructions as if nothing had happened at all.

"So take a look and see if there's something you want to keep. If not, then just put whatever price you think you can get. Don't worry if it seems high. They can always talk us down once everything's out on the lawn."

Was she faking? Pretending that nothing happened, or did Rachel somehow also flicker off for a moment along with the lights? Was it some sort of momentary short-circuiting in her brain? Emma looked at her, but Rachel's face gave nothing away.

Rachel blinked again, then, headed off into the big room, their playroom when she and Sam were kids. She walked with purpose, like she was on her way to a board meeting.

When Emma went into the laundry room, it was as if Grandma were just upstairs. The powdered detergent sat ready on the shelf next to the washing machine. Some of it had spilled over the side, leaving tiny white beads scattered across the floor. Stain remover, bleach, everything ready. It was ridiculous, but for a moment Emma felt bad for the detergent, waiting for the hands that had first brought it home to come lift it up and scoop it into the washer, as if it were a pet who had been abandoned.

"She's gone," Emma whispered into the room, and began assembling the box she had brought in with her.

When she was done, and the box stood there ready to be filled, she felt someone in the doorway. Rachel.

"I think we can get a start on this tomorrow. We've got the clothes done, and files sorted. That's enough for today. I'm going to head home now." Rachel was looking at the ironing board, staring at it with a look that said she wasn't seeing it at all. She was seeing something else.

"You'll be all right tonight? Here alone?" Then a beat later, the question became a statement. "You'll be all right."

Emma nodded. She didn't know this Rachel. The one who stared at ironing boards.

"I'll be fine."

Rachel turned to leave. Emma listened to the sound of her footsteps walking up to the main level. She heard the sound of something thudding down on the floor, then of feet walking into the dining room, then into the kitchen. They stopped directly above. Then Emma heard the sound of water running into the sink, water gurgling down the pipes, water sloshing behind the washing machine and into the floor.

Emma sat in the middle of the laundry room, next to the empty box, cross-legged on the round rag rug. She could go upstairs and say goodbye. Could ask Rachel what was wrong. See if she wanted to talk. Wasn't this what she had been waiting for? Some sign of loss, a wrinkle in the smooth exterior? Yes. So, be there for her, then, she thought and stood up.

But then she heard the front door opening with a squeak. The screen door banged shut behind it. She was too late.

Emma listened as Rachel's car pulled out of the driveway – Rachel who stared at ironing boards. That was it for Rachel's list, at least for the night. Emma was set free.

She went upstairs. The house was silent, except for the hum of traffic in the distance. Emma was standing by the front door, looking out at the empty driveway, when she began to feel a pull toward the park. She put on her coat, and went out the front door, down Garden Avenue and across the street, away from the houses of Parkside Drive, and into the darkness of trees on the other side. The light was starting to fade; the park looked deserted. She knew it was a bad idea to be alone there at night. Being alone in the woods in the country was fine, camping off some old logging road in BC, just Emma and the bears, no problem. But in the city, the parks were full of the potential menace of erratic humans. She'd need protection, so asked the Grandmothers to come with her, wherever it was she was being led, she would need them.

Emma walked through the entranceway to the parking lot, that someone, sometime, long ago, had decided to call Spring

Road. Emma had intended to walk deep into the park, and then turn right, toward the zoo. It was the most likely source of the consciousness that had directed her instinct to head out here, into the night. But instead of being led in that direction, when she reached the bottom of the road, the wind picked up and blew all the trees to the left. Emma headed down the pathway that ran along the back end of the park, next to Lower Duck Pond. Bottom Pond, that's what they used to call it, Emma can't remember why now. Rachel and her used to skate on it in the winters when they were young. Everybody did. Now there were signs: *Beware!* Everything was more dangerous in the city. Lester always disagreed with her about this.

"Listen Emma, I love camping, but I mean there's a reason people gather in urban areas. Human beings live in cities and animals live in nature, that's the deal. They have their turf and we have ours. It's best if we respect that. It's safer that way."

But Emma thought Lester had it wrong. Cities were more dangerous, exactly because they were full of people. Humans were more violent and unpredictable than animals, and stupid, hence the crime rate, and the need for signs.

Emma walked past the back end of the pond, and followed the wind back toward the bike trails. Years of teenagers burning off hormonally-charged adrenaline on dirt bikes had worn the hilly area behind the pond down to a series of smoothed out runs. But that night, the bike trail was inaccessible as a low wire-mesh fence now surrounded the whole area. There was an official looking sign nailed to one of the posts. Emma fished around in her pocket and pulled out a lighter. She flicked it, bent over, and by the light of the flame read the words: *No Access. Closed for woodland restoration.* Emma let the lighter go out and stood back up. She waited. Now what? There must have been a reason she was called here, some purpose behind the impulse that took hold of her and led her to this spot – some fox wanting to talk, or even a coyote. People had reported seeing all sorts of animals in the park over the years. One time there was a beaver loose on Parkside Drive. The news report said that cars swerved to avoid him. The beaver was captured and returned to the pond in perfect health, but one of the drivers ran into a light pole and was sent to the hospital.

Emma hoped it was a deer that had called her, inviting her to share its medicine. She could use a little more intuition, gentleness, and agility moving through obstacles right about now.

Emma gave up trying to figure out what had called her into the park. She was suddenly very tired. Her bones felt old and pulled her down to sitting cross-legged in the dirt on the path.

Who died here? The words Emma had unthinkingly said to Rachel that first day out in the back garden began to echo through Emma's mind. She frowned, annoyed by the distraction. Rachel always took Emma's train of thought off track. The trick with Rachel was to not let her know what Emma was really thinking. *Who died here?* Emma didn't know better back then. With three words, she had gotten on Rachel's bad side, and was never able to repair the damage done. That's why Emma hadn't told her anything about working with animal medicine. Not only was she charging people to tell them what their pets were thinking, but she also offered sessions to help people become more open to communication from animal spirits, and the healing messages they carried with them.

Every animal had something to share, some restorative power, and when you came across one, in real life or even in your dreams, it was that animal – the vibration of what it represented, its essence – attempting to mingle with your consciousness. The universe and everything in it was communicating to us constantly, telling us how to reach a state of equilibrium. A human lifetime was simply an exercise at perfecting balance. That was pretty much the gist of what she told people, the same blurb from her website. Her consultation style was pretty common sense, meat and potatoes totem animal stuff. Almost every culture had some sort of symbolic associations with animals, so it was really just a matter of zeroing in on the client's social and individual mythological context, doing some research, and delivering an interpretation. It wasn't anything magical, or even something Emma invented. It was all over the Internet. But the communication – the ability to listen and know what someone wants, thinks and feels – that was Emma's gift.

Emma knew Rachel would have a field day with the whole spirit animal medicine idea, so she never mentioned it. Being around Rachel required a lot of editing. There were so many things that could trigger her sister into some reactionary response. Emma had learned to protect herself over the years by revealing details of her life selectively. She never told Rachel about the eagle who talked to Emma when she was a baby at the beach. She never mentioned Big Jim, New West, or Foster's house. That whole part of Emma's life she had kept to herself, and thankfully Rachel had never asked.

The park had grown silent. All the birds were getting ready for bed for the night.

Emma held on to the fence, closed her eyes, and remembered back to that day on Columbia Street, walking home from school with Jenny and her grandfather. She had asked Big Jim how he had learned to listen.

"The trick is knowing how to be empty enough to get filled up with something other than yourself," he had told her. "Then you tune-in, like adjusting a radio dial."

Standing there in the park, under the darkening sky, Emma waited. Nothing. She opened her eyes, focused her ears, and commanded all her senses to high alert. No resistance, no resistance…

And then she heard it, *snake* Emma jumped up and stood erect. She heard the word as if it were being said to her, whispered inside her head. The whispering wasn't from an animal, Emma could tell that much. It wasn't an actual snake, proclaiming itself and its turf in the dark, offering its snake medicine up, it was a human voice that said the words. Or voices, rather, as there were more than one. Voices humming like a chorus. Then, at that moment, a picture began to form in Emma's mind, an image of a mound of dirt in the shape of a newly-dug grave.

She shuddered. Either there was some creepy assemblage of telepathic people lurking around in the woods somewhere, or some non-physical entities were trying to tell her something. Maybe it was the Howards, John and Jemima, the benefactors of the park who gave it to the city *for the free use, benefit and enjoyment of the citizens of the City of Toronto forever.* The Howards were clearly generous and kindly people who would likely think nothing of taking a few moments out of their eternal peace, hovering over Colborne Lodge in order to scare the pants off a middle-aged, brown woman wandering around the park in the middle of the night. Emma admired their cleverness and economy in the use of the word *snake* and a picture of a grave. Of course she would know they were talking to her, warning her away. Reminding Emma that she was no longer in the familiar forest of her childhood, she was in a city park, surrounded by the unknown.

It was dark now, no moon. Okay, John and Jemima, I get the message, Emma thought. She turned away from the fence, and walked back down the path, tracing her steps back home.

19.

THAT SUNDAY MORNING on Columbia Street was peaceful as Emma got up out of bed. Nina was still sleeping, so Emma was quiet leaving their room. A dream from the night before followed her as she went down the stairs. There had been a snake, who had winked at Emma from underneath Just Jack's car. She had been about to blow him a kiss in return, but when she put her hand to lips, her teeth began to loosen, then fell out like hail to the ground. The dream followed Emma through the house, tugging at her nightgown as she went out into the backyard to look for Barney. Things for Barney hadn't been going so well lately. His whole face was grey now and his eyes had started to go a bluish white. He never chased the ball anymore when Mr. Purvis threw it. He moved slowly around the yard, spending most of his time sleeping under the porch.

It was the first morning without frost, and the sun was shining strong. Emma had put her rubber boots on before going out, but was still chilly in her nightgown. She looked next door, and was relieved to see Barney in the yard, lying on the warmed patio stones. He lifted his tail, and brought it down hard repetitively, thumping out an angry pulse. Emma closed her eyes, and saw the inside of a veterinarian's office. Oh no. No wonder he was so grumpy. Emma called his name, but Barney refused to turn around. Maybe he didn't hear me, Emma thought. Barney didn't hear so good most of the time these days. The thumping grew harder and his leg twitched. Not in a dreaming chasing squirrels sort of way, but more like he hated the world and would kick you if you were close enough.

Mr. Purvis opened the door, "Okay, okay. But you know we'll be early if we leave now," he said over his shoulder, shaking the leash in Barney's direction. Barney lifted his head, looked towards the door, and lumbered off into the house.

By the time Mr. Purvis and Barney pulled out of the driveway, Emma had forgotten all about the snake and her teeth falling out. She went inside, got changed and had Cheerios with Lester, and then the two of them went out the front to ride around in the sunshine. Emma on the red scooter, Lester on the banana seat bike – back and forth, back and forth, up and down Columbia Street.

Just when her legs started to turn to jelly and her belly started to rumble for lunch, Emma began to feel Barney talking to her, began to hear his little old man voice inside her head. She couldn't see him at first, but then, a moment later, she saw the Purvis car come around the corner. She dropped her scooter and stared. It must be important if Barney was sending her words. Most of the time, he just sent pictures.

Betrayal, Barney said. *I knew we weren't going to the beach. Does he think I'm stupid? No, I was being cooperative. I thought that might make it better this time. But no, it was just the same as always – the smell of unhappy strangers, and being stabbed in the rump. A handful of chew treats aren't enough to make up for that! I'm not going to get any sleep tonight, I know. Not with this completely unnecessary incessantly throbbing pain in my behind.*

As the car approached the house, Emma tried to tell Barney to calm down – that it would be okay. But, it was like Barney couldn't hear Emma at all, even though she was right inside his head, in his body, soaking up every feeling he had, every word and thought that went through his head. The car pulled into the driveway, and Barney and Mr. Purvis got out. Emma was standing on the sidewalk, where Lester had started playing hopscotch. Lester was about to toss his beanbag, when they saw Barney hobble out of the car and follow Mr. Purvis into the house.

Emma picked up Lester's beanbag, and rushed through the rest of the game. She let Lester win, then went through the house and into the backyard to look for Barney.

Barney was there under the porch, but he wasn't himself. He looked over at Emma standing by the fence, but didn't move from where he was. Instead, he sent her pictures of what happened at the vet's office, and another one of him waking up under the coffee table in a puddle of his own pee.

Emma told Barney that he was a good dog, and it wasn't his fault, but he wasn't listening at all.

That's it for me. No more sneaky trips to that place. I've had a good life. When one gets to this point – the accidents on the rug are bad enough. No, it's time.

Then Emma remembered the snake and the teeth, and started to cry. She didn't know why thinking about the dream would make her cry, but she couldn't stop.

Barney stopped talking after that, and stayed under the porch with his back to the fence. Emma sat on the grass, trying to coax him out.

There was the sound of a car in the driveway. A door. Mamma Shirley's favourite 45 played on the stereo, "Midnight at the Oasis." Emma listened as Mamma Shirley sang along. When the song was over, it was quiet again. Emma didn't move from her spot by the fence.

"Come on, Barney, you're a good boy," Emma said as the late afternoon darkened. From Barney, nothing but silence.

Lester called to Emma outside the front of the house, Mamma Shirley joined in from inside, and then Nina's face was at the kitchen window, peering out into the backyard.

"Here she is," Nina said. "She's sitting in the dirt talking to herself."

Mamma Shirley's face was at the window too. Hard eyes.

She frowned. Whatever she said, Emma didn't hear.

Barney, don't be a big jerk. Emma said using her inside words. *You can't just give up. Only a stupid head would just give up.*

The patio door squeaked open. Mamma Shirley. Dinner.

Emma sat at the table with Lester and Nina and Jamie Francis. Mamma Shirley slammed down Emma's plate. "Don't pretend you didn't hear us, Emma. Dinner is at the same time, every single day. I don't have time to chase you down. And no more sitting in the dirt."

"Sorry," Emma said, keeping her eyes down.

After dinner, Emma didn't help with the dishes, and instead snuck back out to the yard to talk to Barney some more. She talked silent, and out loud. She was sweet and mean and whatever else she could think of. Nothing worked. Barney hadn't budged. It looked like he hadn't moved at all, not even to go in for dinner.

She stayed out by the fence until Mamma Shirley yelled out the kitchen window for Emma to stop talking to the damned dog like a crazy person and get her butt in the house.

Emma didn't say goodbye to Barney. She wouldn't. Instead, she went to her bedroom and stood by the window, watching Barney wander around the yard. Emma's plan was to stay awake as long as she could. Barney wouldn't leave while she was watching him. Emma knew that much for sure. She stood by the dresser, looking out into the night.

She could hear Mamma Shirley go to bed, could hear Jamie Francis come in, slam his door, then go quiet. Emma's eyes drooped and her legs wobbled as the night became a deep silence. Her body finally gave way, sinking down as birds began chirping. She could feel a dull cutting pain down the side of her leg as she went. Could feel her head hit the carpet floor, jarring her, but for a moment only. The urge to sleep was stronger than pain.

Later, she heard tires squealing, and for an instant she surfaced, then sank back down.

Then came daylight and Nina, screaming. "Oh my God, she's dead. She's dead!" Nina walked over to the window, where Emma was lying on the floor by the dresser. She gave Emma a little kick with her platform wedgies.

"Ow," Emma said, "Knock it off!"

"Oh my God, I thought you were dead!" Nina said. "I thought, oh my God, now I've got to deal with a dead girl in my room on top of everything else."

Lester bounded into the bedroom. "Who's dead? Who's dead?" he asked, excited.

Jamie Francis followed. "What the hell?" he said, pushing down at his pajama bottom front and rubbing his head. He looked at Emma, still there on the floor. "What happened to your leg?"

Emma looked down. There was a bright, swollen red line running down the side of her leg. Then she remembered the open dresser drawer cutting into her leg as she was falling, falling, unable to stay awake.

"Barney!" Emma screamed as Mamma Shirley and Just Jack also came in the room. Emma got up and was running to the door, when Just Jack blocked the doorway with his big bear chest.

"Barney's dead," he said. "Sorry Emma. I know you really liked the dog, but he got hit by a car. He was there in the street when I pulled in the driveway this morning."

"We almost hit him!" Nina said. "Someone put a tire track right down his middle."

Mamma Shirley, who hadn't said anything this whole time, snapped her head around to look at Nina after that one. "What do you mean we?"

"Don't worry though, Emma," Nina said, ignoring Mamma Shirley. "Jack scooped him off the road and gave him back to old man Purvis, so you won't see his guts all over or anything."

Emma looked at Just Jack. There was blood across the chest

of his shirt, and over his arms. Barney's blood. Emma thought about how everyone was in her bedroom and that should have been a good thing, to have everyone together in her room, but it wasn't good at all. She couldn't breathe.

Emma pushed her way past Just Jack and went out to the backyard. She could hear Mamma Shirley yelling inside the house. "Where the hell were you all night? And what did Nina mean by *we*? I know that you were both out all night. Do you think I'm blind? You came home at the same time! I know, Jack, I know."

Doors slamming and Just Jack exploding like thunder. "You're crazy, Shirley. That's nuts. I told you, I was playing poker. You can call Stu and ask him. Go ahead. I'll give you the number. Now I've had it with the investigation, Sherlock. I'm going to bed."

In the backyard, there was nothing. No noises, no sounds of birds chirping or even the wind blowing in the trees. Emma stood in the grass, listening.

"Hello?" she called into the sun-soaked yard.

20.

RACHEL PULLED THE BENZ off Lakeshore and onto Parkside Drive. She'd had it washed on the way to the house. Sometimes it was best to leave it dirty, because when it was too clean, too shiny, it made her feel embarrassed. Made her think about people living in alleys, eating out of garbage cans. Most days she could get away with not thinking about things like that. We all have a choice in this life. Look at her; she had lots of excuses, lots of reasons to fall through the cracks. She could have made a mess of her life. But not everyone from a broken home grew up to be a broken person. Some decided on something better for themselves. Set their rudder for a better shore and hoisted sail. Straight into headwind, straight into a storm if need be, but onward.

Still, last night something inside her had felt unsettled. A small crack on the surface. Nothing big or dramatic, but still worth watching, like a hairline fracture on a windshield. It was the Easy-Bake Oven that had started it. Emma had been in the laundry room packing things up in there, and Rachel had been in the playroom, although she didn't like to call it that anymore. Playroom somehow seemed embarrassing now. It shouldn't be; everyone was a kid at one time or another. But still, there it was, playroom plus childhood equalled shame.

It had been so humbling, that it should be there in the playroom, behind the old orange sofa that Grandma had refused to throw out. As soon as she saw it, Rachel had remembered

– that was where she had stashed her dad's tie that day so long ago. She had thought about that tie often, had known it wouldn't be difficult to find as Grandma never threw anything out. Luckily she didn't buy new stuff much either, or her house would have looked like an episode of *Hoarders*. She had thought about looking for it often, but somehow, it had always been enough to know that somewhere in the basement her father's necktie was safe.

Perhaps it had been talking about her dad trying to finish the basement before he died that had made her turn the lights off. It was an embarrassing accident. She didn't want to deal with Emma, so it was easier to pretend it never happened. Emma had always been good like that. If anyone ever wanted to play "stick your head in the sand and make like whatever's happening wasn't," Emma was game. She didn't like confrontations. Rachel had only seen her fight for something once in her life. But that had been stupid. Emma had taken on the biggest bully in school for no apparent reason at all. Still, that was it. The only time Rachel saw Emma ever take a stand. So there really was no reason to explain about the lights. It was better to pretend it hadn't happened.

Rachel was in the driveway now. It had only been a minute since she turned off the Lake, but that minute was gone. She remembered what she had been thinking; turning the lights off in the basement, the Easy-Bake Oven, her dad. But she couldn't remember being in the car during that time. Couldn't remember her feet on the accelerator or hands on the wheel. She knew she put the turn signal on, and pulled onto Garden Avenue, then onto Indian Road. She must have done all these things, but all she could remember was that one minute she was on Lakeshore Boulevard, and the next, she was home.

She should have just left the stupid Easy-Bake Oven at the house last night, instead of lugging it up the stairs, hoping Emma wouldn't see, and then bringing it to her condo. She should have never looked inside. The tie was gone. Gone.

Why would Grandma keep the stupid toy all these years in a corner full of old tennis rackets and roller-skates so heavy with dust it was like they had grown moss, yet be bothered to reach inside, pull out the tie and put it somewhere else? Where? Where was it now? Idiotic, that she had brought the dirty old metal oven up the stairs and into her car. Once she had it home in her bedroom, she had opened the door to the oven again to look. Of course it hadn't been there. What had she expected? Magical thinking. Clearly, she'd been spending too much time with Emma.

Rachel pulled the keys out of the ignition, picked up her briefcase, and walked from the car toward old number 66. She brought her laptop from home with her this time. She had been up since six a.m., so she was prepared. She had a new to-do list, and a plan in place for the day. She would leave Emma to continue packing up the house, while Rachel attended to the endless paperwork that needed to be done in order to finish sorting out her grandmother's affairs. She still had to call the insurance company. She had meant to do that yesterday. What happened to the time? That day, too, like the drive from the Lakeshore, was also a blur. She'd have to go by the bank sometime during the day to close the account. She also had to look up the protocol online for cancelling Grandma's health card, her passport, old age pension, and birth certificate. And of course Robertson would have to be contacted to sort out the ridiculous mix up with Wanda and the will. Then later this evening, Sam would be flying in. There was no need to pick him up, as he said he'd take a cab. At least that was one less thing to worry about.

Even before she was up the steps to the house, Rachel could hear voices laughing inside. The fact that Emma was up at all at this time of day was a shocker, but already up and chatting away to someone? Maybe one of the repairmen had come early. Rachel had hired a crew to come by to do the basics, but most of the work she had ordered was for outside. There were repairs to be done to the disintegrating old wood fence, and to the concrete on the walk and the stairs up to the house. The dangling eaves would need to be fixed as well, of course.

She almost knocked. It was the laughter that threw her off. She was on the outside not knowing what was going on inside her own house. Or, at least half of it would be hers soon. She fished in her purse for the key and opened the door.

Emma was wearing Grandma's purple terry-cloth bathrobe again. It slid off one of her shoulders, leaving a wide, deep V in the front, which showed off her cleavage. She was sitting at the kitchen table laughing, and dipping cut up strips of toast into a soft-boiled egg. Soldiers. That's what Grandma used to call it when she made their toast like that. "Take your soldier for a yolk dip," she'd tell them.

Lester was sitting across the table from her. Clearly, he had come to the house like a white knight to save Emma, the damsel in distress. He looked up at Rachel. He was wearing jeans, but no top. That was the worst part. Lester always had a nice chest – not too much hair, but not totally hairless. Some men shaved these days. So silly. What woman wants full body stubble burns? His hair was a mess and that was what really stood out to Rachel. When he had been with her, Lester was always fussing with his hair. He had never let her touch it. She used to call him egomaniacal when they were fighting, and a peacock when things were good. "Oh here he comes strutting his stuff," she'd say, and they'd laugh, just the two of them for a moment, and no one else. In those moments, he was Rachel's boy. Rachel's Lester. Hers.

"Oh shit, what time is it?" Emma pulled the bathrobe up on her shoulders when she saw Rachel come in. No "hello," "good morning," or anything like that, more like she had been caught in the act.

"Hi Lester, how are you doing?" Rachel said, putting her briefcase on the floor and hanging up her coat as if it were another day at the office. Someone had to be normal, show some sense of decorum.

"Rachel!" he said, as if surprised. Oh come on. He knew Rachel would be walking through that door any minute. She bet that's why he kept his shirt off. He knew what effect that would have on her.

"I like how big your eyes get when you look at me naked," he had said to her once, back when they were living together. Rachel had hated him for saying that. It was one thing to be putty in a man's hands, and another for him to point it out. That was then. Time had passed. Rachel was older, wiser, stronger now.

"Don't let me interrupt your breakfast. I've got some calls to make this morning," Rachel said as she headed into the dining room.

"Coffee? You want some?" Emma, overcompensating for her guilt, but Rachel wasn't in the mood. It was too early in the morning for the drama of the Emma show.

"No," Rachel yelled, adding "thank you" as a barely audible afterthought.

"Lester came over late last night to check on me," Emma yelled now from the kitchen. Coward. "He said he wanted to help out today so –"

Let her talk. Rachel knew how to turn it off. She could no longer understand English, she told herself. It was just sound, with no meaning attached. It worked. It always worked. It was a trick Rachel had invented long ago. At first it had been her own thoughts that she couldn't turn off, as they rambled through her mind in the dark of her bedroom during that time after Wanda had left. She had tried to make her mind stop thinking, but it never worked. So she had come to the idea that if she tried, she could convince herself that she was listening to a foreign language, and she could tune it out. It had taken a bit of practice, but eventually she had it down to an art. All the chatter of her thoughts had become noise, like an adult speaking in a Charlie Brown cartoon. Eventually she had also learned how to do it with voices outside of her head. Of course Emma's was the first. *Blah, blah, blah* – oh what interesting sounds. What a musical language. No meaning, no meaning, just sound bubbling in her brain like a creek in spring.

Rachel took out her phone, glad that she had remembered to bring her charger with her this time. She dialed the number to Robertson's office, and had him on the line within seconds. What a difference a day, and modern technology, made.

"I'm sorry, Rachel, there's nothing that can be done about it now. The law's pretty clear." And then, after Rachel suggested incompetence on his part, "These things happen, Rachel. I've been in this situation before, so don't worry. We have an associate who's an ace at tracking people down. I spoke to her yesterday, and told her to go by the house to see you. She's very good. If your mother's out there, we'll find her. And if she isn't, well, we'll find that out too."

"And of course that will be an extra expense on your final bill, won't it?"

"We'll keep it reasonable," Robertson said. "Give us a couple of days, to see what we come up with."

Rachel hung up the phone. She would not be daunted. A dark cloud was only a dark cloud, not a storm. Wanda would be located. The first time she had disappeared, Wanda returned on her own. This time, she'd be rooted from wherever she'd been hiding all these years – whether she liked it or not. The house would be sorted. On schedule.

Emma stood in the entranceway, looking sheepish. Rachel tried not to think of her in bed with Lester the night before, under the covers giggling in the dark house. This house – half hers.

"I just wanted to let you know that the funeral home called just before you came this morning," Emma said. "Well, they said they can't get the minister you wanted. They can't seem to find anyone. But don't worry, because I've got an idea..."

Why hadn't they called her on her cell? Rachel was the executor. They had all her numbers. Cell, home, office. Who calls the home of a dead woman to tell her there's a glitch in her funeral arrangements? The notice hadn't even gone in the paper yet, that was further down on the list. Maybe they could do the funeral early next week. They could do the cremation this week as planned, and hold off a few days. It wasn't like they were going to do an open casket. Lucky for the funeral home, or they'd really get an earful. Could you imagine if that had been their plan? How would they keep her fresh all this time? She still hadn't managed to get over there to sign the contract. Maybe she should just agree to hand all the arrangements over to Sam; she had so many other details to attend to.

Emma stopped talking and sulked back into the kitchen. Rachel heard the table being cleared, dishes being washed, the fridge door opening and closing. Lester left Emma to the clean up, and walked down the hall toward the bathroom. He was likely preening for his next appearance.

An hour or so later, there was a knock on the front door. Emma was closest at the time, but Rachel bounded up and toward the door, noticing how Emma cowered a bit as she passed her. Emma was always so scared of everything.

Through the peephole, Rachel saw another face she didn't recognize. A woman this time, in a light grey business suit. The woman looked professional, hair all pulled back into a neat bun. Likely a Jehovah's Witness coming to convince them all that there was such thing as a God. How could human civilization come so far? We've landed on the moon, sent satellites out to the edges of the solar system. How much proof do we need? All that's up there is space, dust, gas, planets, stars, black holes and dark matter, like a web holding the whole apparatus together. But God? Some guy in a long white beard looking down on us all? No. In thousands of years, not one scrap of verifiable evidence has been found to support their claims, besides the odd face of Jesus, burned suspiciously onto the surface of a tortilla, or a slice of toasted Wonder Bread.

Rachel opened the door. "Yes? Can I help you?" she asked the woman.

"Are you Rachel? Or is it Emma?" The woman removed her sunglasses. They were oversized, like Jackie O's. That should have been the tip off: Jehovah's Witnesses don't wear sunglasses. And they certainly don't come to the door already knowing your name. How did she know their names? Rachel didn't like to be at a disadvantage.

"I'm sorry," the woman said. "I should have introduced myself. My name is Ms. Fletcher. Nina. You can call me Nina. I got a call from George Robertson, and I was in the area. He said we should get started on your case right away."

Rachel blinked in the sunlight.

The woman seemed to be able to read her thoughts. Whoever she was, she was astute.

"Finding your mother so you can settle your grandmother's will," she said. "Oh, yes of course," Rachel said. "That was fast. Yes, it is a rush. Please, come in." Rachel ushered the woman into the house. After that, the two exchanged the requisite pleasantries. It's getting warm outside, isn't it? Can I get you coffee, tea, water? Rachel was relieved when Nina said no. She didn't want to waste time fiddling with coffee filters or tea bags – she wanted to get this show on the road. Apparently, Ms. Fletcher did too, as she looked at the empty kitchen chair. It was the same chair that Lester had been sitting in.

"May I?" She sat down, and opened her briefcase without waiting for an answer. On a pad of yellow paper, Rachel saw the notes. The woman's writing was messy, but still you could make out a few of the words. "Mother." "Wanda." "Dead or Alive."

Rachel sat across from the woman, looking quick at the light switch. She didn't need to touch it; looking was enough. She looked once, only once.

"So when was the last time you saw you mother?" Ms. Fletcher asked.

"When she lived here," Rachel replied, immediately feeling like an idiot when she noticed the look of puzzlement her cryptic statement was met with.

"After she brought Emma back," Rachel tried again. No, no. That didn't help. She was giving this woman the wrong impression and coming off like a flake.

Nina's purse began to buzz.

"Excuse me," she said, adding, "My daughter just learned to text." Nina opened her purse and glanced at her phone. Rachel took the moment to compose herself.

"I was eleven, Emma was ten," Rachel said. "It was 1977." Better. That was better. She started to feel more herself and answered the rest of the questions with her usual level of clarity. Facts, they were Rachel's business. She put together facts and made sense of them. What was the probability that Wanda would be found? It was too early to say. There were too many variables not yet accounted for. One of which was this Ms. Fletcher. So far, Rachel liked her. She was cool, unaffected, and efficient. She didn't try to console Rachel, or heaven forbid, do something ridiculous like reach across the table and pat her hand. No. She was there to do a job, and so far seemed to be doing it well. If appearances were any indication, Ms. Fletcher would up the probability of getting this mess sorted in time considerably.

"Oh my God! Nina? Nina Buziak?"

Rachel turned around. Behind her, Emma was standing in the doorway, staring at Ms. Fletcher as if she had seen a ghost. Buziak? Where did she get that name? And how did Emma have any connection to this calm, competent woman sitting at their grandmother's kitchen table.

Ms. Fletcher's composure faltered for a moment. Her brow furrowed, she took a deep breath as if winded as she looked towards the door.

"Emma," she said. That was all. No emotion was betrayed on her face, yet her voice suggested recognition, and something else that Rachel couldn't put a label on.

"What are you doing here?" Emma asked, now starting to giggle.

Nina was about to reply. She opened her mouth, then closed it again, as she stared behind Rachel to the doorway where Emma stood. Lester was standing next to Emma now. At least he had put a shirt on.

"Oh my God." It was apparently Nina's turn to call out the name of the lord now. It became clear to Rachel that something was going on that she didn't understand. Details and information that it seemed everyone in the room was privy to, except her.

"Lester," Nina said, still staring. "Lester – Templeton? It's Templeton right?"

Lester smiled.

"Yep, that's right. Templeton. It's me."

Emma walked over towards Nina, as if she was going to touch her. Make sure she was real.

"Nina Buziak," she repeated. Rachel was getting frustrated. Okay, clearly everyone here knows everyone's name. Enough already.

"So, you all... You all know one another?" Rachel needed to say something to insert her presence once again into the proceedings. Just when it seemed things were beginning to move forward, that this Nina Fletcher, or Buziak or whatever her name was, actually had the ability to solve the Wanda dilemma and put things back on track, all it took was for Emma to merely enter the room for the whole process to slide into chaos.

Lester beamed. Nina looked decidedly flustered and uncomfortable.

"We all go way back," Emma said, giggling again.

Great, Rachel thought. That made it clear as mud. Way back where? Okay, enough staring and giggling and making no sense. Time to get the morning back on track.

"Anyway, Ms. Fletcher…" was all Rachel managed to get out of her mouth, when there was a knock at the door. "Oh, for Chrissake, now what?" Rachel said, not meaning to say it out loud. She was on her feet, pushing past Lester with a slight shove that felt cathartic, and moving to the door.

The peephole showed two men standing on the porch in overalls. The repairmen. She had been eager for them to come. They were supposed to be at the house half an hour ago. Still, she resented their presence now. It took her from the kitchen, and the conversation that continued on without her. Rachel opened the door and gave the men their instructions: paint the garage, then repair the fence and the eaves. Check back with her after that to see what else. Was she barking at them? They looked frazzled and confused, like they wanted to linger and tell her their life stories. No, instead, they began to ask stupid questions about what kind of paint she wanted them to use, and how she wanted them to secure the eaves. Had she considered replacing them altogether? Because to them, it looked like it would be just as much work to repair what was up there than to tear the whole thing down and start new. Then they began to argue about the possible costs of a new installation versus the relative length of time repairs would likely last until they would have to be done again.

"For fuck's sakes, just fix the thing." Oh. That didn't come out right at all. The men both stood staring at her, speechless. One turned to leave.

"No! I'm sorry," Rachel said, feeling insincere. Apologies in general were a waste of time. If you did something and it was a mistake, it would become apparent by the fact that you didn't do it again. Apologies always seemed like sucking up, a way to get off the hook. "I'm sorry," Rachel repeated. "My mother. Our mother died a few days ago. This was her house. We just want to clean it up enough to sell." She had no idea why she lied. Things were happening too fast. There was no time to think clearly. Instead, she felt like she was flying on instinct, doing whatever her impulses dictated. It seemed as if, with each breath, the probability of her taking a misstep was increasing exponentially.

The men seemed relieved by her explanation, as expressions of condolence passed over their faces. That was worse. She should have left it at the swearing. Now she got pity. Pathetic.

"Sorry," she said again, in spite of herself, then closed the door.

21.

THE FIRST TIME that Rachel heard about Emma was on a postcard from Wanda that arrived out of the blue. It had been three months since she'd left, and in that time, there had been no word, not a whisper of news. Then one day after school, Rachel opened the mailbox and there it was, a postcard from Vancouver.

It was a photograph of a cityscape, with two huge, looming, snow-covered mountains in the distance. British Columbia was pretty, but dangerous. Rachel learned about it in social studies class. There were potential landslides, earthquakes, and tsunamis to deal with there.

Scrawled across the back: *Made my way out here for a break. Will settle in for a bit before I head home, love Mom.* And underneath, PS: *To Grandma, I found her.*

Her. There was a *her* out in Vancouver who Wanda had found. Someone from before, when she left and did something so bad that nobody would talk about it after. No, that wasn't true. Rachel's mind pulled up memories and spun through them for evidence like she was searching a library microfilm. There had been moments, the few times Grandma was allowed to come and visit them over the years, moments between mother and daughter that Rachel never quite understood.

"You should look for her," Grandma had said, stirring gravy in her snowman apron the year Rachel got an Etch-A-Sketch for Christmas.

"You should leave it alone," Rachel's mom replied, her hand slippery with grease, fumbling with the faux wooden handle of a carving knife hilt-deep in turkey.

"If you don't go, I'm going. She needs to know she has family." Grandma had stopped stirring after that, letting the bottom of the gravy pan burn.

Rachel had thought they were talking about her. She was seven, and the day before she had been over to play at her next-door neighbour Julie Yamagata's house. Julie had a type of bathrobe she called a "kimono" with birds and mountains on it that she let Rachel wear. Rachel had figured that her mother and grandmother thought she had gone over to the Yamagata's again, and had fallen so in love with the satiny Japanese robe that she forgot who her real family was. It had been the only thing that made sense at the time. She was a kid back then. She hadn't yet realized the importance of keeping track.

There had been other moments too, when Rachel had wondered if there were more going on in her family than she was aware of. These moments, like little splinters on the surface of their everyday life, seemed to lead into a world that only Wanda and Grandma could understand. Sam had given her the impression that the parent to watch was her dad. But all along it had been her mother's stance on some unseen fault line that sent the tremors through the earth beneath them all. Rachel's father hadn't been the one with the secrets. He had been quiet, but simple. Wanda? Wanda had been the one to watch. It had been the aftershocks of her decisions that tore their family apart.

"Humph, we'll see," was what Grandma said when she finished reading the postcard and put it back down on the dining-room table. Rachel watched from the hall, her fingers itching for the light switch, forcing herself to stand still. It was the worst. The worst news ever possible. The *her* was a little girl. Rachel's sister. Wanda's secret daughter. A few weeks afterwards, when Rachel came home from school, there she was, sitting on the couch. She was almost Rachel's age, with dark curly hair and dark skin. She looked foreign, and wore a silver chain around her neck, with a turtle pendant the size of an egg. She looked at Rachel. Scared. Hopeful. Rachel looked away. She wished they would take the little brown Turtle Girl back home. Rachel wanted her father back, not some stranger who was supposed to be her sister now.

"Rachel," Grandma said from behind her. "Rachel, this is Emma dear. She used to live in Vancouver, and now she's going to live here with us. She is your sister. Well, half sister to be precise. But the point is, she's family now, so we're going to welcome her with open arms."

"Where's Sam?" Rachel asked, refusing to look at either Turtle Girl or her grandmother.

"Rachel, I know it's all very sudden, but you have to…" Grandma tried, but Rachel turned away and left the room in search of Sam. On her way past the kitchen, she stopped. Wanda stopped too, frozen to the spot with one hand holding a jar of mustard, and the other hand propping open the refrigerator door.

"Who are you?" Rachel asked, not giving Wanda any time to reply, instead, she turned away, and stomped up the stairs. When she reached the landing she stopped for a moment then turned to look back down into the kitchen. Wanda the Question Mark was still standing where Rachel had left her, the stupid mustard jar still in her hand, and her mouth hanging wide open.

Sam wasn't in his room, but upstairs was better than downstairs where everything was in the middle of becoming terrible. Rachel went to her own bedroom instead, and took her father's tie out of her Easy-Bake Oven, where she had stuffed it after she had tucked it aside the day they had gone through his clothes. She balled it up, trying to make it fit inside her fist, but her hand was too small. Instead, she lifted her shirt, wrapped it around her waist, tied it and dropped her shirt back down. It reminded her of the time she saw the picture of Muhammad

Ali in the newspaper. His fist was pumped in the air, and his waist was circled with his thick shiny heavyweight belt. *Float like a butterfly, sting like a bee.*

"Rachel!" Grandma's voice was calling. It was okay. Rachel was ready now.

Downstairs there were sandwiches and cookies on the table, like they had company. But Turtle Girl wasn't company. She was staying put whether Rachel wanted her to or not.

"Come sit with us Rachel," Grandma said. Rachel grudgingly shuffled towards the couch next to her grandmother. At the other end was Turtle Girl. Wanda was in the rocking chair, drinking rum and Tab from a coffee cup and lighting a smoke off the end of her last one.

Rachel flopped down, sending a ripple through her grandmother to Emma on the other end of the couch. "Where's Sam?" Rachel asked again.

"Sam's working at the Burger Chef. It's just us girls," Grandma replied.

Rachel looked over to the other end of the couch, where Emma sat wide-eyed. Rachel still hadn't heard Turtle Girl's voice, but you could tell, she was soft. Rachel could take her.

"Where is she supposed to sleep?" Rachel asked her grandmother.

"Sam's moving out, so she can get his room when he's gone, and in the meantime she can sleep in my bed. I'll sleep on the pull out," Wanda replied, puffing.

"You can take the guest room, Wanda," Grandma said "Or stay in there with me. It's a double."

"I'm fine on the pull out, thanks," Wanda said, not looking at her mother.

"Sam's moving out? What are you talking about? Since when? Where's he going?" Rachel wanted them to stop talking about stupid things and get to the point of how exactly her world was being ripped to shreds.

"Oh sweets, don't be upset," Grandma said. "It won't be till after he graduates. He's decided he's going to take a year off before he goes to college and try living in an apartment with some friends. I, of course, think it's a terrible idea, and that he should just go right into school. He could still live away with his friends if he wanted to, and I told him I'd cover the rent and tuition for him, of course, but your mother here just –"

"Yeah, okay Mom, enough commentary." Wanda's rum and Tab was almost done. It wasn't her first. Rachel could hear it in her voice.

"Well, he never told me anything, so I don't know –" Rachel started.

"He told us before he went on his shift tonight. You weren't home from school yet," Wanda said. "He met Emma, too. Right, Emma honey?" Rachel looked at Wanda, looking at Emma. Then she looked at the light switches. What she really wanted to do was set something on fire.

"Um, yes. I met Sam. I guess he's my half brother. I guess." Emma spoke. Her voice didn't match how scared she looked. It was deep like a grown up woman. Sam. *Her* half-brother.

Rachel looked at her grandmother. "Why don't me and you go live somewhere? What about your apartment in Florida?"

Grandma laughed, then covered her mouth, like she didn't mean to, but it slipped out. Still, the laugh travelled, and landed like a bruise on Rachel's cheek. "No, hon, we're all going to stay here together. It'll be good, you'll see."

The last time Grandma had used those words, after Rachel's father died, Rachel had believed them, and they had come true. This time they seemed like flimsy, desperate crumbs for Rachel's hunger for solid ground. There was none. Landslide. Earthquake.

Rachel stayed silent, while Wanda and Grandma made polite talk with Emma.

"Yes," Emma said, "I liked Vancouver, but I didn't live there. We lived in New West, in Foster's – um – in a foster home. There's a river in New West, but to get to the ocean you have to go to Vancouver. I like the ocean better. Um – Yeah." Emma smiled like a puppy waiting for a treat.

Wanda smiled too, put on her sweet listening face, squinting in her own smoke. "And were there any other kids at the, ah, place where you were honey?" she said.

Oh give me a break, Rachel thought. Honey? It was honey now? Oh, wait till she saw. Wait till little Miss Turtle Girl saw what really happened around here when all the new niceness settled down. Rachel almost felt sorry for the girl for a moment. Then, no. She wouldn't be duped. It was a trick of the enemy to get you to feel for them. Then, when you were all suckered in – *wham!* They gave it to you when you least expected it.

"Yes, there were other kids where I used to live," Emma said. "Jamie Francis, who's from England, but that doesn't mean that he's gay, and Lester, who is – um – um – different. And there was this mean girl, who smelled like bacon. She got sent away because of kissing Just Jack in the car. And there was Mamma Shirley, but she wasn't really…"

Well, at least she was a blathering idiot. Rachel knew the type. Eager to please. Easy to manoeuver.

"Emma," Rachel said. Emma stopped mid-sentence. Wanda and Grandma turned to look at Rachel, with a mixture of hope, fear, and warning in both of their eyes. "Emma, how about I take you outside and show you the backyard? Would you like that?" Rachel could play along. She knew the words to the make-nice song as well as anyone else.

Emma perked up like it was Christmas. "Is it okay?" she asked Wanda. Wanda nodded. "Yay, hooray. Thanks, Rachel."

Rachel got up and led the way, thinking, this was going to be a piece of cake.

As soon as they were in the backyard, Emma started chirping up. "Do you guys have any pets here?" she asked, peering around the yard, and then to the yards next door.

"Yes, I have a cat," Rachel replied quickly. "Say, Emma?" She went on, taking a deep breath to steady herself.

"Yeah," Emma replied.

"I really like your necklace. So you met Sam, eh?"

"Oh, thanks," Emma said, looking down at her turtle pendant. "Yeah, I met Sam. He seems nice. He's way older than you are, though. Wow, I just can't believe I'm here. Like, a minute ago I was in New West with Jenny and Big..." Rachel cut Emma short.

"So I just wanted to warn you about Sam. Just so you know." Rachel stopped for a moment, noticing the sparkle suddenly darkening in the little girl's eyes.

"What about Sam just so I know?" Emma asked.

"Well, you have to watch out for him because sometimes he just goes crazy and yells and calls people mean names and, um, smashes things. And throws things at people. Mostly people who try to hang out with him." There, that should be sufficient, Rachel thought.

"Are you sure?" Emma asked, looking out over the garden. "I mean, he was nice to me, and I can usually tell if someone's mean right away."

"No, trust me," Rachel said, following Emma's stare.

"Okay, if you say so," Emma replied.

Easy-peasy, Rachel thought. Emma wandered over toward the end of the garden where Rachel and her grandmother planted the flowerbed after Dad died. The sign they made together: *Rachel's Secret Garden, KEEP OUT!* was still there, though the ink had faded and warped under the Saran Wrap. Emma walked right toward it, and looked down at the forget-me-nots. Rachel put her hand to her waist. The smooth fabric under her shirt soothed her fingers. Emma stopped in front of the flowerbed.

"Who died here?" she asked, bending down to get a closer look.

It was like when someone came up behind you, someone mean, some bully who always tripped you when you were getting off the bus, and all of a sudden they came up behind you and cupped their hands onto the side of your head and all the wind bashed your skull in for a moment. That was how it felt to hear those words from Emma's mouth. How did she know? Rachel pulled the tie tighter around her waist. *Who died here?* How dare she? You want to know? Rachel wanted to yell. You want to know who died here you little friggin' Turtle Girl? We all did, that's who. All of us. And just when we started to come back to life, you show up.

"Get away from my garden." Rachel didn't mean to say it out loud. It just slipped out. It wasn't part of the plan at all. She had snapped like a reflex, jumping like a rubber mallet on a shin.

Emma looked more startled than hurt. She was so doe eyed. Like a dodo, a birdbrain.

"Oh, sorry!" Emma said, jumping back. "I wasn't going to touch it or anything. I can tell it's a special place, it's just I was wondering, cause I... Sorry."

Because she what? Rachel waited, but Emma didn't continue. She stared at Rachel's garden, with her eyebrows furrowed. It gave Rachel the creeps. Emma knew someone had died. How did she know? Maybe she was putting on an act, pretending to be innocent to get Rachel to put her guard down. She wouldn't though. She wasn't born yesterday.

"Yeah, okay. Sorry to yell like that," she said. "I just – I saw a wasp. It was coming right at you."

More jumping back from Emma. She was like a wind-up toy.

"So, yeah," Rachel started up again, leading Emma away from the garden, and towards the other side of the back yard. "What do you think of Wanda?" Rachel asked.

"Well, she's nice. She drinks a lot sometimes and forgets stuff, but her hair is pretty. I think she's just really sad. Does she cry a lot?" Emma asked.

It was something that hadn't dawned on Rachel until that moment. Her mother did cry a lot. Rachel thought it was just that her mother cried more than Grandma and Rachel and Dad and Sam. But now that she was thinking about it, her mother cried more than anyone Rachel had ever known. Sometimes, she cried every morning. Rachel supposed she'd never noticed because she'd thought it was normal. It wasn't though. Rachel wished it would have been someone else, anyone else in that moment that helped her see that there had been something wrong with her mother for as long as she could remember. Emma knew too much for someone so apparently clueless. Rachel promised herself she'd keep her wits about her as long as Emma was around.

"Well, Wanda wouldn't tell you right off. She wouldn't want you to know in case it made you upset." Rachel was flying by the seat of her pants now.

Emma was all ears. "What? What does Wanda not want me to know about?" she asked.

Rachel paused for dramatic effect. "She doesn't want you to know that she's only got you here on a trial basis."

Emma's eyebrows pinched together. "What do you mean 'a trial basis'?"

Rachel knew she was onto something now. "Well, she just wanted to bring you back here to test you out. To see if you could get along with everyone. Me especially. She said that if we aren't happy with you she's going to send you back."

Emma's eyes lit up. "Back to Foster's – I mean to the house on Columbia Street?"

Rachel had to make a quick course adjustment. "No, not that place. No, Wanda would have to send you to a different place. Somewhere in Alaska." Rachel felt a tinge of pride for being so quick on her feet. Even though Alaska was on the coast, it was still pretty far from both Vancouver and Toronto. And it wasn't even in Canada, a bonus.

Emma's face froze. Her eyes looked far away and hollow. She stood there for a moment, looking at nothing; then, her voice was a low rumble. "But I don't want to go to Alaska. I'd rather go back to the house on Columbia Street."

Rachel should have gone with something simpler, like telling

Emma that Wanda was an axe murderer or something. But she wanted a two-for-one, to put a wedge between Emma and her mother, and keep this little Turtle Girl under her thumb. "You can't go back there. It's full now. Some other little girl took your place. All the foster homes in Canada are full."

Emma looked like someone had hit her. She grabbed hold of her turtle pendant and sat down on the ground. "There's a new girl there now? I thought – I thought that Just Jack and Mamma Shirley broke up. They said they were breaking up and that's why we all had to go. But it was me? They just sent me away? Is Jamie Francis still there? What about Lester?"

Rachel couldn't help it. She felt bad for the Turtle Girl. She was in too deep now though. She'd have to see it through. "No, none of your old friends are there anymore. They're all gone too. So the point is that if Wanda doesn't think we get along, she's going to send you to Alaska." Emma was crying now. Rachel couldn't see her eyes, but she could hear from the girl's sniffing sounds. Rachel didn't want to, it was stupid to be so soft in a moment when she almost had everything under control, but watching Emma made her tear up as well.

"Listen Emma," Rachel said, bending down. "I won't let that happen to you. I won't let them take you to Alaska. You just have to trust me, and do what I tell you? Like for one thing, make sure you stay away from Wanda. Don't follow her around and talk to her all the time. She doesn't like that." Rachel helped Emma up. "Now, you don't have to cry. It's going to be okay, you'll see."

Emma tried to smile. "Thanks, Rachel. Don't worry. I won't be trouble. If I can't go back..." Emma stopped for a moment, and Rachel was wondering what she was thinking.

"I was just thinking," Emma said, as if on cue, "that if I can't go back, I've got to make it work out here. I don't want to have to leave again, especially to go live in Alaska. So, don't worry, there won't be any trouble from me."

"Thanks Emma. I'll look out for you. Now wipe up your

face, okay?" Rachel said. Her eyes were dry, but a lump had crept into her throat. She wanted to go inside now, inside and away from Turtle Girl and her contagious tears. Emma wiped her eyes on her sleeve and headed toward the house. Rachel led, without looking back.

22.

WITH RACHEL BUSY with Nina Buziak in the kitchen, and the workmen outside, Emma decided it was time to go up to the attic to take a look around. She knew what she was looking for, and didn't want to hear one of Rachel's tirades if she found it.

The book had been calling to her. Just like it had that time when she first found it in the basement. How had she forgotten it all these years? It had been Wanda's, and then it had been hers – her first introduction into the world of astrology. Before that she had known she was a Pisces, and that she was sensitive and poetic and mystic and scattered. But the book had taken her deeper, into a world of planets and aspects, and all the geometrical patterns created between them. A world where mythology met astronomy. That had always been at the heart of Rachel's objection to anything astrological: it messed around in astronomy's sandbox, and that was in Rachel's backyard. That was her sacred soil, her secret burial ground. Emma thought about that first day when Rachel and Emma had met, and Rachel had taken her out into the garden and Emma had seen it – the little patch of dirt that had held all of Rachel's sadness. Emma hadn't thought, hadn't given enough time for the meaning of the words that appeared in her mind to register before they had come out of her mouth.

"Who died here?" Emma could tell from the way that Rachel wheeled around and glared at her that there would be no magic, no silent talking, no secret world between them. Rachel was scared of that stuff, she'd made that much clear. She was scared of death too. Emma would know better next time.

Emma went upstairs, and into the closet of Wanda's bedroom. On the ceiling of the closet, there was a little square cut-out hole that went up into the attic. She would need a ladder. She couldn't get the one from the basement, Rachel would hear, but she could pull a chair over and stand on it. That should give her enough height to get the cover moved to the side, but then she'd have to hoist herself up there somehow. Maybe if she stood on a milk crate? Had she seen any milk crates in the house?

"I could give you a boost," Lester said, standing behind her.

"Oh Jesus!" Emma put her hand on her chest.

"If you want to get up there," he said. "I could give you a boost. You never know what you'll find in these old houses. I mean, there could be heirlooms, a Picasso, you never know. There's this show where people go around and clean houses out. You wouldn't believe the stuff they find."

Yes. Yes, actually, a boost from Lester would be a big help, would give her just enough extra height to get up there. But then he might want to come up too. No, she wanted to go up alone.

"Well sure, but –" she started, before Lester cut in.

"Can you believe that? Nina fucking Buziak. She looked good, eh?" Lester was on the other side of the bedroom, dragging the big old green chair over from the corner.

"No take that one." Emma pointed to the straight-backed wooden one behind the door.

"Oh. Okay. Yeah, so holy shit, eh? Who would have thought that we'd all meet up here in Toronto after, what has it been? Thirty years?" Lester looked up at the ceiling for a moment, nodding his head slightly as he calculated. "Actually, it's been at least thirty-*five* years. Yep, over thirty-five fucking years, all right." Nina Buziak. As soon as she had shown up at Grandma's house Emma had known that Wanda would be found. It wasn't like with the animals, where images and impressions would float into her mind. It wasn't like words appearing either. No, this kind of knowing came from somewhere deeper. Thoughts and feelings combined into some intangible extra-sensory soup. Like when someone called and you knew who it was before you answered, Emma just knew that Wanda would be found. Who would have thought it would be her childhood tormentor who would finally lead them all back to their mother. Emma thought of Grandma and smiled.

"You want it here, or further to the back? I think it should be further to the back." Lester tried the chair at various angles, settling with its back wedged to the side of the closet.

"We should all go out for drinks. You, me, and Nina Buziak. Fuck. Can you believe it? Who would have thought we'd see her again? Boy, she freaked when she saw you, eh? No way could she forget what a bitch she used to be back in the day. Did you see her face? She would have had no way of knowing what she was walking into when she came to work today, that's for sure."

It was funny now to think of how Rachel had looked in that moment, when it had become clear that they all somehow knew each other. She had looked shocked, like someone had smacked her across the face with a fish. Rachel had been the odd one out, and something was going on that she not only couldn't control, but also didn't understand.

"Unanticipated variables," Rachel always said, "are the death of any attempt at predicting an outcome."

Emma shouldn't have giggled. She knew it wasn't nice, the way she got a kick out of it whenever Rachel got the rug pulled out from under her. It wasn't nice, but it was natural. Everyone had a shadow side; Jung had settled it. And it did do Rachel some good to have her perfectly ordered world shaken up a bit, just enough overturn of the soil that new life could grow.

"Imagine what it must have been like to be her," Lester said, stepping out of the closet. "There you are, off to do your job, just another day, when suddenly your past is standing in front of you. She probably thought she was in *The Twilight Zone*." He laughed, then made a sweeping gesture with his hands, inviting Emma to enter the closet and step up onto the chair.

Lester always loved it when life became unpredictable and squirrely. Lester bored easily, which was one reason for the Rachel, Lester, Emma triangle.

Emma stepped up onto the chair, her socks sliding a bit on the smooth wooden surface. Lester steadied her. She reached up. She was still a good two feet short.

"I've got an idea. Why don't you stand on my shoulders?" Lester said, wedging himself in beside her. "I'll crouch down and you can climb on." Lester shimmied himself into a squat position next to chair, and Emma stepped onto his shoulders. He slowly stood up, and Emma pushed the square wooden cover to one side. Dust and bits of insulation flew out of the dark hole with a whoosh of air. Lester stood with his legs straight, and Emma hoisted herself up and onto the old, wooden boards of the attic floor.

"I'll just get on the chair then and..."

"No. Please," Emma said. "I just want to take a look around by myself. If that's okay."

Silence, at first.

Then he said, "Sure. Okay. Well, sure. Just let me know if you need anything."

Footsteps crossed the bedroom.

"Sorry. Thank you," Emma shouted through the hole.

Lester closed the bedroom door behind him.

She'd try to make it up to him later. Do something, or say something to let him know she appreciated him. One day he'll get sick of this, she told herself. Then I'll really be lonely. Then I'll be free. Better alone already, than waiting for the day to come when he finally left her. Funny, Emma never felt that way about Rachel. With Rachel, it was like a given, no matter how much time passed or what happened between them, Rachel would always be around.

Rachel, the Actuary. Emma had never even heard of the word until Rachel corrected her when she said her sister was an accountant. "Actually, I'm an actuary," Rachel had said. Emma had laughed, liking the sound of the two words together. The actuary sorts through infinite possibilities in order to ascertain what will actually occur. Ha! No way Rachel could have predicted the appearance of Nina Buziak.

Nina Fletcher now, so she had said. She had turned out well, looking all put together and lawyerly. Emma had always thought that Nina would have fallen through the cracks of "the system" as Lester called it. "We grew up in the system," that was what he always said, and every time he said it, it made Emma think of *The Wall*, that Pink Floyd movie. She thought of them at Foster's house like hamburger churning through a machine. That must have been how Lester felt, shuffled from one house to another. Maybe that was why he was the most damaged of all of them. Emma, Nina, even Rachel all had had their lives turned upside down as children, and they had all turned out all right by society's standards. At least Nina and Rachel had. Emma, maybe not so much.

Emma looked into the attic. Darkness.

"Here, you're going to need this." Lester's hand, holding a flashlight, popped up out of the hole in the floor.

"Oh. Thanks," Emma said, guilt rumbling in her belly.

His hand retreated. Footsteps through the bedroom, and the door closed again, softly this time.

Flashlight in hand, Emma made her way to the boxes piled in the far corner of the attic. The circle of light cast before her was dim. The batteries were dying. She'd better get what she came for quick, before they burned out all together. The book was in there somewhere, she could feel it. There were at least half a dozen boxes in the attic. Searching them all would take too long. Emma remembered how the book had called her to it the first time. That time it had been in the basement, in the furnace room. There had been scratching, like a mouse was trapped inside.

Emma stood still on the rough wood floor and listened. Nothing. Then the words from that first *Star Wars* movie echoed in her mind. Obi Wan Kenobi, speaking to Luke in the scene where they blow up the Death Star: *Use the force, Luke. Let go.* Rachel would laugh, but to hell with Rachel. Emma tried to open her senses. She calmed her mind. Still nothing. She'd have to do it the regular way. She leaned over the boxes. The one on the top was the biggest. Someone had done a terrible stacking job. Emma opened the flaps to the box, then laughed out loud. Sometimes things could be easy, she thought. Sometimes there was no need for clues or secret messages. All it took was taking a step forward, and moving into the unknown with nothing but faith.

The books were right there, in the first box she opened. Emma took them out one by one, reading their covers with the flashlight, when *The Secret Garden* jumped out at her. That had been Rachel's. The next book she picked up made her hand tingle. *Mrs. Dalloway.* Emma put that one aside as well. A couple of seconds later she found it, *The Astrologer's Handbook.* She flipped open the cover. The words were more faded now, but they were still there: *I hope this helps you, love Mom.* Grandma's handwriting. It was a message to Wanda. Emma wondered what Grandma had thought Wanda needed help with. Whatever it was, it seemed that the astrology book hadn't done the trick. Emma tried to imagine what Wanda had been like as a teenager. How she and Grandma must have battled in those years. Maybe that had been when the rift started between them. Emma wouldn't know. By the time she had come onto the scene at old number 66, the cracks in the relationship between Wanda and her grandmother had grown into a chasm.

Wanda, the missing mother. Wanda, the ghost. Where was she now? Somehow Emma knew that Wanda was alive. She knew because of the silence. If her mother were dead, then she would reach out to them, to Emma, Rachel and Sam. Even if she had left them behind in life, in death her spirit would move toward them. They were her children, her unfinished business. Emma would feel it if her mother were dead. She knew it in her heart.

Emma took the books she had put aside, tucked them under her arm, and began putting the other books back in the box. She knew she'd still have to haul the other boxes out eventually, but decided not to do it now. Rachel would likely have sorting out the attic somewhere on her list already. Emma would deal with it later.

The old wooden boards creaked under her feet as she headed back to the small square in the floor. Before she could reach it, the light flickered and died. Her first thought was if she were Rachel, that little thing, the flashlight flickering, would have sent her into a tailspin. The second thought was, ouch! Her foot had struck something hard. There was another box in her path. She hadn't noticed it when she walked over to the corner; she'd been too intent on finding the book. She stopped and sat on the old floorboards for a moment, and rubbed her sore toe. As she put the flashlight down on the box that had appeared in her path, it flickered back on again. The box was long and rectangular, with the words: *Do not open without supervision* written across it in black marker. Whose writing was it? It looked like a man's, boxy and angular, but it wasn't Sam's. Emma picked the flashlight back up, held it wedged between her shoulder and her ear, like the receiver of a telephone, and tore the old crumbling cellophane tape off of the end of the box. She opened it, tipping it on end. Inside was a telescope. Emma knew in that moment whose handwriting was on the box. It was Rachel's dad's.

Emma took a breath. She figured Rachel would have kept

her father's telescope at her place all these years. Maybe she didn't know it was up there. It wasn't Rachel who stacked the boxes, that was for sure; the piles were too untidy. Emma pushed the telescope back into the box, and slid it along the floor towards the square of light that led the way back into Wanda's room. She left the telescope there, reminding herself to ask Lester to help her get it down later. Emma put the books in the waistband of her jeans, and eased herself through the opening, feet first. She dangled a couple of feet above the chair for a moment, then, let go. One stocking foot slipped off the chair as she landed, and she fell onto the floor. The attic cover gaped open like a mouth.

23.

SAM FINISHED SCHOOL and by July he and Frank Carpenter had found their new place. Rachel didn't like Emma living in his room. It felt wrong that she should suck up all the air that used to be his. All her life, Sam had gotten the perks of being the older sibling. Now it was Rachel's turn to fill those shoes. Sam's room was bigger. If anyone should have it, it should be Rachel.

So Rachel told Emma to ask Grandma if the two of them could trade. Grandma said, "Suit yourself."

"Emma, you help me move my stuff first, then we'll do yours okay?" Rachel said.

"Sure, Rachel, no problem." Maneuvering Emma was a piece of cake, and as time passed Rachel wondered if the threat of being sent to Alaska should be dropped. Emma seemed happy to go along with pretty much anything. Rachel envied how little Emma thought about life. Anything that happened was all right with her. She was one of those people who would just go with the flow.

When Wanda heard the noise, she came to investigate. "What the heck are you two doing?"

"We're switching rooms," Rachel said brightly, adding, "It was Emma's idea," when she saw the look of mistrust in Wanda's eyes. Wanda looked at Emma, who nodded in earnest agreement.

"Yes, it was my idea," Emma said, unconvincingly.

Wanda looked at Rachel suspiciously, then continued on down the hall.

The two girls lugged Rachel's belongings across the hall. They filled three garbage bags with her clothes, and another one with her dolls and stuffed animals. The final load consisted of Rachel's Easy-Bake Oven, her Barbie camper, and a suitcase full of books – most about science and astronomy.

"Wow, are all these yours?" Emma asked, impressed by the weight of them.

"Yeah, they're mine," Rachel replied. "Maybe I'll let you borrow one sometime. We'll see." The implication of a threat wasn't necessary, but by now it had become ingrained as habit.

"Thanks!" Emma said, with a brightness that left Rachel feeling guilty one moment, then angry the next.

When the girls had finished moving Rachel's belongings, Rachel turned to Emma.

"So that's your stuff?" Rachel asked, pointing to a blue suitcase with wheels on the bottom.

"Yeah, that's it. It'll be easy to move me, eh? Easy-peasy, right?" Emma said laughing.

"Yep, easy-peasy," Rachel replied, reaching for the light switch to give it a flick, as Emma began awkwardly wheeling her suitcase over the shag rug. Two more flicks as Emma managed to get the suitcase into the hall. Rachel breathed deeply, knowing that Sam's old room was now hers. She closed the door without a word, and did a quick inventory of her belongings, just to be sure that Emma hadn't taken anything.

During that first summer with Sam away and Emma in the house with them, life started to settle into a predictable rhythm. Grandma would wake everyone up in the morning and make a proper breakfast of eggs and bacon and cereal and toast, while Wanda would make lunches for herself and the girls. Wanda was back at work again. Not at a homeless shelter this time, and not downtown. The new job was answering phones in a law office above the drugstore in the strip mall four blocks down. Grandma got Wanda the job. The lawyer was a son of one of her friends.

"He's available, you know," Grandma sang to Wanda one day when she came home.

"Please, Mom. The man is as interesting as a cardboard box. Plus, he wears a pen protector in his pocket. And he smells like a wet dog. *I prefer men to cauliflower.*"

"He's an honest, decent man with a good job, Wanda. And he's not married. I believe that would be a novelty for you," Grandma said with a laugh that was more annoyed than amused.

Emma and Rachel went to the same school now, but Rachel was one year ahead of Emma. Rachel had warned Emma to give her space when they were at school.

"I don't want my friends to think that I don't care about them anymore by spending all my time with you. You understand, right?" Emma nodded.

It took a while for it to happen, but eventually word got around Garden Avenue Public School about the new little brown girl in Miss Hamilton's class.

"Did you see her?" Marcia Miller asked at lunch, pointing to Emma who sat alone under a tree in the schoolyard, peering up into the branches above her. "She's so weird. I saw her sitting there one time, and I swear she was talking to the tree. To *the tree* like it was a person or something."

Rachel's face grew hot. She knew the truth would come out sooner or later. "That weird girl is my sister," she said, letting the word hang before continuing. "Well, half-sister really. She came from Vancouver. Wanda – I mean my mom – went to get her over summer vacation," Rachel said, telling mostly the truth, but keeping the fact that Emma had been around at the end of the last school year to herself. She knew Marcia would be either mad or bewildered as to why Rachel had kept the news of a secret sister to herself for so long. Marcia had been Rachel's best friend since kindergarten, and she was the most popular girl at Garden Avenue. She and Rachel had always told each other everything. Now, Rachel needed to worry about damage control.

"She's your sister! Holy shit, are you sure?" Marcia asked.

Rachel laughed for a minute, relieved that Marcia wasn't angry, then stopped. The question was worth considering. Was she sure Emma was really her sister? Rachel decided she would look for proof later. See if she could find a birth certificate or something official that said Emma was who everyone thought she was. Rachel made a mental note to look during her next house inspection.

Marcia was still in shock. "I mean she's *brown*. If you guys have the same mom then that means that her dad must have been a nigger or a Paki or something. Why doesn't she go live with him instead?"

And there it was, the question arising from the dots that Rachel hadn't bothered to connect all summer, the obvious that had once again eluded her – Emma's father. It's not like Rachel hadn't thought of him at all, she had. There had been a flash, a snapshot invented in Rachel's mind of her mom – Wanda – rolling around in bed with some sweaty brown man, someone not Rachel's dad. But that was about as far as Rachel had gone with it. The thought kind of made her nauseous, so she had tried to put it out of her mind. Now she wondered, who was this other father, this man who had made half of Emma, and where was he now? Rachel would have to ask Emma about it when they were at home. She knew Emma would tell her. Emma told her everything. It was like she had no filter. Once a thought came into Emma's head it would end up coming out of her mouth in no time at all. In the meantime, Rachel had school politics to attend to.

"I don't know for sure she's my sister," Rachel told Marcia, jumping on the opportunity to give herself an out. "That's just what they've told me. Maybe she's not though. Maybe my mom and Grandma just made that story up. She doesn't look like me, does she?" Rachel added.

"No, she looks like a black girl or something. I sure hope she's not your sister, cause that means that your mom..." Rachel interrupted Marcia before she went any further. She took out a pack of gum, and offered Marcia a piece, before popping one into her own mouth.

"No, I bet they're lying. They just feel sorry for her, and are probably just saying she's my sister so I'll be nice to her. That doesn't mean I have to go along with it, though. Nobody's gonna make me. I'll do whatever the hell I want. And that's that." Rachel crossed her arms over her chest, and lifted her chin in defiance.

Marcia looked at Rachel skeptically then blew a bubble the size of an orange that popped then stuck to her cheeks before she peeled it off and put it back in her mouth. Rachel knew there were too many holes in the story for Marcia to be convinced. But the good thing about Marcia was that she was easily distracted.

"Hey, is that Mark Gooding over there by the swing set? He's such a hunk, eh?" Marcia's head whipped around towards the playground. Mission accomplished. Emma was forgotten for the time being.

24.

RACHEL TOOK A DEEP BREATH and stealed herself. She was determined to make getting to the bottom of the Nina Fletcher, aka Buziak, mystery her number one priority. Just as Rachel was about to begin investigating the link between them, Nina's purse began to buzz again.

"Excuse me," she said, and then opened her purse to check her phone. She frowned, then began a rapid fire response on the key pad.

Rachel waited. She knew that every second that passed would give her the upper hand. She didn't resent the interruption, as it came with information. In spite of her exterior efficiency and polish, Nina had a weakness.

Nina tried to get back to business quickly, asking the remainder of her questions about Wanda, and making messy notes on her yellow notepad. Rachel let her get on with it, impressed with Nina's professionalism, in spite of her own agenda. It wasn't until Nina began to pack her papers back up in her briefcase that Rachel broached the subject.

"So you all know each other?" Rachel said, as she stood up from the table.

"Yes," Nina replied, offering no further information. Keeping her eyes down.

"How?" It was clear Rachel had the upper hand. "How exactly do you know each other?" It was Rachel's turn to ask the questions now. She was going to get the scoop before she let Nina out the door. No way was she going to spend the rest of the afternoon wondering, nor was she going to stoop to asking Emma or Lester for an explanation.

"I knew them when I was a child. In Vancouver," Nina said, as she stood and walked to the door.

Rachel stood in front of it, resolute.

"You went to school together? Played on the same softball team? What? How did you all meet?"

Nina sighed. Rachel knew she had gone too far. The tone was all right, but the rapid-fire pace of her words came off too aggressive, demanding, desperate. She didn't care. Who the hell was Nina to her, anyway? And who knew? Maybe taking the upper hand, putting Nina at a slight disadvantage would work in Rachel's favor. Maybe it would make Nina want to complete the job that much faster, just to be done with them all.

Nina opened her mouth. She was about to reply, when the door behind Rachel opened.

"Shit, look at that! The old key still works!" Sam stood in the doorway. Rachel looked at him, and then checked her watch. Sam's flight wasn't due to arrive until later in the evening.

"I know, I know, I'm early." Sam threw his head back and laughed, holding his hand out in front of him. "Chill, Rach. It's cool. I was up late last night and thought to hell with bed. Get on the red eye. Sleep on the flight. I got a deal. Saved myself three hundred bucks." Sam put his suitcase down, and stepped back onto the porch. "Figured there'd be no point in calling cause you'd be here, anyway." He looked over to Rachel fondly. "Still the same old Pavlov!" Sam put his right hand straight out in front of him, and his left index finger under his nose. "Still a time Nazi, eh? Hail to the gods of order and scheduling!"

Rachel smiled. Sam could get away with anything, even off-colour metaphor mixing. Sam looked behind Rachel. Now he was the one beaming. Nina. Rachel turned.

"Oh, Sam, this is Nina Fletcher. She was sent over from the lawyer's office. She's helping us track down Wanda."

Sam reached into the pocket of his leather coat, and pulled out a pack of cigarettes.

"Wanda," he said, dropping his bag on the porch. It wasn't a question, but a statement, an uncomfortable fact. He looked up, and suddenly he was no longer Sam the man. As he lit up, Rachel noticed a slight shake in his hand. But, by the time he exhaled, he was himself again.

"Hi Nina. I'm Sam. The brother," he said, as Nina brushed past Rachel to meet Sam's outstretched hand.

"I'm sorry about your grandmother," Nina said. That was all. Sam looked back at her with an expression of vulnerability Rachel didn't remember seeing before. It could have been the mention of Grandma or even Wanda. He could just be into her. But Sam didn't act like that with women he was attracted to. He put on the charm, not this sheepish little boy act.

The moment was over before Rachel could decipher it. Nina was out the door and down the walk. Sam watched her go as he took another puff. Rachel watched him, and realized that she had let Nina go without getting the Vancouver story out of her. Then it hit her.

They must have all been in the same foster home together. Leave it to Emma to make such a simple fact into an epic mystery.

It wasn't until Nina's car pulled out of the driveway that Sam stomped out his cigarette, picked up his carry-on bag and took it into the house.

"I thought you were bringing the real estate agent." Rachel closed the door behind him.

"What, no hug?" His arms were open. Rachel folded into him, then pushed away, laughing as he kissed her on both cheeks, like a European.

"I told the realtor to hold off after I got Emma's message," Sam took off his coat and flung it over the nearest kitchen chair.

"Emma? Emma called you?"

"Yeah, she wanted to give me the heads up on the Wanda stuff.

That we need her to settle the house. She called this morning. Said you were outside dealing with workmen or something."

Of course Emma had called him. It was another obvious stalling tactic. What did she want? To move into the house herself? She and Lester and whoever else they decided to rent rooms out to, like musicians who practiced at all hours of the night, or painters who gummed up the floors, or pet psychics, or astrologers or magic healers. Rachel could see them, sitting in the living room, having a sing-along to "Kumbaya," or a séance, lighting candles and incense, and burning the house down to the ground. No way in hell.

Should she confront her? No. Rachel didn't have the heart for that. She knew how it would go. Rachel would try to stay calm. She would attempt to speak in an even, measured tone, but then Emma would say something ridiculous, and Rachel would lose it. No. They were all under stress and prone to over-reaction. She would talk to Emma later and gently, but firmly, get her back on track.

Sam sat down at the kitchen table, and ran his hands over the surface.

"Listen Sam, you make yourself at home." Rachel caught herself. "Well, of course, you are at home, aren't you?" She picked her purse up off the table and looked at him. "Geez, how long has it been?"

"Five years." He didn't miss a beat. He was always quick. Like a rabbit. Bugs Bunny. Rachel smiled.

"Five years. It's sad that it's…" No need to finish. Cliché. Why did death bring out all the worst clichés ever uttered? "It's good to see you," she said.

Sam stood up.

"I'm beat, Rach. I'm going to take a nap for a bit. I'll be up for dinner. Let's order in. Maybe Amato's?"

Amato's. Ha.

"Well, that's fine. Perfect really, because I have to go out. I've got to go to the bank, to close Grandma's account, then it's off downtown. The life insurance company requires the executor to get the papers notarized with a stamp of authentication before they can be submitted." With her purse over her shoulder, Rachel searched the kitchen for her keys. "It's a ridiculously cumbersome protocol really. I've never seen anything like it. So, I'll be going there afterwards, to the insurance agency." Where were they? On the table? No. On the counter? Maybe somewhere at the bottom of her purse.

"And then, on the way home, I'll swing by the caterers to order the food for the reception here, after the service. And then there's booze. We'll need a few bottles of wine, naturally. And beer. Maybe some rum or rye. I wonder if I can get it delivered." Rachel stopped searching her purse and put it back on her shoulder.

"Oh, and we'll have to figure out the sleeping arrangements. We'll need to be economical with space in case anyone drinks too much and needs to stay over, which is likely. Sheets will need to be washed. And something else. I forget now. It's all on the list though." She stood in the middle of the kitchen and made a three-hundred-and-sixty degree turn. Scanning all surfaces.

"Wow," Sam laughed.

"What?" Rachel looked at him.

"I mean wow, slow down. Seriously. It's great that you've taken all this on. Thanks. But wow. You've got to chill a bit, Rach. There's time for all that. Don't stress yourself. We can help. You're not alone here. We're in this together, remember?"

Rachel felt her eyes inexplicably well up. Not now, for God's sakes, she was wearing mascara. She needed to go out into the world. She turned to the closet, and got her coat. The keys were in the pocket.

"Oh no, it's fine. Really. You know me. I like – I need to be busy. It's good for me." She headed to the door. Sam followed. "And if the workmen knock again while I'm gone, tell them to look at the walkway." She stood at the door.

Sam shook his head. "Rach, I'll be sleeping."

"Right, you'll be sleeping." Rachel stepped over the threshold. "Oh, and Lester's here. You know. Emma's friend?"

"Your friend, too, if I remember correctly," Sam said.

Rachel turned and left the house, stumbling on her way down the front steps. She grabbed the banister and stopped. She took a breath, then continued to her car. She didn't look to see if Sam was still in the doorway. She didn't say goodbye.

25.

RACHEL WAS DETERMINED to not let Turtle Girl ruin her life. Most of the kids at Garden Avenue Public School already thought Emma was a nutcase. Rachel heard some of them making fun of her, especially when they'd see her wandering around the schoolyard alone or sitting under that damned tree, looking up into the branches, and muttering away to herself. It wasn't like Emma didn't have any friends. There was a Chinese girl named Ling Ma that she had started to hang around with, as well as that Indian girl Ina Banerjee, who lived at the corner and smelled like curry. The three of them huddled together at recess. It made sense. Safety in numbers.

Why was it any of her business what Emma did, anyway? It wasn't Rachel's job to be her best friend. It's not like it was her idea to go get Emma from Vancouver so she could come and wreck everything. Why should she have to look after her? Rachel had her own survival to worry about. Just being related to Emma was hard enough. Word had gotten around that they lived in the same house. The word *sister* had even been thrown around. Marcia Miller had a big mouth.

Nobody else asked Rachel about Emma. Most of them were too scared, because Marcia Miller was the most popular girl at school. Rachel was in the in-crowd, so she was protected. For a while, all she had to deal with were whispers by some of the stupid wanna-be girls in Emma's grade. No problem. She could ignore them. But just when it was starting to look like the rumours were going to die down and fade away, the worst happened. At the start of morning recess, she overheard a couple of fifth graders talking about a big fight planned for after school.

"Did you hear?" Marcia asked, when they were standing together at the monkey bars. "It's about Emma. She snitched on Maggie West for killing a Blue Jay with her sling shot, and now Maggie's pissed and telling everyone that she's gonna give Emma what's coming to her."

"Yeah, whatever," Rachel pretended to be watching the group of boys on the other side of the playground.

Marcia followed Rachel's gaze. "I've got some nylons you know. I bought them myself at Becker's when my mom wasn't looking. I'm going to wear them tomorrow. It's going to seal the deal for me."

Rachel turned to her, relieved that the subject had changed. "Seal what deal?"

"It'll seal the deal of officially making me the sexiest girl at school." Marcia stuck out her boobs for emphasis.

"Oh, yeah. That. Sure. It'll seal the deal all right."

Marcia kept talking, but Rachel wasn't listening anymore. Instead she was watching a movie in her head, starring Emma and Maggie West. She knew Maggie from around the halls. She was almost as big as Rachel, and had the reputation of being a scrapper. The scene unfolded: Emma and Maggie standing in the middle of the football field. Maggie, pulling out a pair of brass knuckles. No. Rewind. Where the hell would she get a pair of brass knuckles? No. Maggie, pulling out a knife she stole from her mom's kitchen. Yes. Pulling out a knife and driving it into Emma's stomach. Emma, falling to the ground. Maggie leaving, and Emma alone in a puddle of blood. No, not really alone. Rachel, hiding in the bushes watching. Emma, about to die. Rachel, running over and hearing her whisper her final words: *I'm sorry*. Rachel, deciding she doesn't want Emma to die after all, going to go get help, but then, Emma's eyes rolling into the back of her head. Emma, dead. And Rachel was the only one who could have saved her.

Standing there in the schoolyard, with Marcia Miller going *blah, blah, blah* about nylons and Mark Gooding's ass, all Rachel could think of was what she'd tell Wanda if Emma didn't make it home. What she'd tell her grandmother.

By the end of the school day, everyone knew about the impending fight. Luckily, Rachel saw Emma in the halls before Maggie did.

"Psst, hey Emma. Come here a second," Rachel said, once she was sure that no one else was within earshot.

Emma brightened, and Rachel almost changed her mind.

"What's the matter?" Emma may have been a dough-head, but she was smart enough to know something was up if Rachel was talking to her at school.

"I heard you snitched on Maggie West. That was stupid. She's almost twice as big as you and now she's pissed," Rachel said. "If I was you, I'd go home out the front doors of the school. And take the long way home, okay? Cause if Maggie finds you, she's going to beat you to a pulp."

"I don't care what Maggie does. It was wrong. That bird didn't do a thing to her." Emma's eyes were cold, her mouth resolute. "Maggie's a bitch. She killed that Blue Jay for nothing."

Rachel was stunned for a moment. *A bitch.* Wow. She'd never heard Emma call anyone a name, never mind the biggest bully in Emma's grade. But whatever, whether or not Maggie should have killed the bird wasn't the point. The point was that Maggie West was going to beat the crap out of Emma regardless.

"Are you listening?" Rachel asked. "I said that you need to sneak out today if you want to get home in once piece. You get it?"

Emma eyes started to fill up. "But it was wrong! I don't see why I should have to sneak off. Maybe she doesn't understand. Maybe she just thought it was like a rock or a piece of wood. But it was alive. And she killed it. She needs to understand."

"Jesus, Emma! Are you an idiot or something? Maggie's not going to listen to you! She's going to beat the shit out of you is what's going to happen."

Emma looked down, her voice softer now. "I'm not running away. I didn't do anything wrong."

It was true, but it didn't matter. Rachel's movie played again in her head: the knife wounds, the blood.

"Well if you aren't going to run, then you better try to go for her eyes," Rachel said.

"What?" Emma looked appalled. "I'm not going to fight her! I'm a pacifist – like the Buddha or Jesus."

"Oh for fuck's sakes!" Now Rachel was yelling. "Pacifists get their asses kicked. The Buddha? I bet he got his ass kicked all the time. And look at Jesus – all that turning the other cheek didn't work out too well for him did it? Is that what you want? A permanently kicked ass?"

Emma was adamant. "I'm not running. I'm going to go home the same way I always go. And if I see Maggie, I'll tell her she's a murderer, and she's the one who should be sorry. Anyway, I've got protection. It'll be fine. You'll see." Emma held on to her turtle pendant, and headed down the hall toward the school's back doors.

Shit, this is going to be bad, Rachel thought, following Emma a distance behind. She didn't want to get involved, that was for sure. As Emma stepped out the back doors, a small crowd gathered on the playground. Maggie was standing in the middle of the group with her hands on her hips.

Once Emma was outside, all the attention was on her. Everyone seemed to be holding their breath as she walked toward them, everyone except Maggie, who didn't take her eyes off Emma for an instant. Rachel walked out the door a moment later, and hung back from the fray. She wanted to be close enough to see the action, but still able to get back inside the school fast if she needed to get someone to call Emma an ambulance.

"Hey you!" Maggie West yelled. "You sneaky little snitch! Come over here so I can tell you about how we deal with big mouths in this country."

Emma walked through the crowd, right to where Maggie stood. Rachel was impressed with Turtle Girl despite herself. Huh, maybe Emma was her sister after all.

As Emma walked toward Maggie, one of Mark Gooding's friends started chanting: "Fight, fight, a nigger and a white!"

Emma's eyes were red and she looked like she was going to cry again. But she kept walking. Once she reached Maggie, she started in. "Maggie, I'm not sorry, because it was wrong. I don't think you understand…"

Maggie didn't let her finish. While Emma was starting to launch into her plea of innocence, Maggie balled up her fist and landed a blow full force in the middle of Emma's face. Everyone gasped. Then the playground was silent. Emma just stood there with her hands up around her nose. A flock of geese flew by overhead, and as Emma looked up, blood began to drip down onto her shirt. At the sight of it, some of the girls left the circle whispering. Emma still didn't speak, but she didn't run away either. She just stood there holding her bloody nose. She wasn't even crying.

"See!" Maggie looked at Emma's face, then down at her necklace.

"No!" Emma yelled, too late.

Maggie grabbed hold of Emma's turtle pendant and yanked it off her neck.

Now, finally, Emma looked frightened.

Everyone was so focused on what Emma or Maggie would do next that only a few of them saw Rachel push her way through the crowd. Within seconds she was standing in front of Maggie, looking down at the pendant in the girl's hand.

"Give me that," Rachel said.

"What?"

"I said give that to me you stupid bitch."

Maggie looked at Rachel, then over at Emma. She took a breath and handed the pendant over as she exhaled. Rachel snatched it, turned, grabbed Emma's arm and began to lead her away.

Maggie yelled at their backs as the two left the circle of onlookers who remained. "Everyone knows your mother is a crazy nigger-lover. Everyone laughs behind your back."

Rachel wheeled around again, dropping Emma's arm for a moment, before returning to stand in front of Maggie. Then Rachel reached out fast, before Maggie could see what was coming. She slapped Maggie across the face so hard the sound echoed off the portables, and the force of it left a bright red mark on Maggie's cheek.

"Listen, you little shit," Rachel leaned in closer. "You ever say a word about our mother again, I swear I'll bash your head in, you hear?"

Maggie stood silent, looking small and inconsequential next to Rachel. "I asked you if you heard me." Rachel began to raise her hand again.

"Okay, okay. Yes, I heard you."

"Good. And that goes for the rest of you too." Rachel turned to the crowd. "Anybody bad-mouths my family or messes with Emma is going to have to deal with me." Rachel walked back to Emma, grabbed her arm again, and led her away from the schoolyard.

It wasn't until they were off school property that Rachel let go.

"You're not going to tell Wanda, are you?" There was blood on Emma's shirt, on her hands and around her nose. Her eyes were puffy and red.

Rachel suddenly wanted to fall down. Just fall down on the spot and cry, long and loud. "No Emma, I won't tell. Don't worry. We'll get you cleaned up before Wanda gets home. Just hope Grandma doesn't see us. I'll try to distract her while you wash your face. Change your shirt and give it to me."

"Okay," Emma sniffled. "Thanks, Rachel."

"Yeah, okay. Now stop blubbering. And next time, you do what I tell you, all right?"

"Yep. For sure. Sorry. You were right. Just one more thing I want to ask."

"What?" Rachel sighed.

Emma held out her hand. "Could I get my necklace back?"

Rachel looked into her balled up fist. She forgot she was holding it.

"Yeah, sure." She handed the turtle back to Emma, who held it in her own fist, then pressed it close against her chest.

It was too quiet when Emma and Rachel got home. As soon as Rachel opened the door, they looked at each other. Grandma was in the kitchen, making dinner as usual, but there was no singing. The hi-fi was silent.

Still in the doorway, Rachel put her finger up to her lips and the two began tiptoeing slowly up the stairs.

"Emma? Rachel?" Grandma called out.

"Yeah, it's us, Grandma," Rachel called back from the staircase, leading the way quickly up to the second floor.

Rachel pointed to the bathroom and whispered, "Clean yourself up."

Emma nodded.

When she was gone, Rachel stood in the hallway for a moment, flicking the light switch on and off, then headed slowly toward Wanda's bedroom. The door was open, and it was as if Rachel could smell it before she could see it: the evidence of her mother's escape. It was a smell like milk gone sour.

The drawers of the dresser were hanging open like hungry mouths. Rachel went to the closet. Most of the clothes were gone from the hangers. Two big suitcases were gone, too, as well as the shoes. The bed was unmade, sheets tumbled around each other. Rachel walked toward it and lied down. Just for a moment, she thought, breathing in her mother's sleeping smell. "Off," she muttered into the sheets. "Everything's off now. Mom's off now. Out. Gone."

"What are you doing?" It was Emma, standing over the bed, her eyes wide.

Rachel pushed the sheets away from her face and jumped up. "I'm doing nothing, Emma. For God's sakes, can a person be alone around here for a moment or what?"

"I just – I just thought I heard you in here, and the door was open, and Wanda's car's gone so I knew it wasn't her." Emma looked around her now at the empty closet. "What's going on?" she asked. "Where'd our – where'd Wanda go?"

"How the hell should I know, Emma, what do I look like, a mind reader? I was at school all day with you, remember?" Rachel turned her face away.

"Was it me? She didn't find out about the fight did she?"

"You know what, Emma, maybe she did. Maybe Wanda decided she'd had it with you and all your trouble, because I know I have," Rachel said, scratching at the sheet, absentmindedly.

"Girls, can you come down here." Grandma's voice called out from the bottom of the stairs. Rachel wiped her face with her sleeve, and walked out of the room, passing Emma without a word.

Once they were in the kitchen, Grandma told them to sit down. It was too early for dinner. Rachel knew what was coming. She sat in the chair staring at the fridge, remembering how small it had looked next to the policemen that day they had come to tell her about Dad. Bad news always happened in the kitchen in this house. Rachel remembered how she had imagined stealing the cop's gun and shooting a bullet into the floor. She wished they were here to tell her instead of Grandma. At least then she'd have someone to be mad at.

"I'm sorry, but..." Grandma began, then stopped abruptly. "Jesus God, Emma, what happened to your face?"

"She..." Rachel scrambled for a cover story.

"I got punched in the face by Maggie West. It wasn't my fault. She killed a Blue Jay. For nothing. But Rachel saved me," Emma blurted.

"Always everything at once." Grandma sighed, before she started up again. "So girls. Wanda – your mother. She's gone away for a while."

"Where did she go?" Emma asked, with both hands palms down flat on the table, as if she were holding it in place.

"She's not coming back this time, is she?" Rachel asked at the same time, snapping Emma a look that said that she'd be the one asking the questions.

"I don't know where she went this time, and I'm not sure when she's coming back." Grandma replied. "Really, I wish I could tell you. Rachel, you know how your mother gets sometimes."

"You had another fight, didn't you?"

"Yes, Rachel, we argued. You know I wouldn't just let your mother leave you two like this." Grandma's eyes filled up. It was the first time Rachel had seen her like that, and it made her feel bad for giving her a hard time. For a minute she thought about going upstairs to get her dad's tie. But no, that was stupid. She needed to be strong now, to not fall apart.

Grandma kept talking. Not really saying anything, just making noises to try to make them feel better. Rachel didn't want to feel better. She wanted to take every plate and cup and glass in the cupboards and smash them one by one on the kitchen floor. She closed her eyes and thought about her hand connecting with the side of Maggie West's face. She started to hope that someone would try to mess with Emma again, just to give her a good excuse. Next time she'd keep her hand in a fist instead.

"Did you call Sam?" Rachel stood up. "'Cause he's going to want to know about this. You better call him right away." Maybe if they told Sam, he'd come back home. There was Wanda's room empty now. Sam could move in there. Rachel thought of the alternative, of Wanda's room sitting like an open wound while they all waited for her to come back, and shuddered.

"Rachel, stop that," Grandma said suddenly. Rachel didn't realize that she'd had her hand on the light switch.

"Why do you do that all the time?" Emma asked, and Rachel couldn't help it. She really didn't mean to, but her hand reached out anyway and smacked Emma on the side of the head.

"Rachel!" Grandma yelled, and yanked her hand away. Even though she was yelling, you could tell she wasn't angry by the way her eyes finally spilled over.

Rachel sat down. She felt very tired and way too old for someone who wasn't even a teenager yet. "Sorry," she muttered in Emma's general direction.

"It's okay," Emma said keeping her eyes low. She rubbed her head with one hand, but kept the other flat on the table, firmly planted.

26.

EMMA'S FIRST THOUGHT as her eyes opened the Friday morning of her grandmother's funeral was that she'd forgotten to order the flowers. Her second thought was that she had just been dreaming about Big Jim. She closed her eyes and tried to remember what he had been doing in the dream. The screen was blank; she couldn't conjure any details. But with her eyes closed, she could still see him – his wise, weathered face, long grey hair, blue jeans and denim shirt. Emma opened her eyes. She could tell from the angle of the sun that it was around eight o'clock – she still had a few moments to write before she'd have to get dressed and deal with the flower situation. She reached over and pulled her notebook and pen off of the bedside table.

At the top of a blank sheet she wrote: *Big Jim,* then she put the pen down and stared at the blank page. What could she write? When she thought of her memories of him, the telepathic communication, the animal medicine, and the Chinook legends – was it Chinook or Cheyenne? Emma remembered Chinook, but maybe that was because they were a West Coast Nation. Maybe he was really Cheyenne. Now she wondered if any of it was real. Maybe Emma had imagined all of it, made up an imaginary friend and her kind, wise, old grandad after watching something on TV. Even the turtle pendant they gave her now seemed like a fiction Emma invented to make herself feel loved.

Who cared if she had made it all up? That didn't have to stop her from writing about it. Big Jim and his words had lived inside Emma for years, and for some reason, her subconscious decided that before she said goodbye to her grandmother, she needed to try to get Big Jim down on the page. Emma picked up the pen, closed her eyes and brought him back into focus. Then she put the pen down again, closed the notebook and frowned.

I can't write that, she thought. I can't write what he looks like – it'll sound disrespectful, a stereotyped cliché. Emma picked up the pen and closed her eyes again. Forget the description, she'd focus on what Big Jim had taught her. She thought about how he taught her to call in the Grandmothers of the Elements when she needed extra protection and help. She started to write:

First stand facing north
placing palms down on soil
sending out a call
to the nurturing endurance
of rock steady solid
Grandmother Earth

Then turn
taking in the vista behind
raising hands to the sky
retrieving, receiving
sweet solar blessings
sent forth in careful doses
from the red-hot belly
of feisty Grandmother Fire

Then turn
facing east
inhaling deeply
practising patience

with each exhalation
feeding each cell in my body
the mind-enlivening oxygen
offered by Grandmother Air

Then turn
to greet the current
submerge in surrender
to Grandmother Water
and rise, baptized

Emma stopped writing, frowned again, crumpled up the sheet of paper and threw it across the room. The Big Jim poem was doomed. It stunk of inauthenticity and cultural appropriation. She couldn't write about a tradition not her own. Emma wasn't a medicine man or woman or even related to one. What claim did she have on the information? For a minute it saddened Emma – all those times she'd been called Indian, a Paki, a nigger, and yet still she had no right to speak on behalf of anyone but herself. She'd suffered the racism, but had no claim to any of the perks of belonging. Emma was free to be anything, but she was also rootless. She didn't know what she was, and nothing in her features would give it away for sure. All she knew for sure was she was brown, mixed – a nation unto herself. Sitkum siwash.

Emma closed her eyes, then opened them suddenly. She had almost forgotten – today was a new moon eclipse in Gemini, Wanda's sign. The eclipse wouldn't be visible in North America, but its effects would still be potent. In the old days, people used to cower in fear at the time of an eclipse, but new moons were gentler. They had less focus on the door-slamming finality of a full moon eclipse, and more undertones of possibility and new beginnings. Emma remembered reading that this particular eclipse was forecast to be emotional, escapist but also ultimately healing, due to a square to Neptune, and a trine between Saturn and Venus. A small blessing for the day, but a blessing nonetheless.

By the time Emma finally got out of bed, got dressed and went downstairs, Lester was already sitting at the kitchen table with Sam. They were wearing black suits, drinking coffee and smoking. They looked smart, serious and slightly unscrupulous, like characters in a Quentin Tarantino movie. "Oh hey, Emma," Lester said. "Don't tell Rachel, eh?" he said, holding his cigarette up. Sam just smiled.

Emma poured herself some coffee. "I think she'll figure it out, guys." She opened the window above the sink. "Where'd she go?"

"Coffee cream," Sam said. "It wasn't on her list." He looked at Lester and they both laughed. Emma wanted to punch them. She wanted to punch them both so hard it left bruises. Assholes. Rachel took care of everything for everyone, and there they were doing nothing. Making jokes in their stupid suits.

"We forgot to order flowers," Emma said, joining them at the table.

"Other people send them. I put the address in the obit," Sam said.

"You did? You sent the notice into the paper? I thought Rachel did that." Emma should have known. Every time she got on her high horse, karma knocked her down. Instantly.

"Yeah, she left her list on the table, so I crossed it off. Did it myself. She never even clued in," Sam said, draining the last drops of coffee from his mug. "She's not doing as well as she looks, Emma. When I told her on Wednesday that you and I would look after the service, she didn't even argue."

Emma looked down into her cup, and suddenly thought about Grandma. Then she heard it through the window. A car was idling outside with the radio blaring. Emma recognized the singer's voice immediately. The "Banana Boat Song," by Harry Belafonte. It was a message from Grandma. Emma smiled.

"You'll never guess who called this morning, Em…" Lester said.

"Lester, do you mind?" Sam said, standing up and walking over to the sink to rinse out his coffee cup. "Nina called."

"Nina Buziak?" Emma asked.

"Fletcher," Sam said. "But whatever, yes, Nina. Emma, she found Wanda."

Emma looked at Sam, then at Lester, who nodded.

"Where is she?" Emma asked, sitting down in a chair, putting her palms face down on the table.

Sam sat back down across from her. "She's back out west, Em."

"You'll never guess who she's shacked up with!" Lester said, jumping up out of his chair.

"For fuck sakes Lester, do you mind?" Sam asked. He reminded Emma of a bear for a moment, showing a side of him she didn't often see: protective and territorial.

"Shit, sorry, Sam," Lester said, sitting back down.

"You remember your foster father, Em? Jack Marshall?" Sam asked.

"Just Jack? Yes, I remember him. Why?" Emma felt like she was in a dream. Or like she was watching a movie she had seen before, but had forgotten. Everything was unfolding as if it had already happened, like an extended déjà vu.

"Well, it seems that Wanda and him became friends when she first went out there to get you," Sam said.

"Wanda's friends with Just Jack?" Emma asked.

"They live together," Sam replied.

"Wow." It boggled her mind for Emma to think of the two of them together, but she was also comforted by the thought.

"Well, I told you how him and Shirley broke up after that whole fiasco when Jack made out with Nina. Apparently that's all it was. He never had sex with her, thank God, I mean she wasn't even of age then, for Chrissake," Lester blurted.

Sam shot him a look.

"Okay, okay," Lester said. "Sorry. I'll butt out. Family stuff. I get it." He left the kitchen, and Emma's heart sank. Even with the news of Wanda and Jack settling in her brain, she couldn't help but feel for Lester in that moment. Family stuff. He should be so lucky.

Sam waited till Lester left the kitchen, then he continued. "I know a lot of stuff happened back there when you all lived together, Emma."

"Like what sort of stuff?" she asked.

Sam took a deep breath. "Nina and I have been talking a lot the last couple of days. I called her to see how the search was going. I wanted to take that off Rachel's plate, and saw Nina's number on the fridge."

Emma saw the truth on his face. "You like her, don't you?"

"Yes," Sam said. "I do. I did from the first moment I laid eyes on her. Who knows why or how it happened. What I do know is that she isn't who you think she is, Emma."

"Who is she?" Emma asked, wary.

"She's someone who's been tossed around like garbage from the moment she was born," Sam said. "You know how she ended up in foster care?"

Emma shook her head.

"When she was six years old, she was left alone in her apartment, for days sometimes. She said she'd get so angry, she'd start to throw things off the balcony, and one of the neighbours noticed and called the police."

"She told you all this?" Emma asked. This wasn't the Nina Buziak she remembered at all.

"Yes, she told me a lot of stuff," Sam replied. "Seeing you and Lester again and then learning about Jack out west with Wanda, I think it hit a nerve inside her. I think she told me some things so I would tell you. I think she needed to get it off her chest."

"Get what off her chest?" Emma asked, even though she wanted to change the subject now, and find out more about

Wanda, but it seemed like Sam wanted to tell her everything in a certain order, one bite at a time.

"Emma, I know she was terrible to you. She said she bullied you for years. But what you didn't know is that just before she came to live with you and Lester, she was in an institution. She had been in another foster home before that, and the foster father had been molesting her for years, until one day she had enough and lost it. She stabbed him. With a fork, I think she said." Sam laughed.

"Shit," Emma said. "I remember that story. She told me it was her best friend, some girl named Suzy something or other who got sent to Woodlands. That was Nina?"

"Yeah, that was her, Emma. She's not who she was back then. She has a daughter now too – special needs."

"Nina's daughter is retarded?" Emma blurted out.

Sam shot her a look. "Don't be an asshole, Emma. She's autistic. I thought you were supposed to be the sensitive one out of all of us?" Sam's face softened. "Nina does advocacy work for her. Her daughter is her life now." Sam picked up his cigarettes, and put them in his pocket. "You never know what sort of shit people are carrying around in their hearts, until you give them a chance to tell you who they are."

Emma sat in silence, letting Sam's words sink in for a moment, before she asked, "And what does Nina have to say about Wanda? She's really living with Just ... with Jack now? What about Rachel? Does Rachel know?"

"No," Sam said. "I haven't told Rachel yet. I want to see how things go first. Mom ... Wanda is supposed to be coming out for the funeral today, but it's still iffy if she'll make it. Nina's going to go to the airport and make sure she actually got on the plane. If she did, she get her just in time to make it. Jack's all for it, but apparently Wanda's dragging her heels. I don't want to get Rachel all worked up if Wanda doesn't end up coming. Nina said that she's..."

"She's what?" Emma asked.

"Well, she said Wanda's got some sort of issues with mental illness. You know, it sort of makes sense now. I don't know why I didn't see it before, but she was always sort of all over the place, you know?"

Emma nodded, suddenly remembering the screaming woman she had seen on the streetcar earlier that week. She had been a premonition, a messenger. She had somehow prepared Emma for this moment. Other than the reappearance of Just Jack, nothing Sam was telling her felt like a surprise.

"So let's just keep this between us for the time being," Sam said, standing up from the table. Emma stood as well. "When we're sure Wanda's going to show up, we'll tell Rachel. In the meantime, we'll try to just keep everything chill. Funerals are hard enough, eh?" Sam said, with a laugh, patted Emma on the shoulder and left the room. Emma stood up, alone in the kitchen, letting Sam's words sink in. Wanda had been found, living with Just Jack. And Nina Buziak found her. Wanda would be at the funeral, Emma knew it. That was the message behind the Belafonte song. Somewhere inside her, Wanda wanted to go home.

27.

IT WAS ALWAYS AROUND DAWN when Emma dragged herself out of bed during that last year at Garden Avenue Public School. She didn't need an alarm clock; her body knew what time it was. It had been trained to know that survival meant abandoning the pleasure of sleep and dreaming if it was to make it to school without pain. As soon as she woke, Diana Prince started asking for breakfast, as she stretched out at the end of Emma's bed. Rachel always brought the cat into her own room at night, but Diana Prince knew that Rachel couldn't understand her and Emma could, so she'd sneak over to Emma's room as soon as Rachel was asleep. Emma liked waking up with Diana Prince. It was good to see a friendly face before she braved the outside world.

The echo of Rachel's slap behind the portables had lasted longer than Emma had expected. Maggie West had waited for Rachel to graduate, and then took up the mission of getting her revenge. It was the turtle that had saved Emma that day, and in the days that followed. As soon as Maggie snatched it, Emma had known that she wouldn't get away with taking it. It had been no surprise that Rachel showed up out of nowhere and got it back. Maggie had been cursed.

Jenny didn't use the word curse when she gave Emma the pendant that last time they had seen each other on Columbia Street. Jenny had just said that nobody would be able to mess with Emma if she was wearing it.

"Turtles carry their house around on their backs, so they're at home no matter where they go. Grandpa says that turtle medicine keeps you safe too. I thought it would help you with your new life out east," Jenny had said.

After the fight, Maggie had stayed away from Emma for the most part, but every once in awhile she'd give her a taste of vengeance. Twice during the winter, Maggie the Abominable waited for Emma behind a snowbank, and pounced, shoving a handful of sleet into Emma's face. Once, in the spring, she caught Emma crossing the muddy football field. In seconds, Emma was on her knees in the cold wet earth – the words "nigger" and "dirty" leaving her caked with shame.

After every incident though, Maggie would get hers. The first time, she got the flu. The second time it was the measles, and she was off school for a week. Emma knew Maggie wouldn't get away with pushing her into the mud that day in the football field, and she was right. Three days later, Maggie broke her arm skateboarding. Emma felt a little bad about that one. After all, it wasn't really Maggie's fault. She was a Scorpio.

Astrology was Emma's new passion ever since she found a copy of *The Astrologer's Handbook* down in the basement. Emma had been in the laundry room, looking for her white T-shirt with the big yellow happy face on it, when she an insistent scratching from under the furnace.

"Just a second," Emma said to sound of claws on cardboard as she continued rooting through the pile of clean laundry on top of the dryer. The scratching got louder.

"Okay, okay. Geez Louise." Emma giggled to herself, hearing the echo of Mamma Shirley in the laundry room. Mamma Shirley, the sparkly giraffe lady. She had slowly begun to fade without Emma noticing. All of that time on Columbia Street had become like an old photo left in the sun.

Scratch, scratch, scratch. Emma walked over to furnace, hoping whatever animal it was that was making the noise wasn't injured, or she'd have the problem of trying to save it.

She hadn't wanted any more problems that day. That was why she was looking for the T-shirt in the first place. It had been the kind of day where she would need a smiley face as well as the turtle. Extra protection. A reminder that Emma wasn't a threat – that was what was needed. As soon as she heard Rachel's door slam open against the upstairs hallway wall, Emma had thought smiley face, that would do it.

Emma had bent down, and peered under the furnace. The laundry room exhaled, and Mamma Shirley and her words were gone. The sound was coming from behind the furnace, in a small alcove where Grandma had stacked all the boxes labelled, Wanda.

As soon as she had seen the name, Emma could smell her – that sweet smell of sandalwood and sweat that combined to make "mother" in a way that Emma's memories never could. Memories lied. They told people one thing, but left out important details, as if everyone was too weak to handle it, as if knowing the whole truth would make your brain explode. Memory hadn't trusted her, so Emma had decided that memory couldn't be trusted. But a smell told the whole story. A smell couldn't lie if it tried. Wanda had been there, with Emma in the basement, and there was something she wanted to say.

The moment that Emma found the box where the scratching sound was coming from, it had stopped. She put the box on the floor, then flipped it open with the end of a broom. Instead of some trapped animal, it was full of books. The astrology book sat on top, and as soon as she opened it, she knew it was what had called her. Inside the front cover was the inscription: *I hope this helps you, love Mom.* She had been able to tell from the writing that Grandma had given it to Wanda, but she had also known that in this moment, those words were a message from Wanda to her.

Astrology explained a lot of things that never made sense before. For one thing, it explained Maggie West. Scorpios were famous for holding a grudge, even if you were a Pisces like

Emma, who was supposed to get along with them. No matter what sign you were, when you got on the bad side of a Scorpio, it was only a matter of time until they gave it to you just when you least expected it. *Zap* – a stinger right in the butt.

The only good that came out of Maggie's bullying was that word got out that Emma wasn't afraid to stand up to her. Just like at their first standoff that day on the playground, Emma still didn't run away from Maggie. Sure, if she caught sight of her black fur-trimmed bomber jacket slipping behind some snowy bush up ahead on the way to school, Emma would cross the street. But if she was close enough to see the whites of Maggie's eyes, she'd stand her ground. Even though it looked like bravery, it wasn't. It was faith. She wore her turtle on the inside of her shirt those days.

"You gotta get a back bone, Emma," Rachel had said when Emma had told her about Maggie's tormenting. "Why do you think I never got bullied?"

She had wanted to say, "The reason you never got bullied, Rachel, is because you fit in. You know all the right things to do. You belong." But instead, Emma stayed silent.

"You think it's bad at your school? Ha, I wish I was still twelve years old like you. Wait till next year, and you get to junior high!" Rachel went on to say that astrology was a load of horseshit, but Emma wasn't listening anymore. She knew Rachel didn't believe in the stars, but that was because she was a Virgo. Virgos needed proof.

By the time Emma left public school for Sunnyside Junior High, it started to feel like her troubles were over. For one thing, Maggie West didn't go to Sunnyside. Also, at junior high, there were a lot more kids that looked different. More Chinese kids, Indian kids (from the real India), black kids, and even brown ones like Emma who you couldn't say for sure what they were. Now the big problem was figuring out what to tell people. When she was in New West, everyone thought she was an Indian, and Emma went along with it. At Garden

Avenue Public School, she was black and that was that. But at Sunnyside, some of the other black kids looked at her funny when she talked to the white kids from her old school. At lunchtime, Emma decided to try to lie low. She tried not to make eye contact in the line-up at the cafeteria, and sat with her friends from public school, Ling and Ina. They weren't black, but they weren't white either. Still, one day she heard one of the black kids whisper Oreo, when she was walking past to return her tray. Is that what she was here, black on the outside and white in the middle? Emma wasn't bothered too much about that, though, because whispers were nothing after dealing with Maggie West.

Halfway into the spring of her first year at Sunnyside, Emma started to worry that her good luck was over though. One day, she woke up in the morning, and noticed that her pendant was gone. She had left it on the nightstand, as she did every night, but when she woke up in the morning, it was missing. That day, she asked her grandma if she had seen it, and she'd even asked Rachel about it. But Grandma said no, and Rachel laughed and said, "As if I'd want that thing. Emma, please." Emma felt naked without her turtle – naked and alone. All those years, she had carried her turtle medicine around her neck, along with all her memories of Jenny and Big Jim. It had been so long ago; Emma thought sometimes that she might have made them up. Big Jim seemed more like a childish ideal of the wise-old-man than a real person. His memory reminded her of the eagle who used to whisper to her when she was a baby on the beach. Maybe she had mixed the two up by accident. Or maybe all of it – talking to animals, to Big Jim inside her head, maybe none of it was real. All Emma knew for sure, was that with her turtle pendant now gone, she felt as if she had lost her connection to that time back on Columbia Street, to all the people she used to know, and to the person she used to be.

Emma spent weeks feeling the loss, wishing she had something else to focus her mind on, when she began to learn how to lucid dream. The first time Emma figured out she was in charge of what happened in her dreams, she had been having a nightmare where Norman Bates from *Psycho* was chasing her down Columbia Street. She remembered feeling panicked, as he closed in on her. She tried to think of what she could do to escape. She knew she couldn't outrun him, and he had an axe so she'd get chopped up if she played possum. She was starting to get desperate, and began thinking about how weird it was to have a guy from a movie chasing her down Columbia Street in the first place. Then she heard it, an old quiet voice that reminded her of Barney, whispering: *You're dreaming.*

Then *poof!* Norman Bates was gone.

After that night Emma started to experiment. At first she couldn't remember her dreams when she woke up in the morning. Sometimes, she would wake with no memory of anything other than going to bed the night before, and sometimes she would wake with a head full of jumbled details that were washed from her mind by the time she'd finished showering. Every once in a while, Emma would recall an entire dream, and when she got lucky, she'd remember hearing that warm, familiar voice reassuring her that none of it was real.

Emma decided to do research. She went to the school library, and took out a book called *Lucid Dreaming For Beginners* that said that lots of people knew how to remember they were dreaming without needing a voice to tell them. Anybody could learn how to do it if they practiced enough. It said that the best way to learn how to remember your dreams was by keeping a journal to write them in, so Emma decided to give that a try. Every night before bed, she would write "tonight I will remember my dream" at the top of the page, then, when she woke in the morning, she'd write down whatever she could remember before her feet hit the floor.

By the time Emma was in grade eight and had been at Sunnyside for over a year, she found that she could remember her dreams most nights, yet she still didn't bother trying to talk to Rachel about her experiments. She knew that Rachel would come to the same conclusion she did about pretty much everything Emma said these days.

"You're crazy," is the way Rachel had put it the first time. The two of them had been at the zoo together one Saturday. Grandma had dropped them off in the morning because Rachel was writing an essay on the evolution of the human race and wanted to go see the apes. Emma had said she wanted to come along because she hadn't been to the big new Metro Toronto Zoo yet, but secretly it was because she had wanted to see if any of the animals wanted to talk to her or send pictures to her mind. A chance to talk to an ape was too good to pass up. Ever since she'd read in the newspaper about that grad student in Tennessee who was teaching a gorilla to use sign language, Emma had known that if anyone would have something interesting to say, it would be an ape.

But once Rachel and Emma had gotten to the zoo, everything had become too noisy for Emma to listen properly. She had been able to see pictures in her mind that reminded her of scenes from the movie, *Planet of the Apes* – visions of sad apes in cages, and then snap shots of people behind bars. Gorillas were ironic and bitter. Maybe it was simply a reaction to the suffering of the apes that had made Emma go soft in that moment, or maybe it was because Rachel had suddenly been giving Emma so much attention. She had been treating her like a friend, making jokes, pretending to be a monkey, picking bugs out of Emma's hair.

Or maybe Emma had thought it was safe, because just before they got to the ape pavilion, Rachel had been confiding in Emma about the real reason she decided to run for the head of student council.

"It's not that I give a rat's ass about all that school spirit bullshit, or like I really want to see my face plastered all over the school. Believe it or not I think the whole "vote for me" thing is a little pathetic. But I'm thinking about my future.

Some universities care about that extra-curricular stuff, and when it comes time, I want my pick of the crop. I've got a plan, Emma. I've already started investing some of the money I make from tutoring. I'm not going to be one of those women waiting for some knight in shining armour to come save her. Because you never know what's going to happen in life. Know what I mean?" Rachel had looked up and for a moment Emma saw an expression she had rarely seen on her sister's face – vulnerability. Emma had been so in awe that she kept quiet, not confessing to Rachel that no, she had no idea what she was talking about.

"I mean, let's face it," Rachel had continued, "I've got the brains in the family. I may as well do something with them. And what I plan to do is become an astronomer, or a theoretical physicist, like Einstein, except a woman, and with better hair. Then, once I have a career and discover something amazing, I'll be ready to buy a Mercedes and get married and join the Boulevard Club, and then start having kids. I'm going to have two. One of each."

Emma had been stunned silent. Not so much by the details of Rachel's plan, but by the fact that Rachel had told her about it. Ever since Wanda had left, the rift had deepened between Emma and Rachel. For one thing, it had become clear that the whole being sent away to Alaska story was a lie. Grandma didn't know what Emma was talking about when she finally asked her about it. Alaska. Rachel had made it sound so terrible, but when Emma looked it up, all she saw were lakes, ocean, and mountains. Some of the shots even showed night skies streaked with the green, blue, purple, and indigo. To Emma, it was like a colder, more magical version of home. Emma had been angry with Rachel at first for trying to manipulate her like that, and swore she'd never forgive her until she apologized. Emma had never told Rachel any of this, but she had imagined that Rachel's conscience would catch up to her, and she would eventually come clean. But Rachel had showed no remorse, no matter how long Emma gave her the silent treatment. So Emma had given up waiting for an apology, and accepted the fact that her sister wanted nothing to do with her. Anyway, she had known Rachel couldn't help it because Rachel was a Virgo, and Virgos never believed they were wrong because that would make them feel like a bad person.

So, this confession, this outpouring of Rachel's plans for the future, had left Emma feeling like maybe that day at the zoo was the beginning of a whole new chapter between them. It was in that moment, after Rachel's confession, and joking around with the apes together, that Emma had let her guard down. She had figured it was safe, that Rachel would understand, especially if it was something about how much humans were like animals, since Rachel was writing the essay about it and all. So Emma had spoken out loud the thoughts that entered her head as they stood, watching the apes and catching their breath.

"Oh, I feel bad making fun of the poor guys," Emma said. "They're already upset enough about being in jail."

Emma had known she had said the wrong thing by the way Rachel stopped laughing all of a sudden.

"It's not a jail, Emma. It's a zoo for God's sakes, and as if you know what the hell apes are thinking, anyway." Rachel turned away from the cage, snapping her bubble gum.

Later, Emma had thought that this was where she should have just kept her trap shut, but at the time, she was still a bit dizzy from all the laughing, and all the apes talking at once in the background. She'd hoped that if she was able to get Rachel to understand this once, it might change things between them. Maybe they could even eat lunch together at school once in awhile.

"Well, it's not like I speak ape or anything," Emma had said, "but when they look at me, I can see in their eyes how they feel, and then it's like I can hear what they're thinking inside my head. Like it's my thought, but I know it came from someplace else." It hadn't been until the words left Emma's mouth that she realized how they would sound when they got to Rachel's ears.

That's when Rachel said, "You're crazy." It hadn't been so much the words, because Rachel had said way worse things to Emma before when she was mad, or just joking around. No, it hadn't been the words; it was the look in Rachel's eyes. It was something between fear and disgust. It was a look that had made the hairs on Emma's arm stand up on end. *Woodlands.* They had to have places like Woodlands in Ontario, too.

"No," Emma started desperately. "It's just..."

"It's just that you hear apes talking in your head sometimes." Rachel had stopped laughing.

"Yes. No. It's just that – never mind. You wouldn't understand anyway."

"And why wouldn't I understand? Because I don't speak ape?"

"No. Because you're a Virgo," Emma stammered.

Rachel had laughed then, making circles with her finger at the side of her head. "I leave you to talk horoscopes with your furry little friends here." She had walked toward the pavilion door.

"Where are you going?" Emma asked.

"Going to find a pay phone and call Grandma. I'm going to tell her to come pick us up," Rachel had said with a smirk. "And I'll tell her she can drop you off at the loony bin on the way home."

Emma had stood still and silent as a possum, but inside her head, she was screaming, "*Damn you Rachel. Damn you all to hell!*"

28.

RACHEL PARKED THE BENZ in front of the supermarket. She had planned to go to the corner store to get the coffee cream for the wake, but then she remembered they were out of eggs as well. People would be drinking, so who knew how many would want to stay the night? Best to get stocked up on the essentials while she could.

She had decided to stay over at her grandmother's house the night before. Her reasons were idiotic, she knew, but that didn't stop her. She didn't want Emma and Sam to spend too much time alone together. It wasn't jealousy in spite of how Emma might have perceived it. It was pragmatism, another inconvenient, yet necessary step in ensuring things stayed on track. Who knew what sort of plan the two of them might have cooked up if left alone in the house? It was enough that Rachel had agreed to let them be in charge of the funeral. She hadn't wanted to, but she'd had to. As executor, she had to deal with closing all of Grandma's accounts for most of the week – gas, electric, cable, and on and on. Everything had taken longer than the time she'd allotted. Plus, the insurance people had been impossible. Nothing could move without Wanda. Rachel had tried to explain to them that it was a simple administrative error. She was an actuary for God's sakes; she knew how these things worked. She had respect for protocol. But still, they refused to budge until every "i" was dotted, every "t" crossed. In the end the house would be hers, that much she knew for sure – hers and Emma's.

Inside the store, Rachel stopped her cart in the frozen food aisle and scanned the shelves for orange juice. She tried not to think about Lester, but his face was still fresh in her mind. When she had first gone downstairs to make coffee earlier that morning, there he was, sitting at the kitchen table with his laptop, still in his clothes from the night before.

"I'm a night owl, Rach," he had told her one night when they lived together. "That's when I get creative. During the day, there's too much noise. Not just the noise, but the rumbling. The vibration of the city rumbles right through me. Even with your eyes closed, you can feel it. Some people think that working in a darkroom is like being in some sort of sensory deprivation chamber, but even in there, you can feel it – everybody rushing around. The city's a hustle, I should know. I'm a hustler." Lester had laughed, and run his hand through his hair. "Sure, I can handle the jungle when I need to get shit done, but I can't work on photography in that vibe. I need dead calm when I'm developing. The energy feels clear when everyone's gone to sleep. Maybe I'm tapping into some sort of collective REM consciousness or something."

Rachel had rolled her eyes at that one, which just egged him on.

"You know they've done experiments. I saw this documentary with Emma once – you would have loved it. It was very scientific. There's this bunch of researchers on a mission to prove that there really is such a thing as collective consciousness. The Global Consciousness Project, I think it was called. It used these random number generators, which are totally legit as far as physics is concerned, to see if the power of collective thought creates changes out there, and they found it was true. They wired people up all around the world, and just before 9/11, the numbers shot through the roof. It was wild. Emma wanted to write a poem about it." Lester was in super-animated mode now, pacing the bedroom floor. Rachel was in bed in her pajamas, resenting having to watch the show, and had looked back down to her book.

"No, you don't get it, Rach. It was like people knew beforehand what was going to happen, so it proved *both* the collective unconscious *and* pre-cognition."

Rachel didn't remember the rest of the conversation, but did remember that somehow it led to her and Lester having sex, which in hindsight, made her feel a bit pathetic. At what moment, she wondered, did I give in? Lester was like a black hole – seemingly small and insignificant, yet possessing an unfathomably strong gravitational force. Rachel wonders at what point in their interaction she finally reached the "event horizon" – that invisible line, which when crossed, marked the point of no return. Current theory really had no idea what it felt like to fall into a black hole. Some said you'd become frozen in time at the point of entry, infinitely unaware of your own demise. Others theorized that consciousness would end immediately, as the variations of gravity during descent would stretch the body and mind to the point of spaghettification. From her experience with Lester, Rachel thought it was safe to say that it was possible for both possibilities to occur at the same time.

Rachel opened the freezer door, put the juice in her cart, and crossed it off the list. It still made her wince to remember how desperate she had been for Lester's attention, how hard she had tried to be cool and sexy when she was with him, how much she had abandoned herself. And it had been futile, because in the end, she just didn't speak Lester's language. Emma did. They were from the same distant planet, tuned to a station that nobody could hear but them. Rachel had tried to get on Lester's wavelength. She had gone with him to photography exhibits, dressed all in black, but it had been no use. He hadn't been for her. She had known that from the start really. All the time they had been together, it was like Lester had been on loan to her. A filler to take up the space that Emma had left vacant when she moved back out west. And Rachel had been that for Lester too. He hadn't been her equal. Never could be. And she hadn't been Lester's idea of a dream girl. He'd wanted a Ferrari, but she was a Volvo. Getting him clean had been a project they could both work at together, but once that was accomplished, it was over. They had both just been biding time.

Rachel picked up the eggs, the last item on her list, then pushed her cart to the checkout line. As she waited, she looked at her watch. There was still time. Too bad the liquor store wasn't open yet. She could just pick up the booze herself. Heaven forbid she should run out of drink, with a house full of mourners.

Of course, Lester would be staying the night again. What could she say? He was there for Emma, not her. Still, it irked her that while she was out shopping, he was sitting in her grandmother's kitchen, inserted into the middle of all of their lives. It wouldn't be so bad if she hadn't ever gotten the idea in her mind. Yes, it had been she who had seduced him. She was lonely, and maybe even missing Emma away in Vancouver. Now it was too late. She'd seen how beautiful his face looked when he came inside her. He had seen her naked, time and time again. There was no erasing that. Those moments between them were rocks in the water that Rachel now had to navigate.

"Don't worry about the plans for today, Rach," Lester had said that morning. "Sam and Emma have it sorted. One less thing for you to worry about. Today you can just relax. Let yourself feel." Then he had given her a smile that reminded Rachel of that poster with the cute little kitten dangling from a tree branch. *Hang in there!*

Rachel paid for her groceries, and walked back to the car. Dear God, how embarrassing. Really, how dare he? Who the hell was Lester Templeton to tell her what she should do with herself today of all days? As she put the bags in the trunk, she thought about how she had at least managed to change the subject after Lester's annoying attempts at sympathy.

"You haven't been to bed yet have you, Lester?" Rachel had said.

"Ha, ha. I knew you'd think that. No, Rach," he replied.

Rach. No. She didn't want him calling her that. Rachel. Full name. No pet names.

"I got up a couple of hours ago. I'm an early bird, now. It's partly because of you, you know. Another gift of sobriety, Rach," Lester said, lifting his coffee cup in her direction, before taking a sip.

"Rachel," she replied.

"What? Oh, okay sure. Rachel," he said. "I still get my quiet time in, but I do it in the morning now. Ha, ha, turns out you were right. It's good to do my art early instead of late at night. Then I have the whole day ahead of me to do what I want. Know that my soul has been fed first, you know?"

Rachel got in the car, and drove back to the house. No. Yet again, she hadn't had a clue as to what he was talking about. Or to be more precise, she had known exactly what he was talking about, but she thought it was inane. What grown man talks about feeding his soul without a hint of embarrassment or irony? Self-awareness and maturity were not Lester's forte. Not that Rachel had shown a lot of clear thinking with her choice of Lester in the first place, but it was the nature of the beast. Falling in love was dangerous. You might as well say to someone, will you please inject me with a drug that causes hyperbolic euphoria and then allow me to make huge, life-changing decisions?

Love had baffled Rachel until she learned about oxytocin. Then it had all made sense, but it had also then become clear what a terrible idea romantic love was. Sure, it worked wonders to enhance the possibility of procreation, but in a world already over-populated to a point, which made humans more akin to a weed or a virus than any other animal, help with procreation was the last thing we needed. It was an evolutionary glitch, Rachel thought, most probably caused by the rapid rate of expansion of our cerebral cortex. Humans had become too smart for their own good. Evolution didn't stand a chance of keeping up.

Rachel left Lester in the kitchen without a reply. She had a shower, got dressed, and wrote out her shopping list. It had taken a moment for her to figure out what to wear before she left. At first she thought she'd go for a black dress, but then decided against it. All black was for Italians. Dark brown. Browns were a more subtle way to say goodbye.

29.

AFTER THE ZOO INCIDENT, Emma kicked herself for letting her guard down. She should have known Rachel would make fun of her for saying she knew what the apes were thinking. Some people couldn't be trusted with secrets like that, especially people like Rachel. Emma felt stupid for even trying. Ever since that time in the garden, when Emma had sensed Rachel's grief, and her dead father floating around in the air, it had been clear that Rachel was afraid of anything she couldn't understand.

Every morning at breakfast, when Grandma was reading the news section of the new morning edition of the *Toronto Star,* and Rachel searched for articles on the latest science breakthroughs, Emma read the horoscopes. Everyone knew she believed in astrology, so there was no point trying to hide it. She'd read Grandma's aloud first, which meant reading both the Capricorn and the Sagittarius horoscopes, because Grandma was born on the cusp. Next Emma would read the one for her own sign, Pisces, and then she'd read the one for Virgo. No matter what it said, Emma never read it out loud. Even that time when the stars warned that Rachel's Mars in Aries would be at an antagonistic angle to Uranus in her first house. Emma knew Rachel would say that astrology was stupid, so she kept her mouth shut. She did feel a little guilty though, when Rachel came home at the end of the day with a tensor bandage around her ankle. Emma didn't read Wanda's horoscope out loud either, but she still checked it, trying to imagine how each transit would affect her mysterious Gemini mother, wherever she was.

Emma decided, after that day at the zoo, that it was best to keep her dream journals under her bed. They were filling up quickly. By the time Emma was halfway through grade eight, she had become a whiz at remembering her dreams. She had even gotten to the point where she could control what she wanted to dream that night.

The first time it happened, Emma said to the darkness of her bedroom, "tonight I want a dream that will tell me who I can trust." Then, after Emma fell asleep, there was Grandma, dancing around their living room in a long flowing ball gown, singing a duet into a microphone with a nice looking black man in a red shirt. Grandma was about to introduce the man to Emma, but just as she was taking a breath, Emma woke up.

Although she was happy that she had been able to dream up her grandma that night, Emma didn't realize that the dream was a miracle, until later that day when she came home from school and heard music she hadn't heard before coming from the house as she headed up the driveway. *Day-O! Day-ay-ay-ay O* – a male voice sang through the windows. When Emma went inside, she almost passed out when Grandma came up to her waving a record with the same man on the cover that Emma had seen in her dream.

"Oh, wait till you hear this!" Grandma said. "I know you're sick of Tom Jones, but this Harry Belafonte guy you're just going to love."

"Well, I don't go in for all that psychedelic hippy stuff like your mother was into," Grandma had said once, while they were folding laundry together in the living room. "But I do believe in dreams. And that thing – what is it when you know who's calling before the phone rings? I believe in that," Grandma said.

"You mean psychic powers? Like telepathy?" Emma had replied, rolling a pair of tube socks up into a ball.

"Yes, that's it," Grandma had said. "And I know a thing or two about dreams. Like just before your grandfather died, I had a dream that I was swimming in muddy water," Grandma had frowned and stopped folding. "Your mother was there too," she added, then paused. Grandma had looked away for a moment, then she turned back to Emma and gave her a pretend smile. "I heard one of those psychics on TV say that muddy water is a bad omen. So are those dreams where you lose all your teeth."

"I had one of those once!" Emma let the sheet she was folding fall to the ground.

"And I bet somebody died right after that didn't they?" Grandma had said, picking it up again.

"Yes. Sorry," Emma had replied. "Somebody did. Barney the dog."

"Oh that's too bad, Emma," Grandma had said. "But that's a common one. Someone close to you is ready to pop off, and all of a sudden you're dreaming about all of your teeth falling out."

Grandma was a natural at remembering her dreams, but she had no interest in learning how to control them. "Honey," she had said as she folded the last shirt, "the last thing I want to do when I'm asleep is think. Once I'm out, it's like I'm in a movie theatre. I just lay back and let the show begin!"

Emma's ability to lucid dream was getting better each night, and more and more often she was able to recognize that she was dreaming without waiting for the voice to tell her. She had almost forgotten about the dream miracle of conjuring up Harry Belafonte for Grandma, until she dreamed of Lester Templeton. In that dream, Lester was walking across a football field. It was overflowing with poppies like in *The Wizard of Oz*. He looked pretty much the same as he did at Foster's house, only taller, as if he had been stretched out, or as if Emma were looking at him in one of those warped mirrors in the fun house at the CNE. Lester was dressed all in black, like Johnny Cash. When he looked at Emma, he put his hand on his heart. He tried to talk, but when he moved his mouth only gasping sounds came out. At that moment, she heard the voice that told her she was dreaming, the next moment, she woke up.

The following morning, Emma recorded the details of her Lester dream in her journal and headed downstairs to the kitchen for breakfast. Rachel was already eating her cereal, and Emma watched her out of the corner of her eye while she waited for her toast. She wanted Rachel to leave, so she could tell Grandma about seeing her old friend Lester again. Usually, Rachel left early for a meeting of the science club or the student council, but on that morning, she lingered over breakfast. "Aren't you going to be late?" Emma asked as she cleared away the breakfast dishes.

"No student council meeting today. Didn't you hear?"

Emma looked at her blankly.

"Geez, Emma, get with the program. The Saints play the Riverdale Raiders this afternoon. We've had enough on our plates with the decorations. Don't tell me you didn't notice all the streamers and balloons? The Riverdale student council went nuts when the championship was there last year. It was red and black all over the place," Rachel replied, flipping her hair leisurely before going back to chewing her toast.

Red and black? Hearing those colours gave Emma the same sort of jolt the old toaster used to give before they had to toss it out. Emma almost dropped her dish before it made it to the sink. Lester had been wearing all black, standing in a red field. "There's a football game?" Emma asked. "Today? With a team with red and black uniforms?"

"That's usually how they do it, Emma. Pretty hard to win a football game when you don't have a clue who you're supposed to be bashing around," Rachel said, laughing to herself.

"I'm coming," Emma announced in a voice so loud and uncharacteristically decisive that even Grandma stopped unloading the dishwasher for a minute to turn around and look.

"Huh. Well, that's nice, Emma. Isn't it, Rachel? Nice for your sister to get involved with school events."

"Yep," Rachel replied, not bothering to look up. "That's swell."

Emma wanted to ball up the soggy dishrag and lob it at the side of Rachel's head. She knew it was mean, and didn't want to have that thought, but she did. More and more these days, Emma found herself feeling angry with Rachel. On the outside, she was the same. But on the inside, Emma seethed whenever she was in her sister's presence. She just couldn't forgive her for threatening her with Alaska. And often, she found herself having to fight off an overwhelming urge to do something nasty, like cut all Rachel's hair off in the middle of the night, or throw her homework in the fire.

Emma stood by the sink, dishrag still balled up in her hand. Grandma had gone outside to check on the mail. Rachel got up and put her plate on the counter, not bothering to so much as look at Emma as she walked past and headed up the stairs.

"I'm not going to the game today because I care about that school spirit stuff or anything. I have my own reasons, okay," Emma shouted into the air of the empty kitchen. She knew Rachel was out of earshot, but it felt good to say the words anyway.

All day, all Emma could think about was the big game, and the feeling she had that it was somehow connected to her dream about Lester. She asked around about the Riverdale Raiders. What time would they be coming? What were the names of the players?

"Are you sure you're feeling okay?" Ina Banerjee asked Emma at lunch, while Ling Ma reached over to touch Emma's head.

"Well, she doesn't have a fever."

"Not that kind of fever maybe, but I think she's got football fever for sure. What's his name, Emma?" Ina laughed.

Emma stayed silent, eating the peanut butter sandwich Grandma had made her that morning, hoping the chewing would hide her smile. She knew better than to say anything to anyone this time. If a miracle were about to occur, Emma would be the only one who would know.

After all the anticipation, the big game was a letdown. Rachel was there, hanging out with her gang of popular grade niners. The Riverdale Raiders were there too, and it sent a wave of possibility through Emma to see the colours of their jerseys – a field of poppies and Johnny Cashes. Still, when she scanned the faces of the players, none of them looked like Lester. Emma began to lose faith. Not all of her dreams had come true. In fact, it had only happened once before. Now that she thought about it, she had no idea why she thought dreaming of Lester would make him appear. It was just a feeling she had. But where did that feeling come from? When she tried to recall it, that sense of surety that she would see him that day, she came up empty. Maybe it had only been wishful thinking. Maybe she just missed her old friend and had tricked herself into believing that dreaming of him meant something more.

The Sunnyside Saints scored the winning touchdown. Whoop-ti-do. Emma was looking away from the field, toward home, wondering what Grandma would be making for dinner that night.

"Emma?" A familiar voice asked the back of her head. She turned around. Some boy in black jeans and a red T-shirt was standing in front of her. It took her a moment to recognize the face, but the eyes brought her back. Sad eyes, full of love. Lester.

"It *is* you! I knew it!" His voice was deep now. And his hair was short. No bow tie. Lester, the little boy with the Winnie-the-Pooh suitcase was gone.

Lester was beaming. "I saw you. From across the field. I don't know what it was that made me think it was you. Just had this feeling. And it is! It's Emma. From Foster's house on Columbia Street."

Emma couldn't speak. She could only stare. In a way, Lester was like a stranger. He had a new body now, and his face had lost its childishness, but how she felt around him was the same. It was no different than when they were kids. Instantly, instinctively, all she wanted to do was love and protect him, like he was a wounded animal.

"Are you okay?" Lester asked, snapping Emma out of her trance.

"Oh, yeah. I'm good. Wow, Lester! It's you." Emma began to giggle.

Lester started to giggle too. It sounded funny coming from his grown-up body. Then a look of pain came over his face. He put one hand on his chest, and the other on his knee as he bent down and tried to catch his breath.

"What's the matter with you?" Emma watched as the colour faded from his face.

"Oh God." Lester was still bent down and breathing hard. "I don't know. I was fine until practice. This afternoon. I took a hit. Knocked the wind outta me. Didn't think it was a big deal. But my chest hurt. Like a son of a gun. Ever since. Been getting these pains. Then I can't catch my breath."

Emma watched him, thinking two things almost at the same time. One was that Lester said "son of a gun," which was sort of funny, and made him sound like an old man. The other was that she hoped there was nothing really wrong with him, and how terrible it would be to find him after all this time, only to have him drop dead right in front of her.

"Don't talk. Just give yourself a minute first, okay."

Lester nodded his head, and they both smiled. It was just like old times, Emma telling Lester what to do and Lester trusting Emma enough to comply without thinking. Finally Lester caught his breath.

"I was supposed to be on the field today. I go to Riverdale now, eh? But the coach pulled me. Said I had to take it easy," Lester said.

"Oh, too bad that you didn't get to play," Emma said.

"Ah, to tell you the truth, I don't give a shit. I'd rather be out somewhere taking pictures. Photography. That's what I really like. But my stupid-ass foster dad makes me play football. Turns out I'm good at it. I try to win for the team. They're good guys. I'm not here for me, that's for sure."

"Why does your foster dad want you to play football?" Emma tried to imagine Lester living anywhere other than Columbia Street.

"He thinks that athletics are the only way I'll get into university. I'm like his pet fucking project. I think that's why he adopted me after his wife died. She used to be my foster mom. She was amazing." Lester stopped for minute, like he wasn't going to say anymore, but then changed his mind. "He didn't know what to do with himself, and I became his distraction. Then he got the job out here, and he decided that we'd start a new life where I'd get to live out all his high school fantasies." Lester laughed, shaking his head. "He's not all bad though, and I kinda feel bad for him about losing his wife. Marie, that was her name."

Lester sat down on the bench next to Emma. He kept his eyes down for a moment, then looked up and out over the field.

"I don't have the heart to tell him I hate football, but as soon as I graduate, I'm outta here. Forget this school crap. I'm going to go shoot pictures for *National Geographic*."

Emma didn't know what to say. There were too many questions, too many stories to tell, too much time to make up for. Not enough words.

"Hey, how did it go with your birth mom? How did you end up here?" Lester asked Emma, sitting down in the bleachers next to her.

"Well, after I left Foster's, it was weird at first," she said. "I remember it was the middle of the day when I left the house that last time. The social worker told Mamma Shirley that they would come to get me after dinner, but my birth-mother came by herself instead. You guys were all at school, and the doorbell rings and it was this lady, and her and Just Jack sat together in the kitchen drinking beer all afternoon. I thought she was one of his friends at first, but it turned out it was Wanda. That's her name. I never called her Mom or anything." Emma stopped, and looked at Lester before continuing. What if he had changed? What if he was mean now, or made fun of her?

"What else, Emma?" he asked, his voice gentle.

"Well, after I left with her, I realized that she was like this total stranger, but then like someone I knew too. I'd look at her face, and it was like I could see parts of my own face in there with hers. It was really strange, that and the way Wanda was like a bunch of different people all rolled into one. Sometimes she'd be like a normal grown up, and then sometimes she'd act like a little kid and say stuff that didn't make any sense. We went to live in this house in Kitsilano by the beach with a bunch of hippies. I was the only kid. Talk about feeling like a pet. Nobody had jobs or hardly ever even bothered to wear shoes. And they all smoked pot a lot, and played drums in a big circle in the backyard." As Emma spoke, she realized that it was the first time she had ever told anyone about those days with Wanda. It was also the first time anyone ever asked. "Then we came here, and went to live with Wanda's mother and Rachel. That's her daughter. My half-sister. She's head of the stupid student council. Wanda stuck around for a while, and then she just took off and left us with Grandma. I have a brother too, Sam, but he moved out."

"What a trip," Lester said. "The house in Kitsilano sounds kinda cool. Too bad you guys had to leave BC."

"Yeah, I guess sometimes it was okay there," Emma confessed. "But then you never knew when dinner would be, or even if there would be enough food sometimes. I remember us running out of stuff a lot. And a couple of times they turned all the electricity off because nobody paid the bill. It reminded me of when I was really little, the bits of memories I have about the time before I went to Foster's. I remember feeling scared then too. It wasn't all good."

"Wow," Lester repeated, grabbing at his chest again.

"Lester you gotta get that looked at okay? Like by a doctor."

"It's fine. I get hit all the time," Lester said.

Emma had a bad feeling about the look on Lester's face. There was something about the way the light around him wavered every time the pain seemed to hit.

"Promise me," she said. "Promise me that if you don't feel better by the time you get home today that you'll get your foster dad or somebody to take you to a doctor."

Lester looked up into Emma's eyes, and she saw the same look of love, fear and gratitude that she remembered seeing on his face when they were both little kids. Only this time, there was that darkness around his eyes that made Emma wonder what else had happened to him all this time they had been apart.

"I promise, Emma," he said. "If I don't feel better, I'll go."

After making his promise, Emma took a pen and paper from her bag so the two could exchange phone numbers.

Lester called Emma the next day after school. As soon as the phone rang, she knew it would be him.

"You saved my life," Lester's voice was solemn on the other end of the line.

"What do you mean?" Emma asked, only briefly noting that neither of them had even said hello.

"I did what you said. By the time I got home, the pain was worse, so I got my foster dad to take me to the hospital. You know what the doctor said?"

Emma shook her head.

"They did an X-ray, and told me that if I hadn't come in when I did, I wouldn't have been able to breathe at all after a while. I had a collapsed lung. Can you friggin' believe it? They had to put a tube in my chest to suck out all the extra air. They say I have to stay in at least one more day."

"I'm glad you're okay," Emma said.

"I'm glad I listened to you. I thought it would just go away. If it wasn't for you, I'd be dead right now. You knew it was bad, didn't you?"

Emma nodded.

"And you know what, Emma?" Lester continued. "Maybe four years ago I wouldn't have minded dying, when I was in the last place, the place after Foster's house, before I met my dad. But now ... I mean, my dad now is a bit of a control freak and everything, but for the last three years..." Lester's voice cracked. Emma didn't have to see him to know there were tears in his eyes. "Well, I wouldn't say I've been happy, but for the first time I've felt, you know, normal."

"Yeah, I get that, Lester. The last place was bad eh? I think I know what you mean."

"I don't really think you do, Emma, but that's okay. Maybe I'll tell you about it sometime." Lester laughed. "Or maybe I won't. I don't know. But what I do know for sure is that I'm glad I'm not dead."

"I'm glad you're not dead too," Emma said, hoping he would hear the smile in her voice.

"Thanks, Emma. For everything. I'll call you again soon okay?"

"Okay," Emma said, and then added, "I'll be here," but it was too late. The line had gone dead.

30.

LESTER WAS TALKING AGAIN. Talking, talking, talking, talking. The talking never stopped. And it was pointless, long, and meandering. At least when he was still doing coke he'd sleep for days at a time, but it had been weeks since he'd been clean, and he was getting restless. Rachel just hoped that he waited until she finished her paper before he decided to break up with her. She didn't have time for the distraction; she had a GPA to keep up. The competition at the University of Toronto was fierce, and without a full scholarship, there was no way Rachel would be able to afford the luxury of her own place.

The pieces of her new futon bed-frame lay scattered on the floor. The mattress was flat on the ground, waiting for its home.

"You know this whole futon thing is just marketing, don't you," he said. "Futons. I mean who ever heard of futons ten years ago? Nobody, that's who. And you know why? Because they're crap. Total shit to sleep on. They're fluffy for about a week, and then, if you sweat on them like once, it's like sleeping on a camping mat."

"Yes, okay Lester," Rachel said, reading the instructions, or at least trying to. Her eyes saw the words, and tried to send their meaning to her brain, but she couldn't think, not with Lester's voice booming as he paced the floor behind her. Of course, the futon had been her idea. And, of course, she had been the one to pay for it. "I'll get you back, Rach," is all he had said. Rachel had never asked when that would be. She'd known better. She had known, when he showed up at her apartment that day that if she took him in, she'd be paying his way. She'd known she'd have to take care of him. Feed him. Keep him like a pet. But he had kept his part of the bargain. He had gone to detox. So far, he'd kept his promises.

"Not that I have anything against camping mats. I went all over Thailand sleeping on one of those things. You know there's something very healthy about sleeping on the ground, Rachel. Sleeping under the stars in a little two-person pop up tent. That's all I had for three months, just whatever could fit into my backpack. I thought Emma was going to come too." Lester stopped pacing, and flopped down on the futon.

Rachel tried to turn her ears off and focus. She tried to pretend Lester was speaking a foreign language, but it didn't work; his words still somehow found their way into her brain. Emma. Emma again. No matter where he started, Lester always made his way back to Emma.

He shifted from lying on his back, to his side, propping himself up on his elbow to face Rachel, where she sat hunched over the instruction sheet. The assorted screws and bolts were arranged neatly on top of the square plastic bags they came in, bags that Rachel had sliced open with an X-acto knife.

"I mean she never said for sure she'd come with me," Lester continued. "But I just figured she'd be willing to get away for like at least a few weeks. But no, it was always the band. The fucking band. You know what, Rachel?" Lester said, his voice begging her to turn and face him. She refused and focused on the instructions.

"They're not even that good. I mean, Jamie Francis, he's half-decent on the guitar, I'll give him that, but Emma. Well, her songs don't really make any sense. It's just Emma talk you know. Emma talk from Emma land, and she thinks she's being all enlightening and everything, but really, nobody be-sides me knows what the fuck she's talking about. Not that I'd ever tell her that, mind you. You know how sensitive she is. So, no, I was just the dutiful boyfriend. Lester, can you drive me to my gig? Lester, can you run home and pick up my lyrics sheets? I mean, fuck, lyrics sheets! What the fuck? When is the last time you saw the lead singer of a punk band read their lyrics from a piece of paper? But no, she'd just say that it was fusion. That's what she called it. And that name? Koko and the Talking Apes? I mean, what the fuck kind of name for a band is that?"

Rachel had begun putting the screws into the appropriate slots. But something was wrong. The legs were uneven. The frame wouldn't bend into the L shape of a couch. She had done it wrong. Back to the instruction sheet. A into slot B. C into –

"Okay, maybe it wasn't a bad idea in theory. I mean, okay, the folk music of the sixties, like Bob Dylan and even Joni Mitchell, I mean they were up to something. They wanted to change shit. And punk was trying to do that too. I mean, the whole Sex Pistols, 'God Save the Queen' – was revolutionary, sure. But, I mean, it was still the eighties for Chrissake, everyone was listening to Cyndi Lauper and Bananarama the Go-Go's. Nobody wanted to hear that whole Velvet Underground bummer vibe anymore.

And Emma just doesn't have the edge to pull off an Exene Cervenka or Lene Lovich kind of persona. It's not like she's doing some melodic Laurie Anderson thing, it's just noise. And Jamie Francis can play. I don't see why she doesn't just let him, instead of forcing everyone in the band to do that experimental bullshit. It's just a lot of wanking-off."

Lester sat on the edge of the bed, facing Rachel and making gestures that alternated between masturbation and air guitar. Rachel refused to look. "And there she is, singing off-key and jingling that fucking tambourine. And then, all of a sudden, in the middle of the set, like say, just after some really hard-core song, you know? When the energy is going, and the mosh pit is rocking – at that fucking moment, she'd decide to pull out some stupid journal or piece of paper and start reading her poetry. Jamie Francis? You could see he was pissed." Lester got up off the futon, and sat next to Rachel. He picked up the X-acto knife and began poking the tip into a crack in the hardwood floor.

"Lester, I gotta get this thing together. I have to get back to my paper. I haven't even started, and it's due in two weeks." Rachel looked at him. He dropped the X-acto knife and smiled. He went back to the futon, laid down on his back, and looked at the ceiling.

"Not that I don't think it's any good. I do. Especially that one about the beginning of the universe, where she goes all crazy in the end and starts riffing off T. S. Eliot. That one almost works when she does it with the band. You'd like that one Rach, it's got cosmology in it. I know you dig the stars. I remember when we were back at school you were always up in your room staring off into that telescope. I thought you wanted to be an astronomer. You still have that thing?"

Rachel took a deep breath, and put her hands on her hips. "Listen, Lester, I…"

"I mean as poetry, her writing is pretty good. It just doesn't work as song lyrics. It's too cryptic, and besides the structure's all wrong. None of her pieces even have a chorus. I'm the one who always said that she should write a book," Lester continued, oblivious. "You know, get her stuff published properly. Why not? She could get a book deal. Have some money coming in. Get her name out there. You know?"

And after the paper was due, there'd be midterms. Paper first, though. If she could get the bloody bed together and put in a good three hours of research before she called it a night, there might be a chance to wrap her head around it in the next week. Then three days to write it, four more to edit. The paper was for Nonlinear Equations. Not her best course. Still, there was hope. If he would just shut up for a minute.

Lester was back to standing now and fixing his hair in the mirror she had hung on the wall above the dresser.

"Do you think I should let it grow? I know you like the clean-cut look, but I think it frames my face better when it's longer. Ha! Jamie Francis. Back when we all lived at Foster's – at the house in BC – he used to use a bowl to cut his hair. Going for that whole early Beatles look or something. Emma and I used to laugh!"

Rachel went back to the instructions, but she couldn't focus. She was thinking about her paper again. Too bad it wasn't on Shallow Crust Geophysics because then she could use Lester for research. She stifled a laugh, frowned. It was her own fault. It had been her idea to move in together. He'd been all for it, once she tallied up the money he'd save. And she had really wanted to help him get clean and back on his feet. He was a talented photographer and had just started to get some gallery interest when he first tried cocaine. "It was stupid," he had told her. "Emma had broken up with me again. She totally cut me off this time. Wouldn't even take my calls. I just wanted to feel good, you know?" Rachel didn't usually have such a soft spot for a sob story, but she thought she'd try to help. At first he slept on the couch. That didn't last long.

But what about her? It's not like she was taking Liberal Arts or something. She was a fourth year physics student for god's sakes, with a paper due in less than two weeks, that she hadn't even started. Instead, there she was, on her knees listening to her sister's cast-off, newly-ex coke-head boyfriend, giving her a lesson on the best way to present poetry as the love child of Joni Mitchell and Johnny Rotten. How had this happened?

Lester turned from the mirror.

"You got that eh, Rach? I'm going to go have a smoke. I know you don't want me to smoke inside."

Then he gave her the smile. The little boy smile. The high-school-cream-her-jeans smile. He knew the effect he had on her. She wondered if he practised in front of the mirror when she wasn't home.

"Yeah," she said. "Sure Lester. Go. I got it."

Lester walked over to where she kneeled, oblivious as his bare foot kicked her carefully arranged nuts and bolts toward the wall. He kissed her on the head.

"You know why I love you, Rach?" he asked, standing over her now. "Because you don't nag. Don't try to control me. You let me make my own decisions, you know. Like detox. You let it be my idea. Emma always tried to force me to do what she thought I should do. Always thought she knew best. No wonder it never worked with her. I needed a partner, not a mother, you know? But you. You just let me be, Rach. I love you for that," he said as he turned on his heels and headed out the door.

31.

THE OUTSIDE OF Mourning Glory Funeral Home looked like an auto body shop. In fact, Rachel was pretty sure it had been an auto body shop at some point as four large garage doors made up the front of the building. This was going to be a disaster, Rachel thought as she pulled the car into the lot, imagining an interior décor of grease-stained walls, and gas station bathrooms, a cardboard air freshener in the shape of a pine tree dangling from the soap dispensers. Rachel should have never let Sam sweet-talk her into letting him and Emma take over the funeral arrangements.

"Well, this looks interesting," she said as she put the Benz into park and pulled the key out of the ignition.

"It's fine, Rachel," Emma said, as she got out of the back seat. "Chill. It's going to be great."

"Chill." That was Sam's word. Emma was like a sponge. How many other people's words lived inside her?

Sam looked over at Rachel from the front passenger seat with a pretend stern expression.

"What?" Rachel mouthed to him.

The outside of the chapel was deceiving. Inside, the space had been tastefully renovated, the foyer walls were a cheerful light yellow. The lamps were nice. Crystal. Real? No, likely not, but decent replicas. Light filled the space through sheers over the garage doors, which from the inside, just looked like four large windows.

The funeral director came to meet them. He was handsome. Too handsome to run a funeral home. And too young; he was in his mid-thirties at most. His suit was stylish, his hair coiffed like the guy from the *Twilight* movies. He was a bit too Hollywood for Rachel's liking, but his demeanor, at least, was unobtrusive and reserved. When he shook her hand and offered his condolences, Rachel could feel Emma watching her, scanning Rachel's face for a reaction. Searching for approval. Grandma's funeral or not, it was always about *The Emma Show*. All Emma. All the time.

The inside of the chapel was dark green. It had high, wood-panelled ceilings and large stained glass windows. At least there weren't any depictions of Jesus or Mary or angels. So far so good.

The photos of Grandma were set up in a gallery area off the foyer. The Mourning Glory staff had taken care of that. They had set up a guest book next to the display as well. The urn was at the front of the chapel. It was the same as in the pictures that Rachel had browsed through when she chose it, dark blue with small pink and white flowers. Forget-me-nots. There were two young attendants in crisp white shirts and dark blue blazers standing by the front door, ready to respectfully usher in guests. Everything seemed in order. Ready. Still, there was the service to consider. Emma had moved outside, and was sitting on a bench, writing in her notebook. Lester paced in front of her, smoking, as if there was nothing else to be done. Rachel went toward the doors. Sam stepped into her path.

"No. Leave it, Rach. It's all fine. Chill. Get some tea. There's nothing to do now."

Rachel turned around without replying, and sat on a cream faux-suede sofa. She checked her phone. It was Friday after all, there could be news. But there was nothing from Nina about Wanda. No messages. No e-mail. Nothing.

Sam sat down on the couch next to her.

"It's harder than you thought it would be, isn't it?" he said.

Rachel looked at him, took a breath, and opened her mouth. Then she closed it again, and looked down. Wet dots, the size of dimes, began to appear on her brown skirt.

"Sometimes it takes something like this," Sam continued, looking at his hands, giving her privacy, "to bring everything to a head. It hasn't been easy for any of us, but you, you've been holding down the fort for everyone since Grandma died."

Rachel didn't look up. Her shoulders moved up and down rhythmically.

"But I have a feeling that after today, you'll be able to put a lot of things to rest once and for all," he said, adding, "Dad, Grandma, Mom – all of it."

Rachel put her hands over her face.

"Breathe," Sam said, putting his arm around her shoulder. "Just breathe, Rachel. That's all there is to do now."

Rachel put down her hands, and pushed herself away from him. She looked up, and met his eyes. She opened her mouth, closed it again.

"Breathe," Sam said.

Rachel took a deep breath, held it then exhaled.

"Thank you," she said.

32.

*M*AY 20, 2012

Everyone has their own personal mythology, their own unique view of themselves and their place in the world. If you're lucky, your thought patterns, your system, your lens is something that others can identify, something people can put a label on – Christian, Jew, Muslim, or atheist. Even if they misinterpret what that means, at least people can have a clue as to how you see the world. But if your personal mythology has no official, easily recognizable title, you're screwed. Then, even if you try to explain it to people, there's about a hundred percent chance they'll get it wrong. Because words fail. That's why poetry – it's only through the misuse of words, the breaking of agreed upon customs of sentence structure and grammar imposed on thought by prose – that one can get anywhere near something resembling the truth.

It's like how you become animated, speaking in mime with your hands, drawing pictures in the sky, when you try to communicate with someone who doesn't speak your language. In the end, they may nod and smile to indicate comprehension, but chances are that some subtlety in your meaning has been missed. And when that happens, the mind fills in the blanks. When we input information that is incomplete, or that we don't understand, we make up the rest. It's how our brain was built. If we were in the jungle, being attacked by a tiger,

we wouldn't have time to really examine the charging beast;
tail – check, stripes – check, whiskers – check, claws – check,
teeth ... there's no time for that. So our brain, instead, takes
a quick look for salient features, then says: tiger – run! But
when our brain is trying to grasp the paradoxically complex
subtleties of a human being, this quick recognition method is
ineffective, leads us running down the wrong path.

Who I am
depends on which side of my skin
you stand on, in here

it's all neurons firing
synapses telling stories
blood tracing ancestral histories
races blending in veins
truth obscured by memory

inside all is flux and flow
stillness and storms
contradiction – and at the heart of it

just another mammal
wanting to be loved

outside is all vibration
rubbing up against eardrum
someone's mouth pounds out
enigma

my mind tries it on, pins it
itchy like a label on my lapel

and wonders
if the skin over bone

wrapping around this self
distracts
sends the other off

to question, not who I am
but what.

"What do you think Rachel's going to say if Wanda shows up?" Lester ran his hand through his hair, as he stopped his frenetic pacing and smoking long enough to interrupt Emma's train of thought. She closed her notebook with a sigh, and put it on the bench next to her. She should have known better than to try to write with Lester around. He always interrupted. He couldn't help himself, without attention he withered.

"Seriously, Em. What do you think she'll say?"

It was morbid to look forward to a funeral. But Emma couldn't blame him. She knew that there was a chance that their mother would attend. Sam hadn't heard confirmation from Nina that Wanda was on her way yet, but there was still time. Emma was also eager for the service to start. She knew that their grandmother would have loved what she and Sam had planned.

Lester waited for Emma to reply. She shrugged. Words felt heavy in her throat. Talking felt like too much work. Rachel? Rachel was a work-in-progress. She hadn't liked the look of the place from outside; that much was clear. It had almost been impossible to stop her checking it out beforehand, but the week had kept her busy with executor duties. There were papers only she could sign, things that only she could do – Rachel's forte. So she didn't like the outside of the place? So what? What was more important was the service. What would Rachel think about that?

So, the funeral home was a converted old mechanic's shop. It had belonged to Brad, the funeral director's father.

"*Mourning Glory.* That name's a little cheesy eh? Well, maybe not cheesy, but bland for sure." Lester lit up another smoke. "I thought it was a bit of a fucking cliché, but I didn't want to say anything to Brad over there. Mourning Glory. They should have asked me. I could have given them some ideas. They could have called it something like, the Goodbye Garage, or how about Life's a Gas?" Lester laughed.

Emma smiled, and looked past him. People streamed into the building. Grandma knew everyone.

Mourning Glory. Rachel would call it a cliché for sure. Emma had seen her roll her eyes at the brochure, maybe because there was a typo or grammatical error. But, other than that, she had seemed satisfied enough. Emma had known that Rachel could sense her watching when Rachel went to shake Brad's hand. She had hoped Rachel would feel something in his touch, some energy passed on from all the grieving people he'd connected with in the past. But Rachel's face held steady. She'd left Brad and walked unaffected around the chapel like she was doing an inspection. At one point, she had looked over at the light switch, but her arms had stayed by her side. She had started to come outside for a minute, but Sam had stopped her, and then led her back inside to sit down and do nothing. As Emma had watched her through the window, she realized that it was the first time she had ever seen Rachel just let herself be.

Too bad it had only been for a few minutes – then the first guests began to arrive. Rachel stayed on the couch for a moment, but no, of course, she had to do the greeting herself. A second later, she was welcoming everyone. Gracious and composed.

Emma sniffled into a Kleenex, and listened to Lester talk. From a tree in a yard across the street, a raven cawed. Emma looked up, closed her eyes, and received an image of the mouth of a cave. *Thank you*, she said in her mind, *for the reminder.* Raven medicine was all about entering into the abyss – the great mystery. She had been given a gift by one of the world's greatest magicians – a primordial image to remind her that death was an entrance as much as an exit. It was the great confounder, holding its secrets until the very end. Emma opened her eyes and smiled.

"What?" Lester was staring at her. Emma didn't want to get into an argument about animal medicine – cosmic messages from her furry friends, as Lester called them. No, she decided to move the conversation in a different direction.

"This is all bullshit," Emma said, suddenly standing up, taking up the pacing where Lester left off.

"What?" Lester was losing patience.

"All this death stuff. All this – " Emma waved her hand around like a *Price is Right* girl. "This big Gone Forever Show. Grandma isn't gone. Why am I not allowed to say that? Why do I have to sit and cry and pretend that somehow Grandma isn't like absolutely everything else in the universe? Energy doesn't die; it just changes form. Grandma's body's dead – sure, but that's it. That's all we know for sure." Emma started to laugh. Lester took hold of Emma's arm and led her back to the bench. She sat and he looked at her with an unfamiliar expression of fatherly protectiveness.

You can see it in people's faces sometimes, when they're quiet and unaware, you can see their secret self. It's in the eyes – that ghost that haunts them. Some people's eyes are quiet and sad, and tell you of lonely nights of hopelessness. Some eyes betray fear, showing snapshots of tossed and turned early mornings full of "what if's." Some people's secret faces warn that they would kill you in an instant – if they really wanted to, if they thought they could get away with it – not from malice so much as sheer release. It was usually one of these three – sadness, fear, or anger that escaped from the eyes when people didn't know they were being watched. Those shadow eyes behind people's faces always showed what was unacknowledged.

Rachel's secret face held fear, panic and unrelenting, raw anxiety. She put forward an outside face of being stoic and brave, but her hidden face was ready to crumble under the pressure. Emma thought her own shadow face held indifference. Emma was indifferent the way she turned a blind eye from the complicated – like listening to animals – yet doing nothing to speak up for them. Instead, Emma participated in their suffering by wearing leather, sometimes even eating meat. She was willing to empathize but refused to take action. She could love, but wouldn't commit. Emma lived in a purgatory of faith. She believed in everything and nothing at the same time.

"You need to calm down, Em. Breathe. You're going through a huge loss here. You're losing the one stable parental influence you've ever had in your life. Of course it's going to feel like the rug is getting pulled out from under."

Emma looked up at him. He was right. Some things would never be back, like the smell of Grandma in the house or the sound of her singing off key.

"So don't let it fuck you up too much. Don't get hysterical."

Emma stood up. He was trying, but he went too far – from compassion to condescension. She wanted to smash something.

"Maybe you should do something normal, like greet the guests with Rachel." Lester could teach workshops on how to say the wrong thing, and then say something next to make it worse. That was the last thing Emma wanted to do. Stand there with Rachel like some wax mannequin, pretending to feel things she didn't. No. Emma didn't want to look into all those sad faces and secret eyes, one after another with their endless mantra of, "So sorry for your loss."

She didn't want to believe what they believed. It wasn't new age woo-woo; it was truth. Rachel, of all people, should have understood. It was Rachel who first told Emma about that thermal dynamics law that said energy never dies – can never be destroyed. It was science. Grandma wasn't gone. Not all of her, anyway. When Emma had picked up the music for the service, when she had written the eulogy, chosen the photographs for the gallery, Grandma had been there. She could feel her, in a breeze blowing through the window that brushed against her cheek, in a horn honking at just the right moment. Grandma hadn't gone anywhere.

The raven was back. He sat in a tree, somewhere over Emma's head. She listened for pictures or words from the bird. But there was nothing, just the sound of his call – *caw, caw, caw* – like thunder into silence. Raven medicine rained down – the trickster, the magi, ambassador of the Great Mystery. Gatekeeper to the void.

Emma laughed, putting her hand over her mouth. Lester looked up, grabbed her arm, and pulled her back down next to him on the bench. He looked worried. Be nice Emma, he's trying. He can feel it too, but he doesn't know what it is, so he's scared. He loves you. He's trying. Emma looked at him, and her eyes began to well up again.

"You want some tea or something?" Lester stood up and stretched. It was too much water for a Taurus like Lester. He knew enough to take a break before his earth turned into mud.

"Yes. Sure. Tea." He walked away, looking back with a face full of concern that faded quickly into relief as he headed back into the building.

Emma sat very still, breathing deeply. The raven was silent.

Everyone talks about the miracle of birth, but Emma had never heard anyone talk about the miracle of death – how awe-inspiring and beautiful it is to witness someone you love traverse the space between here and elsewhere. Nobody ever talks about how death seduces with it's beauty, how it humbles, crushes, and uplifts all at the same time. How only in the depths of grief do people call out for answers to the mystery of existence, and how easy it is to miss those answers if you refuse to become quiet and listen.

Emma never suspected it would be the death of the one person she loved and trusted most on this earth that would leave her with the unshakable sense of knowing that no one, nothing could ever truly be lost.

"Oh look, Emma, it's Grandpa," Grandma had said, that

last night in the hospital. She had been scratching at the bed sheets, which is what happened when people started travelling. It had even said so in the pamphlet they hand out in the palliative ward, though they hadn't called it that. The pamphlet had also said that those who are dying will "hallucinate," perhaps thinking that they see the people in their lives who have already passed on.

Emma had known they only say it's a biological process so people won't freak out. Rachel would have, but she had been getting more ice chips to chew on (another suggestion from the pamphlet), when Grandma had first started to talk about what she saw on the other side.

And then, after waking from a short, restless nap, "Emma, it's your little dog!"

"Is his name Barney, Grandma?"

"Barney, yes, that's his name. He's a smart little thing, isn't he? Cute. Barney."

It hadn't been a fair test. Emma shouldn't have fed her the name. If Grandma had guessed it on her own, that would have been something. Statistically significant results, as Rachel would say. Still, Emma knew what she knew, and she didn't want to stand in some stupid funeral receiving line with one pair of sad eyes after another trying to tell her different. She'd rather sit on the bench, breathe, watch the sky and listen for the raven's return.

33.

WANDA WAS SITTING in the corner, by the window of the coffee shop, with her dirty clothes and greasy, stringy hair falling down. Her hair was mostly grey now; the moustache she used to shave and bleach had filled in thick. Her body had too. She had chunked up after they got her meds right and she had stopped her manic marathon walks from Jack's place in Gastown to the beach in Kitsilano.

Jack was over by the counter. He said he wasn't her boyfriend, but he had looked after her for years. Wanda was a lot of work. Every night, after dinner, he put her in his van and took her here, sat her down in a plastic chair, bought her a coffee and spiked it with crushed up meds and four packs of Sweet 'N Low. Before this ritual, she was unmanageable.

While she was waiting for Jack, Wanda turned around in her chair to face an old man eating a bran muffin at the table behind her. "Mrs. Dalloway is shaking me again," Wanda told him. The man stared at her for a moment then went back to his muffin. "A girl can't even have a cup of coffee in peace, you know what I mean? She doesn't ever leave me alone these days. I never used to have to deal with this bullshit, but she follows me around everywhere now. Whenever she's inside me, she shakes my hand when I try to light a smoke. If she does it when I'm drinking, I get soaked."

The man looked up and around the room, at Wanda, then back at his muffin. He stopped eating.

"Jack says she's not real," Wanda continued, her volume rising. "He says that Mrs. Dalloway is just someone I made up in my head, but Jack doesn't know everything. He just acts like he does." Jack looked over from the counter. He was waiting for his change, frowning.

"Like now," Wanda went on. "He's telling me that I have to go back to Toronto. Toronto. I don't want to go there. It's all bad memories and bad mothers back there. I was one of those bad mothers, but that was another life. In this life, I'm good, except for that one time with the brick. Other than that, I just smoke and shake a lot. Jack says the shaking is because of the medication and Mrs. Dalloway is because of what my dad did to me when I was a kid. Jack says that it's his penance to look after me now. Because of the girl from the house, and because of the chef lady he shot."

"Wanda!" Jack yelled from the counter. "Shut up and leave the man alone."

Wanda turned around in her chair. She sat for a moment, shredding a napkin, then leaned back and whispered to the man out of the corner of her mouth. "I told him, bullshit, I don't give a damn what my dad did to me. Maybe he didn't do anything, and Mom was right. Jack says maybe I was just born this way, and it was only a matter of time till I popped."

The old man picked up his muffin and coffee, and moved to a table on the other side of the room. Wanda kept talking. "I said, like a bottle of champagne, and he said, like a jack-in-the-box. He thinks he's so funny. He says it doesn't matter why now, anyways, and tells me to just take the meds and pipe down. He's nice, though; don't let him fool you. He just pretends to be badass because he's so soft inside. We're all soft inside, that's what I think. I never had a skin like other people. Where everyone else gets to have skin on the outside, all I have is raw flesh and nerve endings. There isn't anything else to cover me. There never has been. If you ask me, that's why all the trouble and the meds now and nothing else. Nothing else."

Jack drummed his fingers on the counter. Wanda could hear it like Morse code without even turning around. She went silent for a few minutes, then whispered, "Me and Jack, we know how to go *in and out of each other's minds without any effort.* That's how Mrs. Dalloway describes it."

Jack turned toward her, walked over to the table with their coffees, and sat down. "Don't bother people, Wanda," he said. "Jesus, you want us to get kicked out again?"

Wanda put the napkin down. "Listen Jack, Mrs. Dalloway is driving me crazy. She keeps shaking me, and saying she wants to go to Toronto. She says she never gets to go anywhere, and it would be such a lark and a plunge – but I told her I wasn't going back there and *that's that.*"

"Drink your coffee," Jack said.

"I don't care if they sell that old house," Wanda continued. "It's fine by me. Tell the lady to send the papers here and I'll sign them and mail them back."

"You're going, Wanda," Jack said. "It's your mom's funeral. Nina ... the lawyer lady on the phone said she'd pay for the ticket, all you have to do is get on the plane. I told her she'd better meet you at the airport."

Wanda looked up from her coffee. Jack laughed.

"I know you, Wanda. I warned her. Told her to keep an eye on you or you'd split." Jack laughed again. "Yeah, I warned her. Told her you're a real live wire."

"Live wire," Wanda laughed so hard she almost peed, then, she stopped and coughed for a few seconds.

"It's not your fault," Jack said. Wanda smiled. Jack could be a pain in the ass, but at least he was her friend. He cared, not like some people.

Wanda knew that doctors had told Jack she would never get better, and the cops said they were tired of coming to the house all the time because of Mrs. Dalloway's yelling. The cops had told Jack he should kick her out, and Jack had said, "What do you want me to do? Leave her on the street? They treat dogs better in this country!" As far as Wanda was concerned, all the doctors and social workers didn't know shit. Jack had tried to tell them that Wanda wasn't always like this. She had dreams. When she had first met him, that time when she had come to get the little brown girl, Wanda had told him about her plan to go back to school. She had wanted to be a chef, and work on a cruise ship someday.

Wanda sipped her coffee. She knew Jack would check to make sure she finished it. She felt the urge to talk to the old man again. She turned to look at him, caught his eye, but then he looked away. She wanted to tell him that things had gotten better lately, ever since the cops had taken her away in handcuffs that last time. She had only been in jail for a week before they sent her to the psych hospital. She hadn't minded it there. It was quiet, and she got to make crochet potholders, beaded necklaces, key chains, and dream-catchers. Jack still used the hand-painted teapot she gave him. It was striped with red and yellow and green and black and white and blue, and it was beautiful.

Jack had said he was glad she stopped with all the knitting, because yarn didn't come cheap, and now it was time to stop going to the dollar store to buy all those glass figurines and marbles and bags of smooth stones. He said they were a big waste of money. He didn't have to worry for long though. They wouldn't let Wanda in the dollar store now, even though she didn't yell anymore. They remembered her from the time before. The last time she tried to shop there, the man at the cash looked at her and said, "Oh, no you don't."

Wanda felt her face grow hot at the memory. All she had wanted was to hold the beautiful things for a while. That had been why she had gone back to the house that time. She'd sworn that she never would, but once she had decided to leave Toronto, and go back out west to find Jack, she'd known it would be a good idea to take something with her so she'd re-member what she was leaving behind – the funny boy and the nervous girl, and the little brown one who talked to animals. So she had taken her key and opened the door to number 66 in the middle of the night. She had felt a little bad, like a thief, when she had gone downstairs, and gotten the tie out of that toy oven, and the track and field medal with the red ribbon from the box in the laundry room. The boy had won that one. Wanda remembered that he used to be fast as lightning. She had tried to be invisible when she walked up the stairs. If the mother had gotten out of bed and caught her, she'd be done for.

The brown girl had been sleeping, and hadn't moved a muscle when Wanda walked in her room. She had felt around on the bedside table for the turtle necklace, and after she'd found it, she stood there and listened to the little girl breathe for a while. She'd looked beautiful asleep like that. Everything was so easy when people were asleep.

Wanda had gotten out of the house that night without anyone hearing her. She had all the things in her bag. After that she had left town, and started all over again.

"How did they find me way out here?" Wanda asked. Jack looked away from the window and sighed.

"What did you think? That you were invisible? You get your disability cheques sent to the apartment. There's a paper trail. You should have known they'd come looking for you eventually."

"You're going to come too, right?" Wanda's voice was getting louder again.

"Keep it down," Jack said. "No, I told you. You're going alone."

"I'm going outside for a smoke," Wanda said. She stood up, and bits of shredded napkin fluttered to the ground.

Wanda stood outside the coffee shop, smoking and pacing. Mrs. Dalloway was shaking her hard. Wanda thought she should have been happy that she was going to Toronto, but no matter what happened, Mrs. Dalloway seemed angry all the time. Jack thought that sometimes Mrs. Dalloway went away, but Wanda had just gotten better at hiding her, was all. At first, her anger had ripped through Wanda like lightning. Made her want to tear her eyes out. Wanda had known that back in the old days, they used electric shock therapy. More electricity racing through the veins, like that was what a sick person needed. Good thing they had never tried it on Wanda.

In the beginning, all the lightning had made her throw things. And the voices, there had been more of them, then. She had to do what they said or they wouldn't shut up, wouldn't let her sleep. One of them told her to go buy a dozen ceramic bunnies for the garden. Then Mrs. Dalloway had come in and told her to smash them, one by one, on the backyard patio stones. The voices had told her not to take any more pills, so she had hidden them. But that just seemed to make everyone yell more. The cops had tried to make her go to the hospital to get shots once a month after that. It had stopped Mrs. Dalloway from yelling, but it also made Wanda sleep, all day, every day, for months. She couldn't remember that winter at all. Jack had called it the year she hibernated like a bear. Since then, she let him crush up the pills and put them in her coffee. Mrs. Dalloway hadn't figured it out yet. She didn't trust Jack. She didn't trust anyone.

When he had gotten off the phone with the lawyer lady that day, Jack had been shaking. He kept saying Goddamn, Goddamn, what were the chances, and then he had said he was being punished. Wanda had said that if it was God who was punishing him, then maybe he could ease up on all the damning, but Jack had just walked out the door. He had only been gone a few minutes, and when he came back, he told Wanda her mother was dead, and that she had to go back to Toronto to deal with the house.

"No way, Jack," Wanda had said. "I'm not going back there." But Jack just gave her a look that said she was going and that was that. So, Wanda went outside, smoked cigarettes, and let Mrs. Dalloway shake her and use her mouth to yell at the world. Somebody must have heard all the yelling, a neighbour or something. At least they hadn't called the police on her. They must have gotten tired of doing that. Instead, they had called Jack to complain and he had come outside and told her to shut the fuck up.

Mrs. Dalloway. Of course she would make herself real. That book – Wanda can't even remember the name of the author who wrote it; she only remembers Mrs. Dalloway and the sad, true things she said.

She had the perpetual sense, as she watched the taxi cabs, of being out, out, far out to sea and alone; she always had the feeling that it was very, very, dangerous to live even one day.

When Wanda read these words, it was as if electricity suddenly buzzed through her veins. Yes, Wanda thought, because it is very dangerous, but nobody ever talks about it. Mrs. Dalloway was the only person Wanda had ever known who told the truth about what it was like to be alive.

It was the only book Wanda ever read cover to cover. None of the other books ever called her to finish them. All the other books said: sure you can go and do something else if I'm boring you. And they were, so Wanda did. But Mrs. Dalloway? She dug right in and said, *Wanda you will listen to me from start to finish. You will listen to me until I seep into your pores and you become me. Only then will I let you go.*

Wanda didn't want to become Mrs. Dalloway, but she didn't really mind her so much most of the time. Even with the yelling. Wanda knew that it was because she refused to throw any parties, and Mrs. Dalloway had to do something to cover the silence – just like the mother, with all her music. Wanda supposed it was normal, that everyone needed to do something to drown out the noise of old ghosts rattling their bones. *It was a silly, silly dream, being unhappy.*

Jack came out of the coffee shop. As he walked past her, he said, "Come on, Wanda. Get in the van. We're going home, and then you're going to pack. You're going to Toronto. Get used to it."

The lady from the law office came to meet her at the airport in Toronto. Wanda felt messy when she saw her, like she should have picked out better clothes that morning. They got in a taxi, and the driver didn't know where the funeral parlour was, so they drove around and around for a while. The driver had an accent, and said they could help and look at the map while he called dispatch. Him and the lawyer lady argued about whether or not he should turn the meter off. The lady said her phone was dead, and asked the driver if she could use his. He said no, and she called him an ass. Wanda didn't give a damn if they never found the place. She just wanted them to keep driving.

When they finally found the funeral home, it looked like a big gas station on the outside. *Mourning Glory*. Ha! Whoever wrote that had never tried to forget. Had never wished they could be the one in the casket, instead of the one who had to face all the people left behind.

The service was nice. Wanda saw them right away. All three of the children were sitting together, up at the front. Well, the new versions of them were. It was like a TV sitcom where the kids you once knew had grown up and were now being played by new actors. They sort of looked the same, and if the story was good you went along, but really, you knew they weren't the same people anymore. The lost girl, the brown one, she went up to the front and read a poem. It was a good poem, all about the history of the universe, and how we're all a part of life, and how the poem wasn't really a poem at all – just a test, like they used to do on television, with that multi-coloured bar pattern and that end-of-the-world tone going on and on. The brown girl's words sang, and slid into each other nicely in the ear, even if the poem really didn't make much sense at all.

After that a young man played "Don't Get Around Much Anymore" on the trumpet. He did a good job, too. Wanda remembered that song from the old days. The mother and father, slow dancing in the living room, with Lawrence Welk flickering on the television in the background. The father, laughing and twirling the mother, round and round and round. Those nights they would tell Wanda about what life was like in war-time.

"As soon as you heard the air-raid siren it was lights out Kiddo! Suddenly it went pitch black, all over the town," the father would tell her.

"You should have seen it, Wanda," the mother would say. "We saw an enemy plane explode and break open in the sky right above us."

Wanda didn't know if she had said goodbye to the father the last time she saw him. She just remembered feeling relieved when she heard the news, like a big exhale that let the places he had touched her begin to breathe again. She knew she had been there, at his funeral, but she didn't remember the service. She hoped she wouldn't remember this one either. It was possible. Even when there was someone scratching at the door, you could find a way to keep it closed, and keep what was outside out. It would all feel better when she got back home to Jack's place.

The part of the service when the minister spoke was boring, but after that, there was this feeling of excitement, and a bunch of people came in with big tin drums. A steel band set up in front of the altar, and then the music began: *Day O!* And just when Wanda started to forget about the mother and the father and all the babies that had grown up to become spooky, familiar strangers, the lost brown girl got up and started singing.

It made Wanda want to dance for a moment. It wasn't just her, the music made everyone stand up and sway or shuffle right there, in the gas station church.

When it was over, everyone left the big room with the ashes at the front. That was all that was left of the mother now. Wanda knew she should be crying, but she couldn't. She couldn't be sad to lose someone she had already lost so long ago.

The mother had almost forgiven her. Wanda could feel she had wanted to. Sometimes she was nice for no reason, and would let Wanda do her hair and put on her nail polish. Those times, she wouldn't even get mad if Wanda made a mess, she'd just say: the past is the past and *that's that*.

But when the father had died, everything changed. It was like the mother had thought it was all Wanda's fault. Like she had killed him by being the only person in the world who knew what he was like when there was no one else around. At the reception after the funeral, Wanda remembered catching a glance at the mother. Wanda saw her, standing there with her gardening friends, drinking sherry. The mother had been staring at her with ice in her eyes, and Wanda could hear it – the mother's voice, moving across the room, past all those sad faces in black, back to where Wanda stood. *This is all your fault*, the voice had said.

It was doomed from the get go, everything between the mother and Wanda. She hadn't been thrilled about being pregnant, Wanda knew that much. The mother had said it was all flowers and crooners and tea for two until Wanda came along. Wanda had heard her tell the father one time, "Good thing I never did throw her out the window." And then the mother had laughed. They both did.

Right about then Mrs. Dalloway started to shake Wanda and tell her to snap out of it. She said that everyone was getting up and leaving the room, and it was time for Wanda to go as well. She said to stop wandering off into the memory pit, or she'd forget why they had come in the first place. All she had to do was get through the day, then, she could get back on a plane and go back to Jack's basement apartment in Gastown – their cave, their hole in the ground. Jack always complained about the leaks and mice and mould, but it was home. Wanda could come and go whenever she wanted. Even though she didn't. She just stayed inside and smoked, mostly. But that was better than before, when she first moved out west. Before she tracked

Jack down, and she slept somewhere new every night, and sometimes no place at all.

She wanted to go outside for a smoke right after the service was over, but Mrs. Dalloway pulled Wanda the other way. She had made her put on the necklace and the tie and the medal. She had her around the neck.

Wanda walked over to them. They were standing together, all three. It was time.

She couldn't say anything. She just stood there. Mrs. Dalloway tried to pull the words out of her. Any words. But she couldn't make Wanda speak. It was okay, though. They knew who she was. Even the nervous one, who looked so surprised to see her, knew who she was now.

They looked at the things dangling from around Wanda's neck. The nervous girl, who looked sad and stern with all her hair pulled back, asked Wanda if she could give her the tie back now. Wanda said, "Yes." She gave back the tie and the other things as well. They must have been heavier than she realized, because without them Wanda felt like she was floating. She felt light and soft and warm, and now she was going back home.

Mrs. Dalloway smiled and said, *"An offering for the sake of offering."*

Wanda looked at the children again. "Sorry," she said, then walked away.

34.

THE MORNING OF THE GARAGE SALE, Emma woke up in her old bed at number 66, with Lester snoring in her ear. He had been drunk the night before. They all had. After the service, everyone had gone back to the house for drinks and sandwiches. Rachel had stocked up, so the booze flowed until the birds started chirping.

Emma was in her underwear and bra, the old turtle pendant around her neck. She touched it, and thought for a moment about Wanda. She hadn't been surprised that her mother wasn't well – the yelling lady on the streetcar had prepared Emma for that. What had come as a shock was how old, tired, and bewildered Wanda had seemed. It was as if they, her own children, had become strangers to her now. What had it taken out of her to make the trip back to Toronto? And why had she come? Had it been a sense of duty, or had she needed to say goodbye? Emma had waited after the service for Wanda to join them at the house, but when Nina arrived, she said she had dropped their mother off at a hotel. Nina would go by in the morning to get the paperwork finalized, and then drive Wanda to the airport.

Emma knew that was it. They would never see their mother again.

She sat up, and wiggled herself out from under the covers. She was pinned between the wall and Lester, who was still fully clothed. Emma looked down; her own clothes were in a ball on the floor at the bottom of the bed. She bent over to look at them, and found they were covered in dirt. She tried to remember what had happened. She had danced on the coffee table to Harry Belafonte at some point, she knew that much. She laughed to herself as she remembered that she had also taken the old astrology book out of her room, and had started telling people about how to cast a birth chart. She remembered Rachel playing hostess, and getting mad at Emma for smoking a joint with Billy. Billy the Kid, Emma thought, chuckled to herself for a moment, and then stopped. It was a clue, some piece to the puzzle of what happened the night before. Something about her and Billy being outlaws – not like Bonnie and Clyde, more like Robin Hood. Yes, she had a whiff of it now – Robin Hood and his merry band of Bison. Bison? Emma reached into her memory for more, but her mind just laughed, and sloshed around in the puddle of a hangover that promised to be a tsunami by noon. Harry Belafonte, Billy the Kid, dancing on the coffee table, dirty clothes left in a mound on the floor. Turtle pendant – that was it, the trail went cold.

Emma had seen Billy at the funeral, and wondered who he was – this big, bald, rough-looking guy who had showed-up on a Harley Davidson. When he came to the house and introduced himself after the service, he told Emma that he met Grandma on a plane to Florida once, a long time ago. He had said she had given him some advice on how to get back together with a girlfriend he had cheated on. "I'll never forget," Emma remembered him saying, "I was pounding back double JD's, and she made it so simple," he'd said. "She said, if you love her, you have to beg her forgiveness and hope that she gives it to you." Billy had laughed. "I kept coming up with excuses, trying to weasel out of it, and she kept saying, 'you've got to own up to your mistakes, William, and *that's that*'." Billy had only seen their grandmother once after that, when she had asked him to come scare Sam straight when he was getting in trouble as a teenager.

Rachel had been angry about the pot. She'd said that at least they could have gone outside instead of in the garage, stinking up the whole house. She had even accused Billy of being a criminal. She hadn't minded him so much later, though, when Lester and Sam got into it, and Billy had stepped in and told them both to knock it off.

Emma got out of bed, and stood up. Lester was still asleep. She looked down at him, and remembered how he had flirted with Nina Buziak the night before. Nina had dropped Wanda off at the airport, and then gone back to the house. Lester was standing with Emma at first, saying, "She looks good, eh? Who would have thought she'd turn out to be such a knockout. I wonder if she'd let me take her picture sometime."

"Why don't you go ask her?" Emma remembered saying.

Lester had looked at her, a little suspicious, then he had shrugged his shoulders and off he went. Emma had stood there like an idiot, feeling jealous and abandoned as she watched him flirt with Nina, at her grandmother's wake, no less. So much for the gallant knight, so much for Mr. Save-the-Day.

Emma picked her dirty clothes off the floor and placed them gently over Lester's head, rubbing them together a bit before letting them drop, so some of the dirt fell into his hair. He, oblivious, slept on. Nina Buziak, of all people. At least she'd had the decency to look uncomfortable, and to leave the house shortly after. Emma vaguely remembered crying. She looked in the mirror. Her eyes were small, the skin around them puffy and tight. Yes, she must have cried. She remembered Sam had gone over to Lester, yelling and calling him a slimy little shit. Then, the pushing had started between Sam and Lester until Billy stepped in. After that? Emma couldn't remember. The rest of the evening sank like a stone below consciousness.

Emma looked around the room for her purse, then gave up, and sat on the floor with her back to the bed, rummaging around in her duffle bag for her indigo cotton dress. Already, it was too hot, and she'd be spending the day outside with

Rachel, selling all their memories off to the highest bidder.

Lester began snoring loudly. He had tossed off Emma's dirty clothes and flipped onto his back. Lester. He had to be the centre of attention, always had to be the meat of the sandwich. Emma looked at him again, and had the urge to pull out the corners of the sheet underneath him. Then what would she do? Roll him out of bed, and dump him into a heap onto the floor? Or wrap him up as if she was swaddling him? She wanted to do both.

Outside, the woodpecker egged her on. Emma put her house-coat on and left the room.

35.

RACHEL HADN'T SLEPT at all the night after her grandmother's funeral service. First, there had been the guests to attend to at the reception at the house. The caterers had arrived on schedule with the sandwiches, but there had been two platters of egg salad, only one of roast beef, and they had forgotten the tuna altogether. Then there was Emma, smoking drugs in the house with some Hell's Angel funeral-crasher that she had the nerve to tell Rachel was a friend of their grandmother's.

Whoever he was, like most of the guests, he left just after midnight. Rachel had heard his motorcycle start up as she was taking the empty bottles out to the trash. Emma and Sam were nowhere to be found, so it had been left to Rachel to sort out the guests who remained. There were no takers on her offer to sleepover, so most had been ushered into a series of taxis that came and left in succession until the street grew quiet. The few who had remained lived within walking distance. Rachel had put on a pot of coffee for these local stragglers, and then did one final inspection of the house, collecting anything that had been left out of the inventory of items to be sold.

She had opened the door to the basement, flicked the light switch three times, and then had gone down to check that everything had been properly labelled for the garage sale, working quietly as drunken footsteps above her stumbled toward bed, or out the door. Eventually, the house grew quiet, and

Rachel had climbed up the stairs and gone into her old room, taking off her clothes and leaving them in a pile on the floor. Not folding them was a proclamation: *mourning clothes – I will never wear you again.* She had flicked the switch to her bedroom light three times, and then lay in the dark, eyes open, as glow-in-the-dark planets stuck onto her ceiling shone with silly, brilliant innocence.

It was likely the slam of the screen door that woke Rachel up, that and the sound Emma's singing, loud, slurring and off-key:

Emancipate yourself from mental slavery
None but ourselves can free our kind!

The sound of the kitchen tap being turned on, of the fridge door opening, the cutlery drawer, the tap being turned off, then silence.

She's left the fucking fridge open, Rachel thought, sitting up and reaching in the darkness for her robe. Then the fridge door closed, and Emma thumped up the stairs and slammed the door to her bedroom shut.

Rachel reached for her phone to check the time. It was four a.m. for chrissake. She lay back down, eyes open. She knew she wouldn't be able to fall back asleep. A familiar flush of annoyance throbbed between her temples as Emma's singing echoed in her ears. When her alarm went off at six am, Rachel was relieved, tired but relieved. At least she hadn't slept in. Before her feet hit the floor, she shot a text off to Nina. She wanted to ensure the papers had been signed before Wanda got on the plane. Next, was the garage sale. She could do a lot of the preparation on her own. First, she would drive around the neighborhood putting up signs, then she'd pull the card tables out of the garage and set them up on the lawn. After that, she'd put coffee on for everyone, and paste a smile on her face. Just one more day, and it would all be over.

By noon, many of the big-ticket items were gone. The kitchen table and chairs went for much less than Rachel expected, but they got what they asked for with the couch and bookshelves.

It was a good thing she'd managed to get Sam and Lester up early to move the big pieces out of the house, even if they did both go back to bed immediately afterward. There were at least a dozen people milling around by the time everything was ready to go. Emma, surprisingly, was up early, though for the most part she stayed on the front lawn, mooning around, looking longingly at the sale items with a coffee cup in hand. Rachel felt annoyed at the sight of her, and gave her a wide berth. The sun was high and hot, and that, plus the lack of sleep, left Rachel feeling dizzy and worn.

Emma went into the house, and came out later with sandwiches and lemonade on a tray. Rachel looked at the frosted glass as Emma handed it to her. She wasn't falling for the bait. She'd take the lemonade, but an apology for being woken from a dead sleep was what Rachel was holding out for. I can wait all day, she thought at first, but when she saw the sandwiches, she caved. Tuna fish. A coincidence of course, but it softened the gesture. She looked up at Emma, who avoided Rachel's gaze by looking out at the scene on the lawn.

"I found a can of tuna in the back of the pantry," Emma muttered. "I know you wanted one of these yesterday. Better late than never," Emma let her sandwich sit, and went back to wandering around the yard, as if she were looking for something. Rachel watched her, thinking about Emma's tuna, sitting out in the sun. Emma turned, looking back at her sandwich, as if she had heard.

"I'll eat mine in a sec," Emma yelled in Rachel's direction. "I just want to … I'm just…" Emma stopped speaking, reached across the fold-out table in front of her, and picked up a book. She then turned, and marched over to Rachel as if entering combat.

"What the hell is this?" Emma slammed an astrology book down on the table.

"It's an old book," Rachel said, frowning. It was too hot for this sort of nonsense. A fly began to buzz over Emma's sandwich.

"What the hell, Rachel, I put that aside to keep!" Emma was shouting. People were turning to watch the scene.

"Fine, if you want it, you can have it, I don't really care. It was sitting there on the kitchen counter, so I put it out. You don't have to get so dramatic about it."

"Oh, I can have it? I have your permission, do I? Thanks so much, Ms. Queen of the Universe." Emma stormed up the steps of the old porch, and into the house, the screen door slamming behind her.

Rachel finished off her sandwich, watching as the fly and his new friend strolled leisurely across Emma's. The sun was directly overhead. A news van rolled down the street. A couple of people came up to the table to pay for things. One particularly senile old man told her that he needed new lawn furniture because a herd of buffalo had strolled through his backyard earlier that morning. Rachel looked away, embarrassed. She made the sale and didn't haggle, instead taking five dollars off the ticket price and throwing the garden hose in for free. Grandma would have been appalled.

A few moments later, the screen door swung open and Emma barrelled out, dragging a long box beside her. She dropped it on the porch, and bounded down the steps.

"Here!" Emma pulled a book out from under her arm, and slammed it down on the table, next to the astrology book. It was *The Secret Garden*, the book Grandma had given Rachel just after her father died. Rachel looked up at Emma, then over at the box. "It's your father's telescope. I found it in the attic. I put both of these things aside because I knew that they meant something to you." Emma was crying. It was emotional blackmail, irrational and inappropriate. The events of the day before were clearly too much for her. She hadn't even mentioned Wanda.

"Just settle down Emma," Rachel sighed, thinking that they both really needed to get out of the sun.

"Don't tell me to settle down. In fact, don't tell me what to do at all anymore. That's over now. No more lists, no more directions, no more judgment, no more condescension, no more of your holier-than-thou superiority. I've had it with all that shit." Emma was shaking in a way that conjured an image of Wanda in Rachel's mind.

Perhaps it was a simple matter of not enough sleep and too much time in the sun, or maybe it was something less probable, like a small tear in space-time, or the brief manifestation of a subatomic worm-hole, but for a moment, Rachel was transported back to the gas-station chapel after the service – staring into her mother's eyes as she returned the tie. Wanda's face had looked tired and expressionless, not like she was performing an act of contrition, but like she was doing it because someone told her to. There was a distance, a lack of recognition. Her hair was grey and matted, and the smell in the air around her was rancid, like sour milk.

"Enough!" Rachel suddenly stood up. Everyone was staring now, so what the hell, but standing so fast made her dizzy. She could have sworn she saw a peacock out of the corner of her eye, strolling down Garden Avenue.

Rachel was about to let loose, to give Emma just enough of a blast that she backed off, when Sam, in track pants and his old Rolling Stones t-shirt, suddenly swung open the screen door.

"Nina's coming over soon. She wants to talk to you both." He rubbed his eyes, patted his hair down and attempted to look stern. "I'm going to take a shower," he said, and went back in the house.

Rachel was relieved. Nina was on the way – the wheels were in motion. The papers were signed, and soon Robertson would put the final seal on the will. Soon this would all be over.

Emma got up and took their lunch plates in without a word. The screen door banged shut behind her. Rachel took a sip of lemonade, then she leaned back in her chair and closed her eyes. Was that a sheep bleating?

The screen door banged open again.

36.

"LISTEN, RACHEL, I know you mean well, but you act like you know what's best for everyone, when sometimes you don't even know what's best for yourself." Emma stood in front of the card table, her voice calm and even. She was going to try a different approach. "You think you're objective – you think that the way you see things is the way they are, just because your worldview is reflected back to you in all of its hollow, materialistic glory every time you turn on the TV or open up a magazine. But that doesn't make it the truth."

Emma felt much better now. Her emotions had gotten the better of her earlier. Too much alcohol the night before, too little sleep, and too much sun. Plus, there had been another sound, a buzz of energetic interference that had hung in the air all day like a thundercloud. It reminded Emma of that night in the park, and she wondered, for a moment, if it was the Howards again: John and Jemima, offering their sage advice. Emma tried to tune in the static, but her booze-addled brain rebelled. So, she decided to take a quick moment in the kitchen, to ground herself, and call on the Grandmothers – not for protection, but for guidance.

She had gone back outside afterward, to confront Rachel, again. Rachel was leaning forward, peering out onto the lawn. For a moment, it looked as if she was going to ignore Emma all together. Then she leaned back, and replied with a sigh, "Some of us look at the world objectively, Emma, we weigh the facts and then come to a rational decision." Rachel continued looking out at the scene before her. "And some of us see everything through our emotions."

Okay, touché. Emma could let that one go. She knew she had been a tad dramatic. She felt the weight of the pendant around her neck, and took a slow deep breath.

"Yes, and some of us see everything through our prejudices." Rachel looked up suddenly; seeming surprised that Emma had a response. Emma thought to herself, *the possum has arisen.*

Emma continued, "Sure, you'll measure, analyze and weigh everything, but you'll also throw out any evidence that doesn't prove the hypothesis you've already decided on. You take a situation and view it through the lens of your expectations and your fears. Especially your fears." Emma took a breath and waited.

Rachel stood up with unmistakable annoyance. Emma reminded herself not to enjoy it.

The screen door opened again, and Lester bounded out onto the porch.

"You'll never believe what's going on," he said.

"Oh for God's sakes Emma, can you please keep your new-age psycho-babble to yourself today?" Rachel said, not so much as glancing in Lester's direction. "You're being hysterical. As if you, of all people, have a firm grip on objectivity."

Emma felt a tingling in the soles of her feet, as she grounded herself to the earth. She touched her index finger to her thumb, making a circle that she held up to her eye. "It's like you look at the world through an empty toilet paper roll, and think you've got the lay of the land." Emma let her hand drop to her side, and made an effort to soften her tone. "It's not your fault though, because you're completely left-brained. Or is it right-brained, I forget now. Well, whichever brain it is that controls order and function and compartmentalization and math and linear time, that's you. That's your world, and you can't see beyond it." Emma felt a rush of pride at not stuttering or saying she was sorry, or getting distracted by Lester's impatient shuffling.

Lester tried again.

"No, seriously," he said. "I just heard it on the news."

"And you, you use both brains then, I presume?" Rachel stood with her arms crossed. Emma refused to be daunted. Lester went back inside.

"Yes, I do," Emma replied. "Because I function in society. Maybe I'm not the most glowing success by society's terms, but I function. I dot all the "i's," and cross the "t's" and fill out all the forms. It's a right-brain world." Emma made a mental note to keep her own arms unfolded.

"You mean a left-brain world." Rachel snickered.

"Whatever!" Emma blurted in annoyance, then caught herself. "Listen, I pay my taxes, which if you ask me is way too complicated a process for your average citizen to be expected to complete. And don't get me started on all the contracts and permissions we need to fill out just to exist on the planet today. I mean I can't even order a song online without needing a lawyer to help me navigate through five hundred pages of gobbledy-gook. But that's what they want. They want us to be overwhelmed and to give up so we will be good little sheep. But I'm not a sheep, I'm a turtle, which means I may be slow, but by Goddess..."

"And your point is?" Rachel said, checking her phone.

"My point is that you hide behind your scientific explanations," Emma said defiantly. "What does science know about truth anyway? If, for once, science prefaced all their declarations with: *as usual, we don't really know for sure, because the universe continues to be an unfathomable mystery, but this is what we've found out so far* ... the word 'fact' would be abolished, and the human race would take a giant leap forward in understanding where the hell we are, why we're here, and how this place works."

Rachel continued looking at her phone, shaking her head.

Emma went on, as if she had her full attention. "Science is carried out by humans, Rachel, and humans are subjective. We all see the world through a filter. There's no way around it, our consciousness affects our reality. It's the way the universe works. Physics has already proved it. Call it the uncertainty principle, or the observer effect or whatever it is you guys want to call it, but the truth is the world is the way *we* are, and what we are is whatever we fill ourselves up with."

Rachel sat down, looking decidedly fed-up. "You have a very poetic way of looking at the universe Emma, but it has nothing to do with reality. The reality is that the universe is not some magical place full of rainbows and unicorns where everyone lives forever. The universe is a vast terrain of unimaginable extremes of size, temperature and speed. You anthropomorphize your physical environment as if it's some kind of god. You mix up mysticism with fact. Like when you talk about death, for instance. There's nothing magical about it. Death isn't poetic, it's literal and absolute." Rachel looked up at Emma with an unfamiliar expression of compassion. "I think this whole outburst, this tirade you're on today is all about trying to deny this fundamental fact."

Emma glared at Rachel, and counted to ten. She knew she needed to stay calm and be rational or her message would be lost. She sat down at the card table. "Yes, everything dies, Rachel, but then it's reborn. Plants grow out of decomposing leaves, even stars are recycled from gas and dust made from other dead stars." Emma felt proud to know this last fact, but tried not to let it show.

Rachel nodded her head. "Yes, but that takes energy. It all uses energy that is finite, and one day all the stars will run out of fuel, and the sun will eventually begin to swell and die, taking us and the rest of the solar system with it. And this will happen across the universe, until the only stars left are red dwarfs, burning like coals." Rachel lifted her hand and used it like a scythe to emphasize her point. "And then, when those are gone, there'll be nothing but black holes roaming the universe, sucking up everything that remains. And this will go on for longer than your mind can comprehend, and then, even the black holes will starve, and the universe will be cold, dark and dead. That's where we're going Emma. That's the truth of your magical universe."

Emma thought for a moment. "Well, maybe that's exactly what has to happen before it starts all over again. Maybe it takes exactly that kind of nothingness to coax a universe into being. Maybe we live in a giant multiversal field, where everything blinks in and out of existence like fireflies."

Rachel opened her mouth, then closed it and shook her head.

Emma went on. "And what about that law of thermal dynamics? "

Rachel looked at Emma in surprise for a moment, then smiled.

"The one that states." Emma continued, "that energy is never lost?" Emma felt triumphant, and waited for a response.

Rachel was silent, and looked past Emma toward Garden Avenue. She cocked her head slightly, as if she was listening to something just above the rooftops.

"So, really, how you science people can believe," Emma continued, while following Rachel's gaze. "That there's no such thing as reincarnation is just mind-boggling to me," Emma concluded, taking a breath, and praying to the Grandmothers that her words would flow into open ears.

"For one thing," Rachel began, looking back at Emma again, "it's called thermodynamics, not thermal dynamics, and secondly," she continued, "your whole premise is flawed." Rachel was about to go on when the feeling that she was being watched overcame her. She turned around and looked back at the house. Sam was looking out through the screen door.

37.

SAM WAS STANDING on the welcome mat at the front door in jeans and a T-shirt, towel-drying his hair, and watching his sisters argue. He stepped onto the porch.

"Enough you two. Enough. Just for one day, do you think it would be possible for..." he began, then stood, as if frozen, mouth open, staring at the street.

A panicked reindeer, with antlers as big as baseball bats, ran down Indian Road, and up on the sidewalk. Three men, with ropes and netting, and a woman with a TV camera followed on foot, attempting to surround the animal, as a city parks van and a news truck rumbled behind.

"That's what I was trying to tell you," Lester said, coming up behind Sam to join them all outside. "I just heard it on the radio."

"What did you hear?" Sam asked.

"Someone broke into the zoo last night and set all the animals free."

Rachel looked at Emma.

"Oh shit," Emma said, and then Lester and Sam looked at her as well.

"You're kidding me," Lester said, laughing. "I was wondering where you were last night, and where all that mud..."

"You broke into the zoo?" Sam asked, incredulous, then pulled a cigarette out of the pack in his back pocket, and lit up.

"Yes," Emma said. "I mean no. I mean, honestly, I'm not

sure." She stared after the reindeer, then looked at Rachel, who hadn't said a word. Instead, Rachel looked past her, to where Nina Buziak Fletcher was approaching up the crumbling walk. Nina looked professional and determined, in spite of the circus taking place behind her.

"I heard about it on the way over," Nina said, looking back to the street. The reindeer had gotten its antlers caught in a car antenna, slowing it down long enough for the men with ropes and netting to surround it. Nina turned back to the two women. "The news report said that at first they thought the incident was related to the occupation of the Native burial ground – apparently it's been a year to the day since protesters set-up camp in High Park."

"What are you talking about?" Emma asked, suddenly pulling her gaze away from the reindeer.

"You weren't here," Lester jumped in. "It was all over the news last year. There was this huge protest in the park over the land, you know where the BMX trail was? Well apparently they were riding right over this Iroquois burial site called Snake Mound, and so a bunch of Six Nations Grandmothers decided…"

"Snake Mound?" Emma asked, her eyes wide.

Rachel interrupted, looking at Nina. "There's a problem with the will, isn't there?" Emma, Sam and Lester looked at Nina as well, and waited.

Nina took a deep breath. "I didn't think it was appropriate to get into it yesterday," she began. "But your mother wouldn't agree to sign the papers to let you sell the house."

Rachel stood up. She could feel heat from her belly rise up into her face. She opened her mouth to speak.

"Wait, Rachel," Nina said. "She didn't agree, but she isn't going to stop you either. She waived her rights to the house all together."

Emma stood up as well, backing away from the table, until she was leaning up against the outside wall of the house. She watched, as the reindeer was led, reluctantly, inside the van.

Nina continued. "Which means the determination of what to do with the house is up to the two of you. You have to decide. Together."

Sam looked at Rachel, who watched as Emma ran her hand back and forth over the stones, absentmindedly, like a child. Rachel thought of the tie, neatly folded and placed into a zip-lock sandwich bag in her purse. Then she thought of Wanda, returning it to her. She had looked like a derelict when they saw her at their grandmother's service.

Rachel felt dizzy again, so she sat back down in a lawn chair. A strand of hair fell loose from the bun that was unraveling at the back of her neck. She pushed it back behind her ears, and shielded her eyes with her hand. For a moment she considered taking out Grandma's green visor, which she had tucked away, right next to her father's tie in her purse.

Nina walked over to where Emma was standing. "Your mother also had a message for you, Emma," she said. "I have to say, I'm not sure I understand it, but I'll pass it along, anyway."

Emma waited.

"She said Mrs. Dalloway thought you should know that Wanda doesn't remember much about your father. All she knows for sure is that he loved animals."

Emma slid down the bumpy wall, and sat in the flowerbed. She put her hands over her face and her shoulders shook in a way that made it unclear if she was laughing or crying.

"We can keep the house," Rachel said suddenly.

"No," Emma said, as she slowly stood back up. "It's time to say goodbye. We're selling it, and *that's that*."

It was only a few hours later, after Nina and Sam had gone to lunch, and Lester had gone back to his apartment in Kensington market, when a police cruiser pulled up in front of old number 66 and stopped. Two uniformed officers stepped out, and started up the walk toward where Rachel and Emma sat at the card table. One of the officers tripped and stumbled a bit on his way up the walk, grabbing on to the arm of the other officer for a moment to steady himself.

"I think I'm in trouble," Emma said, standing up, brushing imaginary dirt off of her indigo dress.

"Don't worry," Rachel said, standing beside her. "We'll get it sorted."

38.

NATURALLY, IT HAD BEEN Emma who let all the animals out. As the squad car pulled up to the curb, she had a sinking feeling in her stomach. She still couldn't remember convincing Billy to join her in her caper. She couldn't remember getting on the back of his motorcycle and taking him on a tour of the park. She couldn't remember showing him the Snake Mound burial ground, or telling him about the Howards, or taking him past the children's playground, and explaining that it had been fenced off for reconstruction after a suspected arsonist left it in ashes.

Emma couldn't remember getting Billy to drive over to the little High Park zoo, or how he had stopped her when she tried to hop the fence to "go say hello." Emma didn't remember Billy deciding it was time to go home after that, and depositing Emma on the doorstep of 66 at around two am. Nor did she remember only pretending to go back in the house, and instead, returning to the zoo on her own. Sadly, she also didn't remember the joy in her voice as she belted out the words to Bob Marley's "Redemption Song," just before unlocking all the gates to the pens, and leaving them wide open.

Emma didn't remember any of these things but still, in her gut, she knew. She had been the one to let the animals run free. Later, the incident will make her laugh to herself, and even feel a twinge of pride in her actions, though it will take her some time until she gets to that point. First there will be charges laid, and lawyers to consult, and a court case to attend, and then sentencing. It won't be until Emma has finished her community service that the whole episode will settle into a memory that makes her smile.

Naturally, Rachel took care of everything. The settling of the will, the sale of the house, as well as arranging Emma's legal defense. Still, the whole week could have left Rachel in much the same frame of mind that we found her in if it weren't for one small momentary lapse, one moment of forgetfulness, which became the catalyst for everything.

Rachel blamed herself, of course. She should have double-checked that the garage was empty. After all, it was she who had plugged in the Easy Bake Oven on the day of the garage sale. Some haggler was hell-bent on a discount, unless Rachel could prove it worked, so she had taken the old oven into the garage and plugged it in. Then she and the potential buyer had argued for fifteen minutes, the result of which was his walking away. Rachel had been annoyed, and must have walked away as well. It's impossible to know for sure, but it was easier to blame herself. If someone else had been responsible for burning old 66 down to the ground, she'd never be able to let it go.

It's a shame the house didn't make it. It really was the most beautiful home you'd ever seen. I can almost feel those stones now, just thinking about it. Obviously, they cancelled the sale, and the new owner's money was refunded. The lot was sold eventually, and a new house was built on the land. But it looks nothing like the old number 66.

Emma took her cut of the insurance settlement and used it to revamp her website, attend the Animal Communication Symposium and to pay for advertising in those free magazines you get at health food store. It surprised Emma, as much as anyone, that the story of the grieving pet psychic who emancipated the animals from the High Park zoo attracted so much attention. She was interviewed on radio and television news shows. A group of animal activists even created a Facebook page to share her story. Emma became a hero, and was booked months in advance for her animal communication sessions. The news stories never mentioned the fact that Emma offered animal medicine consultations as well, but people must have found out through her website. She didn't have as many of these clients as she did for her pet psychic business, but the ones who did come to see her left knowing that Emma truly had a gift, and they were finally one step closer to healing whatever it was that ailed them.

As for Rachel, the biggest change came from something seemingly inconsequential. It wasn't as if her life transformed overnight, or as if anything really earth-shattering happened at all. She didn't suddenly decide to become a Hari Krishna or to climb Mount Everest or train for the Boston marathon. What she did do was start a garden, right there, on the balcony of her condo. At first it was just tomatoes, basil and parsley — practical plants that would help her save a bit of money on groceries. But then she planted some sweet peas, and built a trellis for them to climb. She bought a lavender plant, and kept her patio doors open so its fragrance could fill the condo when it bloomed each spring. And when the nights were warm and clear, Rachel would take out her father's old telescope, and sit out on her aromatic balcony, renaming stars.

Epilogue

The World Began With A Whisper

by Emma (aka Koko)

Once upon a time ago
back thirteen point seven
billion years
so were told

the universe gave birth.

Out of gas and dust
and cosmic clouds
chaos created
Gaia divine
a Goddess
we call Earth.

Now before I get this going
let me start by telling you
that this is not a poem
about the saving of the planet.

For since the earth's formation

there've been at least four mass extinctions
near complete annihilations
of all living populations.

Until her atmosphere was altered
through the flux of evolution
through single celled mutation
and organic procreation
in ecosystem synchronization
and symbiotic combination.

Like a phoenix
the garden of Eden
resurrects
in tune with her seasons

only recently becoming ripe
for varied forms of earthly life
and human habitation.

So simply put
the point of the poem
is that the earth was alive
before she was home.

The universe is hostile
and our dependence on the planet
infantile.

There's only
twelve thin miles
between us and
bombardment by
galactic debris

harmful radiation
and the icy cold hands
of infinite
                  ------------------------ space ----------------------------

This planet
our mother
encompasses you
our biosphere
our home, her womb.

(if it weren't for photosynthesis
our brain could not consider this)

This poem...
(this is not a poem
it's a thought
like matter
only less static)

Could it be
possibly that we
are one and the same thing
as earth as life as earth

and that we have been sleeping?

Like the Buddha
before his becoming
like Christ before
awakening

or like when we believed that the earth was
flat
like when we believed that the earth was flat

like when we believed

(of course, up until
that smarty pants Copernicus
shook it up in the 16th century
the idea of solar centric system
was considered crazy blasphemy)

I mean
perhaps we
have made a grave

underestimation
of the entire situation.

(with dozens of microscopic creatures
who now call home to you
can you say for sure that it was nothing
when Horton heard a *who*?)

But this poem/non-poem
does not propose that with
Gaia as our gracious host
we are planetary parasites
earth our hearth and domicile.

Instead
it stands
hands gesturing wildly
in street corner sermon
uncertain it will be believed
yet continues it's oration

The living earth
is a single system

a biodiversified creation
each of us stems
from a single seed
connected despite
species transmutation.

(so rather than just freeloaders
perhaps we're planetary creations)

James Lovelock told the world of this
through a paper he called the Gaia hypothesis.

Perhaps Blake, cummings, Krishna Murti
Hildegard, Joan of Arc, Rumi,
(among the many poets and mystics
who really seemed to *get it*)
knew of our relation
our situation

knew the source
of all divine
and their place
as a piece
of the planetary pie.

That is
if this
was a poem
to begin with

which it isn't
it's just a thought
nothing
but thought.

A versified voodoo creation
from the core of the central nervous system
of
the witch hunts are over
come home
of
perhaps we're all just the same thing
of
synaptic communication
of
spiritual communion
of
if the universe is expanding
doesn't that mean
that we were all one
when it began its beginning?
of
no, it can't be, it makes me dizzy
of
how long can you hold out?
of
I'm a poet, not a planet
of
this is ridiculous, I'm going home
of
there is more to haven and earth, dear Horatio
of
but T.S. called us Hollow Men
of
not with a bang
of
this is a test
this is simply a test
all thinking taking place
is being simulated for test purposes

of
this is the way
this is the way
            this
        this
this is the way
of
            life is but a dream
of

                    this is the way the world
                            begins
                        the world begins
                        the world begins

                    this is the way the world begins
                        not with a bang
                            but a
                        wide open mind

            (and the whisper of the words)

                            meditate
                        deliberate
                        consider

Acknowledgements

It is a pleasure to be able to acknowledge and thank the many people who supported me through the process of writing this novel. First and foremost, much gratitude and love to my Wonder Woman, Luciana Ricciutelli, Editor-in-Chief of Inanna Publications, for her patience, wisdom, and "dear-heart" encouragement. Also to Elizabeth Greene, whose generous guidance and support, helped me to see my blind spots. Without their belief in this book, I would be lost.

I am also deeply appreciative the University of Guelph's Creative Writing MFA program, where I had the opportunity to work on the manuscript. Much love and gratitude to Kathryn Kuitenbrouwer, my thesis advisor and mid-wife, who generously offered her knowledge and encouragement, and to Jeanette Lynes, whose kindness and faith in this story, as well as my ability to tell it, were precious in the early stages. I would also like to thank the wonderful staff and instructors I worked with in the program: Catherine Bush, Meaghan Strimas, Lynn Crosbie, Michael Winter, and Russell Smith. Also my brilliant fellow students, especially Matthew Harris, Kathy Friedman, Leesa Dean, Adam Honsinger, Naoko Kumagai, Ayelet Tsabari, and Nick McArthur.

Much love and gratitude also to my long-time mentors, Lillian Allen and George Elliott Clarke for their nurturing, generous support and guidance over the years, and to Austin Clarke for being the first to encourage me to give fiction a whirl. Also key during the early stages were: Marilyn Biderman, Mari Floros, Marianne Micros, and Olga Petrik, who all went above and beyond in their assistance and support.

Thanks to Jessica Thompson for her encouragement and inspiration, to bill bissett, for introducing me to the phrase "gone to spirit," to Eric Verspoor and Professor Robert K. Logan for assistance and support around the science details, to Mona Rizatti and Dominic Dileo for helping me understand the realities of living with mental illness, and to The Taiaiako'n Historic Preservation Society for preserving the legacy of Snake Mound.

Much gratitude to Lindsay and Nicholas Bradford-Ewart, Meghan Armstrong, and Cameron Maitland of Farmer Vision (farmervision.ca) for their generous belief in this novel, and for creating such an inspired and beautiful book trailer.

Thanks also to my beloved friends for all their faith and support: Seth-Adrian Harris, Clara Blackwood, Adebe DeRango-Adem, Brenda Holden, Maureen Taylor, Missy Marston, John Balabik, Wakefield Brewster, Katherine Bitney, Sheila Stewart, Heather Birrell, Patti Ann Trainor, Jo Citro; my WordSpell Sisters: Alyssa Ginsburg, Vanessa McGowan and Barbara Erochina; also to Tanya Neumeyer, Joanna Zofia Poblocka, Ingle Madrus, Dahila Riback, Jem Rolls, Charlyn Ellis, Brigitte and Sue Lessard-Deyell, Debi Torbar, as well as my lovely friends and former students, Lana Kouchnir-Kachurovska, Laura Kelsey Ridout, Kanwal Rahim, Jessica Gatoni, Rimsha Ahm, and Ayse Kapakili. Much gratitude also to all the colourful characters of my Canadian Spoken Word family, and to the late Frank Plummer, who always encouraged me to follow my dreams.

Special thanks Kimberly Gail (Roppolo) Wieser for her support and friendship, and to the late Eugene Blackbear Senior. Eugene was one of the forty-four traditional Cheyenne chiefs, and was for a number of years until his death, the oldest living Southern Cheyenne Sun Dance Priest, as well as an Arrow Priest, and a Sweat Lodge Priest. He was a Native American Church Roadman for over fifty years, and played Chief Spotted Elk in *Last of the Dogmen.* May his legacy live on...

I am also deeply grateful for the encouragement and support of my family: the McDougall clan (east and west) and the Thompson tribe, especially Gail Durham, Chris Thompson, Pat and Dave McDougall, Lisa Graham and Kyle McDougall. And special thanks to Kristi McDougall for donating her time and talent by providing me with such lovely author head shots.

Finally, I would like to thank my grandparents, Mary and William McDougall for their unending support, encouragement and love, and for sharing their passion for the written and spoken word.

Notes on quotes:

Henry David Thoreau: *Walden* (1854)
Virginia Woolf: *Night and Day* (1919)
Jon Brion: "Over Our Heads," *I Heart Huckabees* soundtrack (2004)

Other Woolf quotes appear throughout the book in the form of italicized dialogue by Wanda. All these quotes are from *Mrs. Dalloway* (1925).

Photo: Kristi McDougall

Andrea Thompson is one of the most well respected poets in the Canadian spoken word scene. A popular performer at venues and festivals across North America, Thompson's work has been featured on film, radio, and television; and included in magazines, literary journals and anthologies across Canada for over two decades. She is the author of a volume of poetry, *Eating the Seed* (2000), and co-editor of *Other Tongues: Mixed-Race Women Speak Out* (2010). In 2009, she was awarded the Canadian Festival of Spoken Word's Poet of Honour: For Outstanding Achievement in the Art of Spoken Word, and in 2005, her spoken word CD One, was nominated for a Canadian Urban Music Award. She is currently teaching Spoken Word through the Ontario College of Art and Design University's Continuing Studies Department in Toronto.